When Freedom

is

Promised

Chrissy Garwood/Chrisolite Books
29 Weston Hill Road,
Sorell, Tasmania, Australia, 7172
www.chrissygarwood.com

Direct quotations from Scripture are taken from the World Wide Bible (WEB) and are available in the public domain. Other verses are written from memory and are not direct quotes.

Book Layout ©2017 BookDesignTemplates.com

Cover Design: Belinda Pollard

When Freedom is Promised/ Chrissy Garwood —1st ed.

ISBN: 978-0-6485434-4-2

When Freedom is Promised

A River Wild Romantic Suspense Novel

Chrissy Garwood

Chrisolite Books
Sorell, Tasmania, Australia

I dedicate this book to my little brother Peter
Garwood. It has been amazing to see him grow up
into a wise friend who is bold enough to speak
words of lasting truth into tricky situations.

Contents

Dismay – Lose Courage

ജ ☼ ങ

Matthew 5:42 Give to one who asks,
and don't turn away someone who comes to borrow.

ജ ☼ ങ

Abigail stepped onto the playground, clutching the crumpled map. Principal Melrose led her across the paved area and pointed towards the landscaped expanse she should patrol. She nodded, adjusting her broad-brimmed hat again.

"Here's my number," he said, returning her phone. "Now, there's no reason for you to be anxious. Most of these boys won't even notice your injuries. When the rumours spread that you survived an explosion, it will be easier for you. It's every junior boy's ambition to blow something up."

Abigail turned to gaze over the playground. He didn't seem to notice his words were making her feel worse.

"You're an experienced teacher," he concluded. "And the boys here are well-behaved and self-disciplined."

She caught the look that suggested he was thinking: "not like your last school". What would he say if he knew the truth?

"If you encounter anything you can't manage, call me." He smiled, and then abandoned her without a backward glance.

Abigail sighed. Would "well-behaved" be how she described these students at the end-of-day debriefing? Or "self-disciplined"? Her playground duty covered the remotest areas of the Boys Junior Campus. She scanned the space before her, familiarising herself with the landmarks.

Above the dull roar of passing traffic, she heard shouting, like the crowd at a country football match. Unable to identify the source, Abigail frowned. She surveyed the grassy expanse separating the junior campus from the senior school. The Melbourne skyline beyond helped remind her she was a stranger here.

She silently prayed as she left behind the towering red-brick school buildings. She stepped onto a broad path that wound through leafy garden beds. She was a long way from the quiet outback school where she had known every face. There she could watch over the whole dusty playground from the shady comfort of the veranda.

Her prayers shrank to a feeble repetition. *God has not given you a spirit of fear. God has not given you a spirit of fear...*

Students in groups of two or three hurried past Abigail. They all wore the *St Jerome's* uniform, the navy and gold blazer over a white shirt with knee-length shorts. She might have been invisible to them, one lone female amid a sea of boys. Occasionally, one of the teenagers jostled her in his haste. Then an exclamation rang out, "Sorry, Miss."

As she turned the corner, a lanky, breathless boy confronted Abigail. He skidded to a halt before grabbing her arm.

"Miss! Miss! You have to come! They're going to kill each other!"

Abigail shook herself free, and increased her pace. The boy ran backwards to confirm she was following him. The path curved around a stand of trees. He was chattering non-stop, disregarding his surroundings. His distraction was a disaster in the making. She recognised him from the class she had taught before lunch. Marco Fontana, 8E Maths – talkative, but bright. A "scholarship boy".

"Slow down, Marco. You're not making any sense. And do watch where you're going."

The path sloped down to the oval. It was there she discovered the source of the excitement. A crowd of boys in the shade of an ancient oak tree formed a makeshift arena for two combatants. There must have been at least a hundred excited students present. Now she understood why so many boys had run past. She stopped, fumbling for her phone.

"There's a fight," she said, when Principal Melrose responded to her call, "near the far oval, under an oak tree. I need help." Abigail ended the call, thrusting her phone into her pocket. She grabbed the whistle she wore around her neck. Blowing the whistle loudly, she ran across the open space. Her short legs struggled to keep up with Marco, who jogged ahead.

This fight was not her first playground conflict. Except she was more used to scuffles between scruffy little children. Would the same strategies work here? What was she to do with this crowd of spectators? Abigail blasted them with her whistle.

She pushed her way into the circle, shouting as she went. "Let me through! Let me through! Anyone still here when the principal arrives will be in big trouble."

The crowd parted. In the centre, two boys wrestled, thumping each other with their fists. Abigail blew her whistle again. The crowd pressed in behind her. She held up her phone to show that she was videoing the gathering. The spectators fell silent. A few of them slunk away. The others waited to see what this new teacher would do next. Abigail circled the protagonists, trying to make her presence more obvious.

Finally, they noticed her and stepped apart. She had to look upwards at these boys. Faced with their defiance, her resolve wavered. Their bloody faces betrayed the seriousness of their dispute. They panted, glaring at each other. Abigail took off her sunglasses and frowned at them. She put her hands on her hips and tried to make herself more imposing.

"You're in trouble now, Kidman," one of the injured boys snarled. The other boy roared in protest and lunged forward as Abigail moved between them. The aggressor shoved her out of the way, and she flew through the air. The awestruck spectators stepped aside. She hit the tree with a thud.

Her scream echoed across the oval.

As darkness overwhelmed her, Marco's concerned face replaced the sky.

"Miss! Miss! Are you okay?"

☽ ✿ ☾

"How long do I have to stay here?" Abigail asked the nurse who was checking her blood pressure. The wall clock read five o'clock.

"Doctor is waiting for the test results to confirm there are no internal injuries. As soon as they arrive, he'll talk to you about what happens next."

The reluctant patient frowned. Not so long ago, a different hospital had released her. What might this new doctor have discovered? She hobbled from the bed, gasping in pain as she searched for her phone. Someone had delivered her luggage to the hospital.

Her fingers snagged a set of keys. Without looking at them, she recalled the information on the tag that listed the time for accessing her rented apartment. Abigail prayed for a speedy release. That morning, she had checked out of her hotel. Her appointment with the apartment caretaker had passed half an hour ago. Every detail of this forced move to Melbourne fed her anxiety. Why hadn't the people who organised everything remained to help her?

Tucked into her phone case was an important card. Abigail studied the information again. This was her lifeline, her only way of contacting the people who insisted she would be free from danger here. She climbed awkwardly back onto the Emergency Room bed to wait.

ꙮ ☼ ꙮ

Dr Anderson looked up from the medical report. The exhausted doctor was nearing the end of a long shift. The female in Cubicle 14 had been reticent to talk about anything other than her immediate injuries. He nodded grimly to the nurse. Together they went to speak to the patient. The nurse swished back the curtains and then re-closed the gap after they entered.

The doctor scrutinised the overweight patient. While he knew nothing about her history, he could see it was not a happy story. Her frizzy hair looked like someone had tipped bleach over it, then tried to repair the damage by attacking it with blunt scissors. Her skin was mottled and blotchy – she said it was from a chemical burn. Her only redeeming features were the brown eyes that stared at him from her round face. She had acknowledged her indigenous heritage on the forms. Yet, she would not meet his eye when he attempted to build a connection by talking about his traditional country.

"There's no record of an Abigail Golding at any of the Sydney hospitals," he began. "I've found no information about you anywhere. Why have you lied about your identity? It's obvious you've experienced significant trauma recently. Your broken nose wasn't reset properly, and those scars look less than six months old."

She held out her stubby fingers, thrusting a business card towards him. Her eyes were bright with pain. "Ring this number."

ꙮ ☼ ꙮ

The taxi stopped outside the white apartment building. The driver paused only long enough for Abigail to drag her suitcase out before racing away. The four-storey building stretched all the way to the dead-end, rising above the street. In the gloom, Abigail considered the peeling paintwork and the neglected garden. She knew her apartment was on the third floor. Her hopes for an elevator faded.

Abigail shuffled forward, each step a painful reminder of today's ordeal. As she walked, she thought of all she had endured to get here, and tears pricked her eyes. When the doctor had returned from making the phone call, he'd handed back the card without comment, then exhibited an eagerness to be rid of her. It took only fifteen minutes for him to approve her release. Another hour passed as she sat on her suitcase waiting for a taxi. Then the taxi became snarled in traffic. She had begun to doubt she would ever get to her destination.

Abigail pressed the buzzer beside the main entrance. Nobody came. She turned the handle. Pushing the door open, she stepped inside. The foyer was well lit, making the caretaker's apartment easy to find. Beside his door was a notice which defined the hours he was available. It was long past that now. Abigail knocked on the door. An ancient man cracked it open. When she held up her key tag, he pointed to the stairs on the right.

"You were supposed to be here at four-thirty," he grumbled. "You can find your own way." The door closed with a bang.

Abigail staggered up three flights of winding stairs. She paused, dizzy and breathless. A passage stretched left and right. A third option lay straight ahead. There were doors on both sides of this shorter hallway. The decision to step forward proved to be another discouraging mistake.

Abigail dragged her suitcase back to her starting point. She looked both ways. A single row of doors stretched to the left.

In the distance, there was another set of stairs, and a second side hallway. Abigail headed in that direction. After checking the third door, she knew she had made another wrong turn. She retraced her steps to the right, where a single row of doors stretched to the windowless end wall. Abigail checked the first number and counted the doorways ahead. Her apartment must be the furthest one. There were seven doors. She groaned. The overhead light had blown. Her end of the hall was in darkness. As she approached, the air throbbed with loud music. It came from behind her immediate neighbour's door.

Abigail put the key in her lock and entered the dark apartment. The curtains were drawn. She located the light switch and flicked the lever. Nothing happened. Using her phone as a torch, she went exploring. The open plan living room was separated from the small kitchen by an island bench. She could see the refrigerator door was open. That was not a good sign. She had been told all she needed to do was walk into the furnished apartment. Abigail slumped onto a lounge chair, covering her face with her hands. Waves of self-pity washed over her. She abandoned herself to the tears.

Finally, Abigail came to her senses. She was hungry and thirsty. No good would come from moping in the darkness. Walking across to the curtains, she pulled them apart. Lights from a nearby shopping centre shone into the room. Her apartment was immediately opposite an entrance. She stood at the window watching the cars on the main thoroughfare. She could see three sets of traffic lights. The lights cycled through the changes. Four lanes of traffic stopped, waited, and then cars and trucks zoomed away. Next, she identified the train station a few blocks away. In the dark, the station lights seemed so distant.

Closer to home, pedestrians hurried from the shopping centre. Her stomach rumbled. She hadn't eaten since breakfast. Did she have the energy to go out? Looking at her watch, Abigail realised it was too late to visit the supermarket tonight. The tears were back. She brushed them away.

The thumping music from next door intruded into her thoughts. At least there was someone at home in that apartment. Abigail rummaged in her handbag for her teacher mug. Together with her supply of teabags, this should have remained at school. She stepped into the hall, snibbing her apartment door lock open, ready for a hasty retreat.

Cautiously, she approached the next apartment, mug in hand. After rapping loudly on the neighbour's door, she waited. The music continued to boom. She rapped again. The door flew open to reveal a familiar figure. The boy from school – the one from the fight – the teenager responsible for her latest injuries.

The wounded teacher and the battle-scarred student stared at each other. A look of horror appeared on the boy's face. He swore and disappeared. Abigail stood frozen in the open doorway. Pressure increased behind her eyes. A strange prickly sensation began in her legs and spread throughout her body. The mug slipped from her hand, but she was powerless to do anything.

"Who was at the door?" a voice asked. The boy didn't answer. A thin, red-haired man with a kind face appeared in the doorway. His eyes widened. Before he could say anything, her legs folded under her. Abigail pitched forward into his arms.

Disarm - Overcome Hostility

ஐ ☼ ை

Romans 12:13 Offer hospitality to the saints who are in need.

ஐ ☼ ை

When Abigail opened her eyes, she was lying on a couch. She cried out in alarm and tried to rise. The red-haired man squatted beside her. He gently pushed her back against the cushions.

"Lie still. My name's Freddie, Freddie Kidman. Should I call an ambulance?"

"No! No ambulance. I've only just come from the hospital." She flapped her wrist to show him the plastic armband.

Freddie reached towards her bruised face. She flinched, and her eyes closed. His fingers lightly brushed away a tear. Abigail held her breath. She hadn't seen a mirror, but she must look a mess.

"Have you been in an accident?"

A shuffling noise behind Freddie drew Abigail's attention. She opened her eyes. The boy was standing on the far side of the room. Both his eyes were blackened, and his face was swollen. Freddie followed her gaze. "Do you two know each other?" he asked. Then he seemed to understand. He rose to his feet. "You're the teacher Butch knocked out? What are you doing here?"

"I-I – umm – next door."

"You're the new neighbour?" Freddie squawked. The boy thumped the wall and swore again.

Abigail lowered her eyes, pushing herself upright. Her head spun as she set her feet on the floor. "I'm sorry. I've had a bad day. I don't hold Butch accountable. I was an idiot to get too close to the fight. I didn't know he lived here until he opened the door. There's no power in my apartment, and I've been holding out for a cuppa..."

"That explains the mug," Freddie responded. "You won't be using that again. It smashed when you dropped it. It must have been a shock when Butch opened the door. Butch, put the kettle on. Then come and apologise." The boy grunted. "Are you hungry?" Freddie asked. "We're about to eat. There's enough for three."

"Why are you being kind to me? Your son doesn't want me here."

"He's not my dad!" Butch snapped.

"This is my nephew, my sister's boy. Butch is always in trouble, which is why he's been sent to live with me. I'm supposed to be a calming influence, but it hasn't worked."

∞✿∟

Freddie regretted saying he would sleep on the couch. It was four o'clock, and he was still awake. Abigail must be shouting in her sleep. Freddie stood outside the closed bedroom door. He imagined his new neighbour lying in his single bed. He was curious, but also afraid.

Everything about this woman warned Freddie that danger accompanied her. But he couldn't stop thinking about her softness as she fell into his arms. Butch said Freddie was "mental" for insisting Abigail stay here. Freddie had not been satisfied with her assurance that she was okay. She didn't look okay. He couldn't send her to that empty apartment.

And now this nightmare told a darker tale. Something very bad had happened to her. Before she came to Melbourne –

before she crossed paths with Butch. Either she was very unlucky, or—

Freddie caught his breath.

God. You're in this. I know You are.

It had been a long time since he last prayed.

I hope You're listening?

Once he started, the words poured out of him:

Everything was okay. I'd moved on, made a new life. And then You do this. My brother Sam said You had a plan. And whether I like it or not, You'll keep working in my life until I acknowledge I still need You. Well, You have my attention now. First, You send me Butch to turn my life upside down, and then You send me this woman...

ॐ ✿ ॐ

Waking in an unfamiliar room, Abigail leapt out of bed. The room swayed, and she sank back onto the covers. Memories from the previous day tumbled over each other. Why had she allowed that kind stranger to talk her into staying in his apartment? She looked around his room. The bed was near the window. A large desk dominated the wall closest to the door. It housed an impressive collection of computer hardware. Freddie said he played computer games. She thought about that as she stood again.

She had slept in her clothes.

She walked to the bookcase. It was filled with video cases. She studied the titles: sci-fi and thrillers, plus dark comedy. Abigail sighed with relief. The absence of pornography was inconclusive evidence, but she desperately wanted Freddie to be someone safe.

The apartment was silent. Abigail cracked open the door and peered out. The room layout seemed to be the same as her apartment. She tiptoed to the bathroom and locked the door.

When she re-emerged, music was playing. She went toward the sound. Butch was in the kitchen with his back to her, cooking something. The aroma of bacon wafted across the room. Abigail baulked.

"Freddie went to work; lef' me in charge," Butch grumbled, turning to talk to Abigail. "I'm cookin' breakfast. I hope yer like—"

She bolted for the bathroom. She made it in time. When she finished vomiting, she stood and washed her face.

"How far gone are yer?" Butch asked from the doorway.

"I-I don't know what you mean."

"Mum chucked like that when she was pregnant. Couldn't stand the smell of bacon. Or drink coffee. Stopped chuckin' when she got rid of it."

Abigail stared at him in despair. She unconsciously wrapped her arms around her lower body. She hadn't told anyone. She had hoped her generous size would make it possible for her to hide her unwelcome pregnancy. Wrong again.

"What happened to the farva?" Butch asked. "Didn't he wanna baby? Mum slept around, so she dunno who the farva was. You're not pretty enough for that."

"I'm leaving now." She pushed past him to escape the bathroom. She headed for the further door. Butch ran past to bar the way.

"You can't go yet. Freddie'll ask what happen. It's no use me trying to lie for yer. He'll see right through me. He'll wanna know what I done to upset yer, and I'll hafta tell 'im yer secret."

"What makes you think I care whether you tell him or not?"

"Oh, you care alright. You're a lousy liar. You want 'im to like yer. He likes you enough already. He'd sleep with you if you asked. That'd fix everyone's problems. Let him think the baby's his."

Abigail staggered. She tried to push past Butch, but he was taller and stronger.

"Eat some toast before yer go," Butch insisted, taking her by the arm and leading her back to the kitchen. "Move in with Freddie, then they'll let my sister Nikki come live here. 'Cos Freddie's single, they think he's a pervert."

"I'm not moving in with Freddie," Abigail said quietly, "and I'm not sleeping with him."

Not with him.

Not with anyone.

Ever.

She accepted the mug of weak tea Butch pressed into her hand. She stood at the counter, watching him cook the toast.

> God, how did I get myself into this mess? Please, get me out of it.

"If we're gonna be friends, tell me yer real name," Butch announced.

Abigail gripped her mug. "I've told you already. Abigail Golding."

Butch laughed. "Las' night, as you came round, Freddie ask yer name. You shook yer head an' says, 'It's a secret.' Then you blinked, looked at that hospital armband, and says, 'Abigail'. Freddie knowed you lied."

There was no way she was going to tell him her real name.

"Why the fake name, anyway?" he continued. "You in witness protection?"

The colour drained from her face. Oh, no. That strange sensation again. He stared at her.

"I bet yer hidin' from a gang of paedophiles, 'cos yer rescued some little kid..."

The mug smashed on the tiled floor. Hot tea splashed her legs. Butch shoved a chair under her and pushed her closer to the table.

"Sheesh! What's with the mugs? That's the secon' one yer dropped." He peered into her face. "I guess right? That's why I'm here too. Mum sold Nikki an' I got mad an' maked off with my sister. They wanted me, too, but I'm too strong to let anyone try that with me. I'm big enough to fight back."

He wiped the spilled tea from the floor. Abigail rested her head on the table as she waited for the dizziness to pass. She thought about what Butch had said.

Was God behind this coincidence? The only way she would ever find out was to accept the offer of friendship from Freddie.

Disrupt –
Break Normal Routine

🙨 ☼ 🙙

Matthew 6:34 Don't worry about tomorrow.
Today has enough trouble of its own.

🙨 ☼ 🙙

Freddie had left a note to say her apartment's electricity was now turned on at the meter downstairs. The hot water hadn't heated sufficiently for Abigail to shower in her apartment. Unfortunately, her aching muscles needed heat. With heavy feet, she returned to Butch to borrow his bathroom. This time, she locked her apartment door and brought her suitcase with her.

When Abigail came out of the bathroom, Butch had another revelation: "Two men come lookin' for yer. That ol' caretaker told 'em about a new tenant. Said they was police, but I didn't believe 'em. Asked for Lou-ise Sil-ver-ton. Said they'd tried your apartment first. I told 'em I dunno no 'Lou-ise Sil-ver-ton'. Told 'em only Uncle Freddie's girlfrien' Abby was here, looking after me 'cos I'm suspended from school. Asked 'em if they'd wait an' show Abby their ID. That got rid of 'em. They had a photo of yer with long hair, makeup an' all. Almost didn't recognise yer, but your eyes was still the same. Something happen to yer face since that photo? Left this number to call if I seed you."

Abigail reached for the card. Her hand was shaking. "Are you sure they weren't police?"

"No ID. And their clothes was all wrong. I've seed enough police to know the difference."

"How did they find me?"

"Where did you stay before you come here? If yer stayed in a hotel, would be easy to track ya. Yer too short'n'fat to hide. Did you use a taxi las' night?"

Abigail nodded. She dropped onto the couch, her head in her hands.

"They dunno yer new name. Maybe they believed me? We'll come up with somethin'. Yer short enough to be a kid. Put on this hoodie. I watched 'em drive off, so let's go shoppin'."

Abigail frowned at the skull design on the hooded long-sleeve shirt.

"Look, I'm grounded," Butch said. "Freddie said, 'cos I'm responsible for yer injuries, I have to babysit you till yer well again. You said yer needed somethin' from the shops. Wanna go on yer own? Freddie said I could go with you. If you changed yer mind about shoppin', we can sit here, and I'll ask more questions."

He grinned at her.

‿✿⁀

Freddie leaned on the work counter. He picked up his phone. Should he call Butch and check that Abigail was alright? He shook his head. That would only encourage Butch. Why did the boy think a romance between his uncle and this teacher was a possibility? Freddie rubbed his forehead. The headache wouldn't stop bothering him. Perhaps he could call his employer to say he was unwell? Again, he reached for the phone, and then stopped.

Today was the one day being absent from work would raise too many questions.

"I'm going across for my security review," his assistant, Blake Remington said. "Evie's on her way to cover for me."

Freddie nodded.

Blake crossed the car park between the service station and the main *Romano* compound. That double-storey black building dominated the streetscape. The bright red logo – a red sports car – stood out in sharp contrast.

The *Romano* building had been there for decades. When the son of the original owner took over, he added the car park and service station. Sebastian Romano was an astute businessman. His employees called him Boss, and he expected absolute loyalty.

Before Butch arrived, Freddie had been the perfect employee. He never took time off...

In recent weeks, how many times had he been called to school to bail Butch out of trouble?

As Blake neared the side entrance to the workshop, two women paused to talk with him. The smaller one, wearing the distinctive red *Romano* shirt, was the Boss's wife, Evie. They had married a few months ago, in August. She would be coming to the service station to make sure the end-of-month records were accurate. And she would take over customer service when Freddie's turn came for his interview.

The other woman was her bodyguard, Jenny Prescott. Evie never left the *Romano* building alone. A few weeks before her wedding, she had been abducted. The details of her rescue were a closely guarded secret. Evie said God had taken care of her.

Freddie frowned. Was that when God started intruding into his life again? He busied himself while he waited for her arrival. Usually, he looked forward to chatting with Evie.

"Hello, Freddie." Evie's soft voice sounded cheerful.

"Hi, Evie." Freddie kept his head in the cold drinks cabinet. He continued restocking the bottles. Then he turned aside and tidied the chocolate bar display.

"Is something wrong?"

"N-no-o," he stammered, finally looking at her. Out of the corner of his eye, he saw Jenny staring at him. "Actually, I have a headache. I thought about calling in sick but with the security review today..."

"What have you got to hide?" Jenny asked scornfully. "Of all the *Romano* employees, you're the easiest one to check out. You come to work at six in the morning, clock off at six in the evening. You walk home to play computer games until you start the process all over again."

"I've got Butch now," Freddie told Jenny. "That boy is more difficult than I expected. Not even swapping schools has made a difference."

"Marco told me there was trouble yesterday," Evie said. "He wanted Sebastian to take him to the hospital to make sure the teacher was all right."

Freddie frowned. He had forgotten Marco would have told her everything. He picked up his water bottle. Would Evie notice his shaking hands?

"What have you done?" Jenny said. "You think Piper and Romano are going to discover something, don't you? If they do, you're out of here, like Mike Kelly last month. He was selling information about Evie to a journalist."

"I-I haven't done anything. I-I w-wouldn't do anything to jeopardise Evie's safety."

"Then you've met someone, and they have a wicked past," Jenny persisted.

Freddie pretended he was busy. He glanced at Evie.

"Leave him alone, Jenny," Evie said. "You know Piper and Sebastian run the monthly review like an interrogation. It must be intimidating to face them, and poor Freddie isn't feeling well."

"It won't be long before we find out," Jenny said. "Here comes Blake now. Off you go, Freddie."

Freddie collected his four-page questionnaire from the counter next to Evie, and moved towards the door.

"I'll be praying for you," Evie called after him.

He tried to walk across the car park as if this was an ordinary day. Each step intensified the pounding in his head. As he entered the workshop, two Rottweilers ran over to inspect him. When the guard dogs had first arrived six years ago, he had been frightened of them. But Tiny and Fifi were friendly. A "Hello Freddie" chorus began as he passed old friends. He had been a mechanic here before the Boss made him the service station manager. Freddie breathed in the oily smells. He thought about how much the workshop had changed. The Boss had upgraded all the equipment, and there were more employees now.

The staff facilities were on the far side of the workshop: the break room, locker and change room, and the laundry. There was also a private gym, but Freddie had never used it. He knew the Boss spent hours there, maintaining his strength. The Boss had impressive muscles. He had once told Freddie exercise helped keep his mind sharp and was good for stress.

Piper Maxwell greeted Freddie at the door. "Take a seat. You know the drill." The Boss employed the ex-military man as his security consultant.

Freddie handed Piper his questionnaire, then moved around the couch to sit in his customary seat. The man didn't even look at the questionnaire, and Freddie relaxed a little. There were two coffee tables in the central space. The Boss and his deputy, Dave Henderson, sat opposite Freddie, on an identical black leather couch.

An unopened bottle of soft drink sat in front of Freddie's position. He picked it up. Condensation had pooled on the tabletop. He stared at the mark. He rocked the bottle in his hands before placing it back on the table. He took a deep breath and looked up.

The silence lengthened. Freddie met his employer's stony gaze, determined not to look away. Sebastian Romano was an intimidating man, a giant covered in extensive tattoos. There was a ragged scar on his forehead, another reminder that this interview was not to be taken lightly. This man had served a lengthy prison sentence. Freddie wasn't usually afraid of him, despite Romano's violent reputation. The Boss had always been fair with his employees. Freddie received a generous salary in exchange for his loyalty.

Piper took his seat beside the Boss and began asking Freddie a series of questions.

"Do you give your permission for this interview to be recorded?"

"Yes."

"How long have you worked here?"

"Ten years."

"In that time, have there been any allegations or complaints made against you?"

"No." Freddie shook his head and picked up the soft drink bottle.

"Has anyone approached you seeking information about your employer, or his wife?"

"No." Freddie uncapped the bottle and took a sip.

"Are you happy here?"

"Yes. I love my job. I don't want to work anywhere else."

These were familiar questions. The answers came easily. But the next ones could change everything.

⁣✿⁣

Abigail followed Butch out of the supermarket. He carried the shopping bags. Butch had insisted on paying. Freddie had left enough money and strict instructions. They emerged from a different exit onto the footpath outside the shopping centre. They stood at a set of traffic lights, where a crowd waited for the signal to change.

On the other side of the street was a massive two-storey black building. She caught glimpses of activity through openings in the wall facing the street. It seemed to be an auto-mechanic workshop. *Romano* was the legend painted across the only window. The walk signal lit up. Abigail hesitated as the other pedestrians surged forward. Butch grabbed her arm to prevent her from falling. Together, they were swept across to the other side. Abigail looked towards their apartment building, but Butch led her in the opposite direction.

"Where are we going?" she asked, struggling to keep up. Every muscle ached.

"You should exercise more." Butch laughed and kept moving.

"I do exercise," Abigail protested. "You seem to have forgotten what happened yesterday."

The boy halted. "Sorry," he said. She had the hood pulled down over her eyes. He stepped closer. "Thought it was just yer head. Where does it hurt?"

Everywhere. But she wasn't going to tell him. She studied the footpath.

"Hey, Butch," a voice called out. "Why aren't you in school?"

"Babysittin'," Butch shouted back, turning towards the black building. "Hey, Leonardo, meet Freddie's new girlfrien'. Abby, this is Leonardo Fontana, Marco's bruvva."

Abigail looked up. A young man wearing black overalls stepped through the gloomy doorway. Leonardo smiled as he wiped his oily hands on a rag. "Hey, Abby. Lucky you, spending your day with Butch. Looks like he's been fighting again. Can't keep Butch Cassidy out of trouble. Speaking of trouble, Butch, does Uncle Freddie know you're out with his 'girlfriend'?"

"Jus' gonna check in with him now. Talk later." Butch chuckled, moving on.

Abigail trotted after him. "You can't tell people I'm Freddie's girlfriend."

"Alright. Next person we meet, I'll tell them yer some stranger who slept in Freddie's bed las' night."

Abigail groaned. "You wouldn't!"

He didn't answer. When they arrived at the service station, Butch confidently entered the building. He walked to the counter. Abigail shuffled behind him, her hands in the hoodie pockets, her head bowed.

"Hey, Evie. Where's Freddie?" Butch asked.

"He's in the main building," a gentle voice answered. Abigail raised her head. A beautiful dark-haired woman smiled from behind the security panel – this must be Evie. "He should be back soon. Marco told me about the fight yesterday. I'm very disappointed to hear you've been in trouble again."

"I was pro-voked."

"Aren't you going to introduce us to your little friend," another woman asked. Abigail looked for the second speaker. This blonde woman's eyes were hard. She came across from the magazine display to stand beside Butch. Abigail looked down at the floor.

"Call 'er Abby. She's got another name, but it's a secret."

"Why is her name a secret?" the unfriendly blonde asked.

"What kind of trouble have you gotten into now?" Evie said at the same time, shaking her head. Her long dark hair shimmered with the movement. Abigail felt a stab of envy.

"Abby said not to tell anyone she's Freddie's girlfrien'," Butch said in a conspiratorial whisper. "She's worried what people will fink if they know she slept in 'is bed..."

Abigail turned away in embarrassment. She wrapped her arms across her chest, holding back unexpected tears. The hum of the refrigerated drinks cabinet intensified. Her heartbeat pounded in her ears. Her face burned, and then a cool chill made her shiver. Pins and needles in her extremities foretold another embarrassing fainting spell.

Evie appeared from behind the counter. Gently, this woman pulled back the hood. Abigail blinked, and tears rolled down her cheeks. When Evie reached out to touch her bruised face, Abigail crumpled to the floor.

"She does that a lot," Butch was saying when Abigail regained consciousness. "Not sure if it's from the fall yesterday, or 'cos she's pregnant."

If Abigail could have reached Butch, she would have tried to silence him. Her intention must have been clear because he stepped back.

The two women helped her up and took her behind the counter. There was a small office hidden from view. Abigail collapsed onto a swivel chair, which tried to throw her onto the floor. Evie grabbed the chair to save her, before passing her a bottle of water. While Evie waited with Abigail, the other woman talked to Butch. Abigail tried to listen.

"Don't worry about Butch," Evie said. "Jenny's a professional. She'll deal with him. And I'll talk to Freddie. I can't believe he came to work and left you with Butch." She shook her head, and then her eyes widened. "But Freddie doesn't know about the baby, does he?"

Abigail stared at Evie. "Freddie's not the father." Tears fell freely at her confession. "I only met him yesterday..."

"Shh," Evie said soothingly, gathering Abigail in a gentle hug. "God has brought you to me. I'm sure everything's going to be alright."

⁚✿⁛

Piper's voice seemed more menacing.

"Have you made any changes to your domestic situation? Any problems or concerns we ought to know about? Any new relationships you should declare?"

Freddie took another sip from his drink. He cleared his throat and put the bottle back on the table. Wiping his damp palms on his jeans, he glanced towards Dave Henderson, who leaned forward. Dave was taller than Freddie, but small in comparison to the other two inquisitors. The silence grew. Dave smiled as if to encourage Freddie.

It was easier to talk to Dave. Freddie kept his eyes focused on him. Freddie had been an apprentice for Dave's father. Mr Henderson Senior had arranged the transfer to Melbourne after Freddie's father turned up at Freddie's work in a drunken rage. That was the last time he had any trouble at work.

"B-Butch," Freddie began. "My n-nephew seems to attract trouble—"

Piper's phone beeped and the security agent leaned over to check the message. He smiled. "Let's take a little walk. On the way, you can tell us about Abby."

"Wh-why are y-you asking about Ab-bi-gail? I-I only met my new n-neighbour y-yesterday," Freddie spluttered as he stood. He followed them from the room.

"That's not the story your nephew's telling. He's at the service station introducing your new girlfriend to Evie."

"What? She's not my girlfriend. Just someone I met last evening. I don't even know if her name's Abigail."

"But she's the reason you're on edge?" Romano asked.

Freddie nodded. He started talking. By the time the four men arrived at their destination, he had unburdened himself of the whole story.

Discern – Identify or Detect

ॐ ☼ ॐ

*Romans 8:13 Selfish desires lead to death,
but allowing the Spirit to put selfishness to death brings life.*

ॐ ☼ ॐ

Butch and Jenny were waiting outside the rear entrance to the service station. Abigail was nowhere to be seen. Freddie had always kept his emotions in check, and was unprepared for the surge of adrenalin that flooded his system. He shoved his nephew against the wall. Surprise registered on the boy's face, and Butch did not attempt to defend himself.

"What kind of idiot are you?" Freddie asked. He shook the stocky teenager. Strong arms grabbed Freddie and pulled him away.

"Violence is not the answer," the Boss said. Freddie lowered his eyes to the ground, unable to meet anyone's gaze.

"Dave," the Boss continued, "take Butch back to the workshop. Keep him out of trouble. His uncle needs time to calm down."

"Freddie, I'm sorry," Butch said. "I thought bringin' her here was the smart thing to do. Men come looking for her. They knocked on our door, and I says only yer girlfrien' was with me. I waited till they was gone, 'n' I got her a hoodie for a disguise. I jus' wanna make sure enough people know the cover story. I come here to explain."

Butch was crying now. Freddie didn't know how to respond. Dave led the distraught teenager away.

Piper opened the door and went in. Romano looked at Freddie before following Piper. Freddie stood frozen in place.

Jenny Prescott came to him, and punched him on the arm. "Time to face the music."

He accompanied her inside. The space behind the counter seemed over-crowded. Piper stood immediately inside the office. The Boss waited outside the door. Abigail was seated on Freddie's chair. Evie had her arms around the woman. Evie whispered something to Abigail and then stepped aside. Abigail stared at the two imposing men, her face screwed up and wet with tears. She looked past Piper and the Boss towards Freddie. "I'm sorry."

Piper loomed over Abigail. "Butch said men came to the apartment looking for you?"

She nodded.

"Would they recognise you if they saw you?"

"Butch said they had a photo," Abigail said. "But it was taken – before. No, I don't think they'd recognise me."

Piper turned and signalled to Jenny, who left via the rear entrance. Through the reinforced glass, Freddie watched her pacing as she talked on her phone.

"The people who arranged the apartment for you – do you have their contact information with you?" Piper held out his hand. Abigail extracted a white card from her phone case. With a trembling hand, she passed it to the security consultant.

"What's going on?" the Boss asked.

"Romano, take Freddie back to the workshop. Keep him and his nephew with you until I tell you otherwise. Get someone else to work here. Freddie's going to be taking some well-earned leave."

Piper turned from the Boss to address Evie. "Are you still meeting with Marilyn for lunch? Take your new friend Abby with you. We can't send her back to the apartment until we know it's safe."

Piper turned back to the Boss. "Jenny's organising back-up. She's more than a match for anyone who might come looking for Abby in the meantime."

He turned back to Abigail. "Time for introductions. I'm Piper Maxwell. Does *Operation Phoenix* mean anything to you?"

Abigail blinked and looked away. She nodded.

"What name have they given you?"

"Abigail Golding. Do you know about me?"

"Not yet, but I'll be accessing the information as soon as I get back to base." Piper leaned even nearer.

Her eyes closed.

Freddie stepped forward, but the Boss held him back.

"Your face has taken a beating," Piper said. "That nose wasn't reset properly. The scars look like they're a few months old. Someone did a terrible job stitching them, unless you didn't get help in time... but these bruises are more recent. How did you get these new injuries?"

Evie answered this question. "Abigail is one of the teachers at *St Jerome's*. She was the teacher hurt when Butch got into a fight yesterday. Freddie knows nothing about any of this. He only met her last night when she came to his apartment looking for help."

"And how do *you* know this?" Piper asked, his eyes narrowing as he studied Evie.

"If you'd looked at Freddie's completed form, you would have noticed the new neighbour declaration. He didn't supply a name. Sorry, Freddie, but I looked through your answers. I was curious about why you seemed anxious. I guessed about the school bit. It seemed too big a coincidence. Marco had described the injured teacher. Then Abby-Abigail turns up."

Piper frowned. "Too many coincidences," he grumbled. "Next, I'm going to find out Abigail knows about the 'river wild and dangerous'."

Unexpectedly, Abigail cried out and hid her face in her hands. Everyone looked towards her.

"I think you have your answer," Evie said, as she knelt beside Abigail.

"Will someone please tell me what's going on?" Freddie asked. "What's *Operation Phoenix*? Who are these men who came to the apartment, and what do they want with Abigail? And why is Piper asking about a river?"

"God has given Piper a puzzle to solve, and each piece comes with a reference to a special river," Evie said. "I've suggested he add questions about the river on his questionnaire, but he's refused to listen. Piper won't admit God's in charge. He still thinks he can solve the mystery on his own."

Disturb - Alter the Position

ꙮ

*Ephesians 2:10 Through Christ we are created to do good works
that He prepared in advance.*

ꙮ

Freddie stumbled when the Boss slapped him on the back.

The older man laughed. "Love makes a fool of every man."

It was difficult enough keeping up with the giant's powerful strides as they walked across the car park to the *Romano* workshop. "How can I be in love? I've only just met her," Freddie said. Jenny had already shepherded Abigail and Evie away.

"You can keep your job, but only if you promise never to see Abby again."

Freddie stopped walking. He couldn't believe Sebastian Romano, a man he greatly admired, would expect him to choose. It was like he was seeing his hero for the first time.

Romano paused and smiled down at him. "There's your answer. Yesterday, you wouldn't have hesitated. You love your job. You tell us that month after month. But you don't love it enough to risk losing a possible future with Abby. Your heart has already decided for you."

"So, what do you want me to do? Give up my job on the unlikely possibility that I'm falling in love with her? What if she leaves and I never see her again?"

"I'm not the one to give advice," Romano said. "I refused to believe I could fall in love. I almost lost Evie before I had a chance to tell her how I felt. If God hadn't stepped in, she'd be dead."

Freddie stared at him. He had been present the night Romano first met his wife, though no-one realised the significance until later – Romano hated women, or so everyone had thought. The next day, Evie had been critically injured in an accident.

Romano had then surprised everyone by announcing his intention to marry Evie. In keeping with his character, he had followed through that declaration with determination. Evie's presence had brought many changes to Freddie's employer, and to the workplace that was Romano's kingdom.

She had been transformed as well, losing her shy awkwardness. Now Evie was a confident, beautiful woman.

Did the Boss see parallels between his own story and Freddie's encounter with Abigail? The giant resumed his march, slower this time because Freddie managed to keep up.

"I'm not like you," Freddie said. "Abigail's in danger. I'm not strong enough to protect her."

"You're more like me than you think," his employer said, slapping Freddie's shoulder again. Freddie looked at Romano, uncertain whether to be frightened or reassured.

"God had to talk to me about my desire to protect Evie. The more strategies I put in place, the greater the danger became. My enemies seemed to multiply. In the end, I had to accept that God could do a better job."

Could this conversation get any worse? First, the topic was love, and now Romano had brought God into it. Freddie kept quiet. Romano didn't pause when they entered the workshop. No-one broke the ominous silence. Freddie glanced sideways and caught someone staring after them. Romano marched forward, relentlessly steering Freddie towards the gym. He felt powerless to resist.

Romano pushed Freddie towards the treadmill. "Before you try to tell me you don't exercise, I know you walk to and from work every day. So, switch this machine on and start walking. You can set your own pace with this control." Freddie peered at the buttons. "It's not a race. You want to wear yourself out, not do yourself harm. You should still be able to talk. I'll send someone to keep you on task."

Romano activated the treadmill and demonstrated how the machine worked. After he dismounted, Freddie placed his feet on the moving belt. When he stumbled, Romano grabbed him. Freddie flinched. His heart rate rocketed as his mind threw him back to his childhood. The surge of adrenalin overruled the years of safety. It had been a decade since he escaped his abusive father.

What explanation was there for this terror? Freddie knew all about Romano's violent history. Twenty-six years in jail had hardened his employer, rendering him inflexible but fair. Yet the past six years had brought Freddie a sense of security. The tattooed giant had won his trust and loyalty.

Neither man said anything, but Romano put more distance between them. For a moment, Freddie thought he may have wounded his invulnerable employer. As he puzzled over this, he lost his concentration.

Without Romano's assistance, he flew off and hit the rear wall. He scrambled back to his feet and remounted the treadmill. His white knuckles gripped the chrome handles.

The giant did not refer to the incident. Instead, he pointed to a digital screen. "Here's the reading that tells you how far you've travelled. When you push this button, it will set the lap marker. Increase your speed as you gain confidence and keep going until you can't walk any further. Then push the button. Give yourself a ten-minute breather and then walk the same distance back. If I don't think you've taken my challenge seriously, I'll make you start over."

Freddie's emotions were out of control. Listening to Romano's dispassionate explanation, his fear morphed into something else.

"I want you exhausted to the point of resenting me," Romano concluded.

Freddie was there already. He glared at him, but kept his feet moving.

"I'd take you out and drop you somewhere, and make you walk home," Romano went on, "but I don't know that we have enough time. You need to be here when Piper reports back."

"Why do I have to do this?"

"You had trouble sleeping last night."

Freddie opened his mouth to protest that assumption.

Romano continued, "That won't be a problem tonight if you do as I say. Physical exhaustion should give you a few hours of peace."

Romano left without another word.

As he laboured on the treadmill, Freddie tried to guess who would be sent to watch him. His headache intensified. He walked a lonely three kilometres before anyone entered the room. He glanced up when Leonardo, the youngest apprentice, came to deliver a bottle of water. The nineteen-year-old was Evie's nephew, the son of her sister Sofia.

"Thanks," Freddie said, slowing the treadmill so he could drink.

"Don't slow down," Leonardo warned him. "That machine has a memory to analyse workouts. The Boss will check to see if you slacked off. He likes his victims to take themselves to the edge, and then more. While I stayed here when Mum was in Thailand, I joined him for a workout. Afterwards, I thought I would die. Evie said the Boss punishes his own body to keep his mind strong."

"You don't call him Uncle," Freddie said, in need of a distraction. "What's it like being related to him?"

"I'm still adjusting. He treats me like he did before, when I'm in the workshop. Only, now, there are times when he'll call me over to do something out of the ordinary. Like watching you. He told me I should keep you talking to take your mind off the challenge he's set you."

Freddie didn't respond.

Leonardo moved a bench seat and placed it closer to the treadmill.

"What happened this morning?" Leonardo asked. "Butch is cleaning out one of the storerooms. We've been told to leave him to do the job alone. What trouble's he in now? Does it have anything to do with the girl he tried to pass off as your girlfriend?"

Freddie almost fell off the treadmill. "How many other people did Butch talk to?" he muttered as he rebalanced himself.

"Hey, don't let it worry you. We all know not to take any notice of anything Butch says. I'm guessing he thought you'd be at the servo. He must have tried his con with Evie, and she called his bluff. That explains why everyone went over to the servo, but I can't work out why you're here on the treadmill."

"I lost my temper with Butch," Freddie said. Just thinking about the incident made him angry. Freddie adjusted the treadmill to take advantage of the boiling rage. "I haven't allowed myself to get angry for a long time. Romano wasn't happy that I resorted to violence."

Leonardo leaned forward. "Since when do you call him Romano?"

"Since he asked me whether I still want to work here."

"He threatened to fire you?"

"I'm going on leave when he releases me from here," Freddie conceded. "He's waiting for Piper to report on whether Abigail is a security risk. If she is, then I'm gone."

"Are you telling me she really is your girlfriend?" Leonardo shook his head. "I didn't think you were interested in dating anyone."

"I'm not. This is one big misunderstanding."

"Then tell the Boss, and get it sorted."

"Have you tried reasoning with him?" Freddie asked and kept walking. "He thinks I'm already in love with Abigail, and I should trust my future in God's hands."

Leonardo looked as uncomfortable with the God talk as Freddie was feeling. The teenager jumped when his phone beeped. Was the timing a coincidence? Leonardo looked at the message.

"Ah!" Leonardo said. "Reinforcements have arrived. I have to go, but don't let that persuade you to slow down."

Leonardo ran for the exit, leaving Freddie to worry what he meant by "reinforcements". A few minutes later, the door opened. A stranger wearing a business suit walked in. He looked about forty years old. At twenty-eight, Freddie suddenly felt young and inexperienced.

"Freddie," the stranger said as he approached, "I'm Pastor John Edwards. Romano asked me to come and see you. He said you have a personal problem that may impact on your work here."

John stood in front of the treadmill and waited patiently for Freddie to answer. Freddie recalled where he'd seen him before. This was the minister who officiated at Romano's wedding.

Freddie ground his teeth, desperate to avoid causing offence by speaking his mind. Why would Romano summon this stranger, except to follow up on his lecture about God?

When Freddie made no reply, John moved to the bench seat that Leonardo had vacated. He unbuttoned his jacket and sat down. He said nothing more. The ease with which this man accepted the silence only intensified Freddie's irritation. He glared at John.

The treadmill hummed. His legs continued to move, but they were hurting now. Soon, he would have to stop.

There was something melancholy in the way John sat on the bench. The pastor looked as if he had troubles of his own. Freddie liked to watch people. Now his mind looked for other signs. They were both about the same height, but John's slumped shoulders were broader. He looked as if he, too, was a stranger to the gym.

John's wavy brown hair was longer than Freddie remembered. The skin on his face was peeling as if he'd been sunburnt. Romano had made an emergency trip to Thailand last week. Maybe John Edwards had gone too? Romano obviously had influence over this religious man.

"What did Romano want you to talk to me about?" Freddie asked.

John almost convinced Freddie his answering smile was genuine. "You can talk about whatever you want. All Romano asked me to do was sit here and listen."

"And then what will you do? Will you report what I say to Romano?"

John sighed. "I will tell you the same thing I told Romano. Whatever you say remains between us. Unless you tell me something that indicates someone is in danger, or a crime is about to take place."

"How can I believe anything you say? It's obvious that you do whatever Romano tells you."

John shook his head. "Romano's a powerful man, but God is greater. Romano made the request, but I'm only here because God confirmed I should come. God said I would learn something about my own challenges by helping you deal with yours."

Freddie wrestled with John's honesty. He made up his mind and slapped the lap button with his hand. He stumbled from the treadmill, reaching for the adjacent wall in exhaustion. He finished the water, dropped the plastic bottle, and slid down the wall to sit on the floor. John seemed unmoved as he waited.

"Ten years ago, I told God I was done with him and I walked away," Freddie began, watching John closely for his reaction. "At first, I waited for God to punish me, but nothing happened. So I took that as permission to get on with making a new life for myself. Years of silence from God and then, suddenly, He's back. Why couldn't God stay out of my life? I would have been content if everything had stayed the same."

The way John lifted his head seemed to question Freddie's declaration. "What makes you think God is back?"

"Too much has happened in such a short time. And there are too many coincidences," Freddie muttered. "If only I could go back and do things differently."

"We don't usually get that luxury. Perhaps, if you start your story at the beginning, that will help you decide what to do now."

With a frown, Freddie searched his memory. He pushed ten-year-old recollections to the back of his mind. The present was crowded with enough possibilities. His nephew's arrival had opened old wounds, but perhaps he was already expecting trouble before then? When had the vague discontent with his solitary existence begun?

Fragments of conversations came to him. He examined them closely before he settled on a recent event. Freddie's headache intensified. Was it a coincidence this memory included his previous encounter with John Edwards?

"Something happened at Romano's wedding," Freddie began. John leaned forward. "I was sitting with my work friends. I'm used to them ribbing me about not drinking alcohol, but then someone made a joke about why I was single. They said I should stand up with the women to catch Evie's bouquet. I laughed it off, telling them catching a bunch of flowers wouldn't be enough incentive. I said the unlucky woman who convinced me to marry her would have to turn up at my door and throw herself into my arms. They thought the idea was hilarious. Until now, I haven't thought any more about it."

John said nothing.

Freddie frowned again, reaching for his discarded water bottle. "I remember how they laughed when Evie's sister, Sofia, caught the bouquet. Someone said I'd be in trouble if she turned up on my doorstep wanting to get married. Neither of her husbands lasted very long. Leonardo told them to stop disrespecting his mother; everyone went quiet about it."

Was it Freddie's imagination, or had John gone pale beneath his tan? Perhaps it wasn't Romano who had compelled this unassuming man to go to Thailand. Had John Edwards crossed Sofia's path at the wedding and fallen for that worldly woman's charm?

"You're in love with Sofia Fontana," Freddie announced. "That's why Romano sent for you. He knows you want to rescue her, but it could cost you everything. God is messing with your life too."

"You have it all wrong," John said. "I'm the one who messed up my life. Now I'm waiting for God to show me how He can fix it."

Freddie glanced away while he considered that response. His eyes locked on the water cooler on the far side of the well-equipped gym, next to the locker room door. It reawakened his thirst.

He pushed himself to his feet. Every muscle ached. Slowly, he approached the water cooler. Waiting for the bottle to refill, Freddie's discomfort reignited his desire to flee. He needed to get away from this place. It was then he saw the choice before him.

John Edwards had not moved. What was to stop Freddie from exiting via the locker room? He would be through the other doors and past Reception before anyone could stop him.

The temptation grew. He turned off the tap, took a sip from his bottle and glanced over his shoulder at John. Did Freddie have the courage to leave? Romano expected absolute obedience. If this was a test of loyalty, then a small act of defiance would be costly.

Freddie remembered the last time he had walked away from everything that mattered. Ten years suddenly felt like a life sentence. Tears pricked his eyes, but he was determined to keep them hidden. He made his decision.

With renewed purpose, he returned to the treadmill. First, he wound back the speed so he could step onto the moving belt. Gradually, he increased the tempo. Then he activated the counter. The digital screen began counting the distance remaining.

His previous walking had taken his thoughts to a dark place. Now he had to find the courage to return to the light.

"Tell me your story, John," Freddie said, "then maybe we'll be able to work out what God wants us to do next."

Display - Make Evident

🟘 ☼ 🟒

Romans 15:1 (WEB)
We who are strong ought to bear the weaknesses of the weak,
and not to please ourselves.

🟘 ☼ 🟒

On the second level of the nearby shopping centre, Abigail sat in a padded booth in the corner of a café. Her mind swirled with confusion as she huddled in the shadows. If only she had a sketchbook and pencil.

Abigail's quick character sketches were insightful. She was certain she could capture the qualities that assured her she could trust Evie. She might also gain an understanding of the terror Jenny inspired.

Abigail folded her hands together, pressing them on the tabletop to keep them still. Drawing in public was forbidden. Her creative gift drew too much attention, making it easier for her enemies to find her.

Abigail squeezed her eyes shut and bit her lip. Enough, she told herself. Don't let the darkness win. She wasn't allowed to draw, but no-one could stop her using her imagination.

Reopening her eyes, she looked across the café to where Evie stood at the counter. That gentle woman would be at home in a pastoral setting, beside a tranquil pool. There should be a bubbling waterfall, a flowing stream and beautiful flowers. She would be smiling, serene and at peace, surrounded by the animals of the field. Abigail's imagination supplied the details.

In her mind, pale-skinned Evie wore flowing robes, brilliant colours to celebrate her dark-haired beauty. Abigail considered her dreamlike scene and discovered an unexpected detail. There was a crown of white roses on the imaginary princess's head.

A movement captured her attention. Abigail looked at Jenny. In a blink, the artist added a warrior-maiden to the imaginary scene. Jenny stood watchful, looking for danger. No harm must reach the beautiful princess. Abigail's imagination painted Jenny in darker tones. She added spiky blonde hair and blue Celtic tattoos that stood out against her pale skin. She dressed the lithe bodyguard in black leather leggings and a belted tunic. There was a spear in her hand, a broad sword with a jewelled pommel at her hip, a bow and quiver of arrows across her back. The stillness of her pose belied her readiness to attack.

What kind of trouble was this woman expecting? The bodyguard moved towards the princess, throwing a glance in Abigail's direction. The vision trembled as reality returned.

Jenny stood with Evie at the counter. They both turned to greet a brown-haired woman who appeared beside them. There was also a child, a miniature version of the new woman. Evie's smile brightened as she hugged them both. Jenny was watchful but unconcerned at this intrusion. Evie pointed towards Abigail. The child skipped over.

Abigail watched the girl intently as the real world faded again. She smiled in wonder.

"Hi, I'm Lilly, and I'm five." Her loud voice broke the illusion. "I've been to the dentist, and now Mummy's buying me lunch. Then Mummy's taking me to buy new school shoes. What's your name, why are you so brown, and what happened to your face?"

Abigail gasped.

"Lilly, mind your manners," another voice said. "Hello, Abby. I'm Marilyn Henderson." The woman lowered herself onto the seat beside Abigail. She held out her hand. Abigail accepted the formal handshake, self-conscious after Lilly's comments. Marilyn's grip was firm and confident, the perfect accompaniment to her smile. Abigail couldn't help staring. There was something special about this woman. Could she see into her troubled soul? Abigail blinked.

"Evie said you've had an eventful few days," Marilyn continued. "There's no need for you to answer any of Lilly's questions. You can sit here and say nothing if that's what your heart tells you to do."

Lilly plonked herself beside her mother. The pink backpack slipped from her shoulders, and thumped onto the table. The girl unzipped it, producing a teddy bear which she sat on the table in front of them. Next, Lilly brought out a colouring book and a sparkly pencil case. The backpack fell to the floor. Lilly chattered as she flipped the pages of the book before making her selection.

"Mummy says I can have ice cream if I sit and colour quietly," Lilly told Abigail. "And if I do an extra good job, I can have a sundae with topping and sprinkles and lollies."

The child opened the pencil case and took out her pencils, lining them up carefully on the table beside the book. "What's your favourite colour?" Lilly asked Abigail, who reached out and touched a pencil. "Pink?" Lilly grinned. "Mine too."

Abigail watched the child colouring in, and her tears overflowed. She looked away. Evie turned from the counter. Jenny was also on the move. Catching Abigail's gaze, Jenny nodded to her before disappearing from view. Evie brought over a tray of soft drinks, which she placed on the table. Taking the seat beside Lilly, Evie distributed the drinks.

"Dry ginger ale for you and me, Abby," Evie said. "I've found it helps settle my stomach. I'm guessing you know what

I'm talking about? Nausea was my first sign three weeks ago. My twins are due in the middle of May."

Evie paused, allowing space for Abigail to speak. Instead, Abigail nodded. She cupped her hands around the offered glass and took a polite sip.

"I've been sick since the beginning," Abigail conceded.

"How long have you been teaching at *St Jerome's*?" Evie asked.

"Yesterday was my first day. I haven't made a good start. I replaced a teacher who had a car accident, and now they have to find a replacement for me too."

"What subjects do you teach?" Marilyn asked.

Abigail hated deception. "Here, I'm teaching Maths and Science for the year sevens and eights."

"And that's how you know my nephew, Marco?" Evie asked. "He was very upset about what happened. He wanted Sebastian to drive him to the hospital to find out how you were."

"Marco lives with you?" Abigail asked. "He doesn't live with his mother?"

"He's only staying with us for a few weeks. His mother, my sister Sofia, was on holiday in Thailand when her fiancé was killed. Marco will return to live with her after she's recovered from her injuries."

Abigail shivered. Another heartbreaking story. Was there no peace left in this world? Silence descended. A glance between Marilyn and Evie reminded Abigail her presence was an intrusion. Abigail took up the paper serviette Evie had placed before her and folded it into an origami crane.

Why had she agreed to come with these women? She remembered her confusion while recovering from her blackout at the service station. The paper crumpled between her fingers, the crane misshapen. Powerful men had crowded around her, while the kind neighbour cowered in their shadow. Gone was the peaceful confidence from Freddie's face. Abigail knew she must be compliant, to save him from further embarrassment.

"Here is the waitress with our meals," Marilyn said. As the tray was unpacked, Marilyn noted the extra plates. "Someone must be hungry today. What happened to Jenny? It's not like her to leave us for so long."

"Two of Jenny's colleagues will be joining us," Evie said. "Piper messaged to say they were on their way. Jenny stepped out onto the concourse to meet them."

Abigail looked at the huge sandwich Evie put in front of her. Evie added a bowl of garden salad, then took half of the wholemeal sandwich and put it on another plate.

"I know you said you weren't hungry," Evie told Abigail, "but you should have protein. You need something substantial to keep your blood sugar up. I can only manage half a sandwich. You will help me if you eat the other half of mine. Eat as much as you can, and you may be surprised at how much better you feel."

"Uncle Seb tells Evie that all the time," Lilly piped up, waving her ham and cheese sandwich at Abigail. "He gets really bossy if Evie leaves anything. Today, we're all eating healthy 'cos fried food makes Evie sick."

Marilyn leaned over and whispered to her daughter.

Abigail kept her eyes lowered. She took a small bite of the chicken, cheese and avocado sandwich and chewed carefully. Evie chatted with the others as they ate.

"Here's Jenny now," Evie announced.

Three women approached their table. Jenny's companions were remarkable in appearance. They might have walked out of a comic book. Both of the unfamiliar women carried themselves like champions.

Abigail imagined them wearing armour and wielding ancient weapons. Now she understood the need for the largest booth, twice the size of all the others. It had a reserved tag on it for a good reason.

One of the champions was exceptionally tall. She wore her reddish-blonde hair in a thick braid, pulled back severely from her square face. Her glare was fierce. She resembled a Viking shield-maiden. The other woman was shorter, broad-shouldered and muscular. More like a Mongolian warrior princess. Her skin was dark like Abigail's, and her eyes shone like polished ebony.

Abigail's artistic fingers twitched, longing to borrow one of Lilly's pencils. Again, she remembered her changed situation. As she stilled her fingers, her curiosity was replaced by another emotion. These women, with their savage self-assurance, emphasised Abigail's shameful vulnerability.

"Evie Romano, this is Sigrid Ericson," Jenny said, introducing the taller woman first. "And this is Xanda Jadaran."

Evie smiled and welcomed each woman. "This is my friend Marilyn Henderson, and her daughter Lilly. And here is our new friend Abby..."

Evie paused and looked to Abigail for confirmation.

Abigail blinked. "A-abigail G-golding."

"Nice to meet you, Abigail," Xanda said in a deep voice, sliding along the padded bench to sit close to her.

Abigail's heart raced. With all that extra room, there was no need for this woman to be so near. Sigrid sat beside Xanda while Jenny moved to Evie's side. This felt like setting up a chessboard for battle.

Jenny allocated the remaining sandwiches. Abigail nibbled cautiously, while Xanda studied her. Abigail's throat closed. Unable to swallow, she put down the half-eaten sandwich. She looked across to Evie apologetically. She coughed, and Xanda pushed her drink into her hand.

Evie was sympathetic. "It takes time to get used to people watching you eat."

"And knowing where you are all the time," Jenny added, nodding to Xanda who removed a white box from her pocket. She placed it on the table. Jenny opened the box to reveal a plain silver bangle nestled on the satin lining. "Put this on," Jenny commanded. Abigail hesitated.

"Don't be frightened." Lilly bounced on the seat and held out her arm to wave a similar bangle. "Evie has one, and so does Mum. Now you can be in Evie's special club."

Abigail stared at the child. Xanda removed the bangle from the box. The armband had an almost invisible hinge. Xanda flipped it open to wrap it around Abigail's chubby wrist before clicking it firmly into place.

"Don't go anywhere without it," Jenny growled. "Even sleep with it on. Only take it off to shower. If anyone asks, it's an ordinary piece of jewellery."

Abigail looked at the bangle. It sat beside the plastic wristband the hospital had told her to wear for forty-eight hours. What had these women committed her to?

೮⟡ೞ

Freddie was still waiting for John Edwards to speak. The pastor sat on the bench, looking at his hands.

"If I didn't have these blisters," John said, holding up his palms, "I might convince myself this whole mess was a bad dream. I'm watching you suffer on the treadmill, and you have my sympathy. Piper and Romano tested my limitations while we were in Thailand. I'm sure they regretted taking me when they realised I was going to slow them down. I struggled to use a machete when we were making our way through the jungle to rescue Evie's sister, Sofia.

45

"All the time, I was asking God what I was doing there, and I'm still trying to make sense of it all. You mentioned coincidences. Then you shouldn't be surprised that my story starts at the same wedding. While your friends were tormenting you about being single, I was arguing with Sofia. She was angry with me because she didn't want Evie to marry Romano.

"I kept bumping into Sofia everywhere I went. I thought God wanted me to help her. I wasn't looking for romance. I'm divorced and raising two children.

"Piper Maxwell – you know Piper?" John paused for confirmation. "He works both sides of the law. He came to warn me off because Sofia was his cousin's fiancée. But he was too late. One of her friends was murdered, and someone tried to assassinate her fiancé. Then Sofia got into trouble in Thailand. Piper and Romano took me with them, so she would have someone sympathetic to take care of her."

John shuffled his feet. "I didn't know I was half in love with her already. Now I can't stop thinking about what it felt like to have her in my arms—"

Freddie swore, missed a step and flew off the treadmill. "I know exactly how you feel."

Dispose – Deal with Conclusively

୧୦ ✡ ୧୦

Deuteronomy 8:3a He humbled you, teaching you hunger, and then He fed you, so you might learn that His word will sustain you.

୧୦ ✡ ୧୦

Romano stepped quietly into the break room and watched Freddie and John. They were silent. Neither noticed his presence. Romano considered the reasons for bringing this pair together. It had been Evie's idea.

Romano was learning to appreciate Evie's quiet wisdom. She was certain God was at work here. His curiosity stirred. What would Evie discover about the new woman? He sent a quick prayer heavenward.

> Here I am again, God. I still find it daunting to approach You like this, but Evie says You're always listening. Thanks for the assurance that You know everything.
>
> When Freddie showed up this morning, I expected some domestic crisis. There have been plenty of those since Butch arrived. But nothing like the trouble we have uncovered.
>
> You know who Abby is, and what danger she brings with her. Please guide Piper as he seeks answers. Evie insisted I involve John in this, and I have to trust that she's listening to You.
>
> Thanks for the reminder that You're in charge. Help me to stop worrying about the unknown details, and teach me to trust You more.

Freddie and John sat on opposite black couches. The silence suggested they had shared their stories and talked about their struggles. Freddie was wearing fresh clothes, his hair damp from a recent shower. He sat with his eyes closed and seemed physically spent.

Romano moved to the coffee machine and pulled out four cups. He prepared the beverages with the confidence of a barista. He heard movement behind him and turned to find John watching him. "Is there news?" John asked. Freddie opened his eyes and looked around the room, finally fixing his gaze on Romano.

"Piper's on his way," Romano said. "Jenny and Evie are keeping Abby busy. Two *Maximum Security* agents have joined them in case there's trouble. I've asked Dave to keep everyone away from the break room until I give the signal. That way, we can hear what Piper has to say without any interruptions."

"What kind of trouble?" Freddie asked.

"Piper's radar lit up as soon you walked in for your interview," Romano said. "He didn't even look at your questionnaire. He knew something was wrong. Then we arrived at the servo to find Jenny already in action. Interrogating Butch and making snap decisions. Piper's response when he set eyes on Abby told me her appearance took even him by surprise."

"Piper doesn't like surprises," John added.

"I thought Piper worked for you?" Freddie said. "You talk as if he's the one giving the orders."

"It suits him to let everyone think he's following my orders," Romano said. He passed a steaming cup of coffee to each of them. "I've been too focused on my corner of Melbourne, but Piper has a global reach. John and I learned that much when we went to Thailand."

"When did you realise he was playing his own game?" Freddie asked.

"After Evie was kidnapped," Romano said, placing the other cups on the table. He remained vigilant beside the closest door. "I talked to John about my suspicions. It was only when Evie's sister, Sofia, was targeted that we discovered something bigger was going on."

"How do you know you can trust Piper?" Freddie asked. Romano looked to John to answer this one.

"Freddie, you talked to me about the coincidences that brought Abigail to you," John began. "Piper's becoming concerned about all the coincidences that surround him. Like you, he's beginning to think God is after him."

"He's in trouble then," Freddie moaned. "God doesn't let up until He has you cornered with nowhere to go."

Only Romano had noticed the security consultant slip into the room while Freddie was speaking. Piper's expression was stern. Romano slapped him on the back to announce his presence, then rounded the nearest couch and took a seat where he could watch both the other men. Piper sat beside him.

"It's too early to write me off," Piper growled, accepting the coffee. An uncomfortable silence grew. Romano waited to see who would give in.

"What did you find out?" Freddie asked.

"First, let me explain how I knew where to go for the information," Piper began.

Freddie's mouth dropped open. He seemed surprised that Piper was talking directly to him.

"Last week, I was approached for a list of possible safe-houses. I knew the apartment next to Freddie had been vacant for a while, so I put it on the list. When he arrived at work with all the hallmarks of a major crisis, I immediately knew the source of the problem.

"It was obvious that witness protection had made a problematic placement. Something must have happened between Freddie and the new neighbour. Of course, I knew nothing about the agency's intention to place their witness at *St Jerome's* school. If they had provided that information, I would have steered them away from this locality. Abby's arrival at school made encounters with Marco and Butch inevitable. That would lead to Evie getting involved and more trouble for me."

Neither Romano nor John took the bait. Freddie was apparently too stunned to say anything.

Piper smiled before continuing. "Two things about Abby's placement raised alarms. First, she was provided with inadequate supervision. Left to settle into the apartment without help. If she had been managed properly, Freddie would never have met her. The agency would have recognised Butch from the incident at school. She would have been placed elsewhere."

"And the second?" Freddie asked.

"Someone appearing at the safe-house a day after placement indicates a security breach. It doesn't matter that they don't know her new identity yet..."

"So, who is she?" Freddie asked.

"Not anyone you would have heard of," Piper replied. "An ordinary woman who realised a serious crime was about to be committed. She stepped in to defend the potential victims. She did the right thing by reporting what she had seen and heard to the police. It should have ended there, but the criminals discovered her identity. She was forced into hiding until it is time for her to testify in court."

"There's a lot you're not telling us," Freddie said. "She has terrible nightmares—"

"The people looking for her are determined to ensure she never testifies," Piper said bluntly. "There's been more than one attempt to silence her. The witness protection team keep moving her on. Unless someone identifies the security leak, she doesn't stand a chance."

"So, what are you going to do?" Freddie rose to his feet. "Are you going to let evil win, or are you going to bring Abigail some justice?"

Piper stood, towering over Freddie, but the service station manager held his gaze. John also rose and walked around to stand beside Freddie. Piper turned toward Romano.

"The usual arrangement?" Piper asked. "You agree to pay for my team's expenses and follow my instructions precisely?"

Romano nodded.

Piper faced Freddie again. "Before I tell you what I require, Freddie, you need to know that Abby is pregnant. This child is a constant reminder of the evil she is trying to escape. She may be permanently scarred, incapable of love, and unable to trust you."

Freddie's face went white. John lowered him back to the couch.

"I-it d-doesn't m-make any d-difference." Freddie shook himself and glared at Piper. "What you want me to do?"

Piper remained standing. "Freddie, you're going to give Abby up."

John restrained Freddie from leaping to his feet again. Freddie threw off his hand but indicated he would sit still and listen.

Piper continued. "I want you to act like you're angry but compliant. Make it clear you're unhappy with the injustice

Romano has meted out. You need to behave as if you're trying to win back your good reputation and save your job.

"Romano's going to give you other work to do, away from the service station. He'll spread the story that you're being disciplined for the trouble Butch has brought to the workshop. You can't tell your nephew the truth. Let him think you're annoyed because he humiliated Abby in front of Evie. Butch must think he's ruined any chance you had for a relationship with Abby."

"How is this going to help Abby?" Freddie asked.

Piper glared at Freddie. "Her enemies must think she's isolated and friendless, while all the time she's watched and protected. This will be a closely guarded secret. Tell no-one."

Piper turned towards John. "That prohibition goes for you too, John. By choosing to stand with Freddie, you've volunteered to be one of my players. I need you to stick close to Freddie to keep him sane, and focused on the end game. Romano and I won't have any direct contact with him until the danger is over. Any information for Freddie will have to come from you. I know you have a problem hiding the truth. Your cover story is that Evie has asked you to counsel Freddie about his anger problem."

Piper took his seat on the couch beside Romano. The instructions continued. "Romano, get Dave to discuss Freddie's violent attack on his nephew with the other employees. Convince them that Freddie's gone rogue and is in danger of losing his job. Make it look as if Evie stepped in to plead on Freddie's behalf, but you want nothing more to do with him."

"What's this 'other work' you want me to provide for Freddie?" Romano asked.

"Good question." Piper smiled. "Do you remember your Aunt Constance's apartment? She's been dead for months, and you still haven't cleared it out. It's in the same apartment block where Freddie lives, one of the older ones on the ground floor. If you'd been to visit it, you'd know it has private access to both the street and the rear garden. With security cameras already in place, it's a much better hiding place should Abby need to disappear. Freddie's going to clear out your aunt's possessions and then redecorate it.

"This reminds me, Freddie. Your long-lost cousin Sigrid is moving in with you today. How you manage to accommodate her into your small apartment is your problem. You might need some new furniture, but your guest will take care of that. Ask Romano if you can be his tenant when Aunt Constance's larger apartment is ready. That will give you an incentive to finish the work faster."

"How am I supposed to convince Butch about a long-lost relative?" Freddie asked, his head falling forward into his hands. His physical exhaustion was obvious.

"Leave that to me," Romano said, rising to his feet. There would be time to talk with Piper after John had removed Freddie from the premises. Romano strode to the door leading to the workshop. He stepped into the open space. The two guard dogs came running to greet him. He gave them a firm pat and settled them at his feet.

With a mighty roar, Romano shouted: "Butch, come here!"

The dogs barked in excitement, leapt up and began searching for a reason for the alarm. All activity in the workshop came to a halt as everyone turned towards the rear storeroom. Cautiously, the boy's head appeared, and then he stepped into the open. The dogs raced over to meet him, and the teenager hesitated.

"Bring him to me!" Romano bellowed. The dogs shepherded the running boy towards him. Everyone watched his progress. There had only been a few occasions when Romano had raised his voice.

"Freddie's in big trouble because of you," Romano roared. "Take him home. I'm sending John Edwards with you to make sure nothing else happens on the way."

Butch was speechless. Romano continued. "After the prank you played this morning, I wanted to get rid of you both – Evie's upset. But she asked me to forgive you. Keep Freddie out of my way, until I calm down. Piper tracked down some distant relative of yours. She's coming to stay with you to make sure Freddie doesn't try to hurt you again. Now go."

The boy was frozen to the spot.

Romano gave him a benign shove and left him with a parting warning. "Stay. Out. Of. TROUBLE!"

John emerged from the break room supporting Freddie. Butch rushed over and added his muscle to get his shattered uncle out of the building. Butch looked back over his shoulder. Romano hid his laughter at the boy's eagerness to escape. It had been a long time since he had played the role of an angry enforcer.

Romano remembered the attitude that had brought him through twenty-six years of prison. Not once had he surrendered control to those who wanted to dominate him.

He turned to look over the workshop, where his employees were resuming their work. Romano would have to rebuild the comfortable peace that characterised this workplace. Evie's expertise would be essential to accomplish that.

He signalled to Dave, who was already marching towards him. Romano ushered him into the break room, where Piper was making more coffee. The door slammed behind them.

Disfigure - Spoil the Appearance

ဢ ☼ G

*Ephesians 1:18a May the eyes of your heart be enlightened,
so that you may experience the hope of His calling.*

ဢ ☼ G

The waitress had cleared the plates from the café table, and Marilyn and Lilly had left.

Everyone stared at Abigail.

"What cover story did they give the school to explain your appearance?" Jenny asked.

"A student experiment that went wrong in the science lab," Abigail said.

"And what really happened?"

"Apart from the beating? Someone took a disliking to the colour of my skin, and tossed industrial bleach over me. I was screaming, and a bystander turned on the fire hose and saved me. The doctors said I was lucky I didn't lose my sight."

"Have you tried covering the damage with cosmetics?" Xanda asked.

"My skin is too sensitive."

"And is that why they didn't fix your broken nose?" Jenny continued.

Abigail shook her head sadly. "It helps disguise me..."

Sigrid snorted. "I bet a man told you that!"

"But surely they could have done something about your hair?" Evie said. "There's a hairdresser here that takes walk-ins. I went there when I needed to cover up the scar from my accident. We could take you there now."

Abigail went rigid. She imagined slipping from her seat and cowering on the floor under the table. Evie reached out and patted her hand.

"Something has to be done," Evie said. "Your hair makes you stand out in the crowd, which is the opposite of what you want if this is your disguise. I'm guessing that the bleach burned your hair, but I don't understand why it's so short on this side. Did you try and fix it yourself?"

Memories choked Abigail's voice. "S-someone tried to cut it, but I-I couldn't handle it. It was like it was happening again. I screamed so much, the neighbours called the police. I had to move house because of it. Afterwards, I felt terrible. I knew these people weren't trying to harm me, but I couldn't stop myself. They said I needed to see someone specialising in trauma recovery. In the meantime, I would have to learn to deal with it."

"Butch said the men who came looking for you had a photo," Jenny reminded Abigail. "When they work out their mistake and find someone who can describe you now, your hair will be a defining feature. We should do everything we can to make it harder to track you down. Your enemies appear to be both resourceful and persistent."

"I don't think I will ever be safe again. I didn't expect to escape from them the first time," Abigail confessed sadly. "They said they were going to kill me."

She sniffed, and unfolded her origami crane to blow her nose on the napkin. "I didn't realise the trouble I was in. I told the police what I knew, and thought everything would go back to normal. But they found out who I was and where I lived..." Abigail took a deep breath. Her voice faded to a whisper. "I tried to defend myself, but there were four of them..."

Dispel - Drive Away

ঙ ☼ ন

Ephesians 3:20
He can do exceedingly more
than we ask or think,
working within us with power.

ঙ ☼ ন

Abigail lurched between Evie and Xanda as Jenny drove like a maniac. The unfamiliar landscape passed in a tinted blur. Their dark van turned into a side street more like a construction site than a row of warehouses. The whole area was being redeveloped.

Jenny acted as if she owned the road, narrowly avoiding a collision with a huge truck. The roaring engine and screeching tyres went unnoticed beneath the industrial clamour. Jenny raced towards a high metal fence that barred their way at the end of the street. At the last minute, the van squealed to a halt.

Sigrid leapt from the front passenger seat. The sound of the slamming door was muffled by the external din. She ran to the heavy gate and began to drag it open. Jenny didn't wait. When there was a gap, Jenny sped up. As they whizzed past, Abigail glimpsed Sigrid dragging the gate closed behind them. Now, the dark van was hidden inside the solid perimeter fence.

Abigail faced forward again. Jenny zoomed towards a large grey building that squatted beside an empty car park. Jenny swerved to follow a painted sign pointing towards the delivery bay.

Rounding the corner, Jenny rushed toward a roller door that was rising too slowly. Abigail cried out and threw her arms over her head.

Jenny laughed as she jerked the van to a stop. "Everyone out."

Abigail opened her eyes. The van was parked inside the empty warehouse. Xanda wrenched open the passenger door and dragged her out. Abigail's whole body was shaking. Evie scrambled after her, seeming almost as nervous as she was. Thumps from the van's rear compartment were followed by Jenny's reappearance with a large bag. The shadowy space was growing darker. Abigail looked to where the roller door was closing again. A dark figure slipped under the door with seconds to spare.

"Hey!" Sigrid shouted as she scrambled to her feet. The thud of metal on concrete as the door dropped into place rang out in the enclosed space. The noise from the neighbourhood construction faded to a dull clamour. "When did this turn into one of your commando training exercises?"

"Wouldn't want you to get soft," Jenny laughed. "Follow me."

Evie caught hold of Abigail's arm, and they clung to each other. They hurried to keep up with the bodyguard. It was so dark they might lose Jenny in the gloom. The building's exterior windows were shuttered. Fractured beams of dusty sunlight fell from somewhere overhead. The sound of Sigrid and Xanda's footsteps brought up the rear.

Jenny produced a small torch and located a locked door in a concrete wall. She pressed her hand to a black metal box set at shoulder height. A row of blinking red lights flashed on. One by one, they turned green.

Jenny pulled the door open to a dark room.

It seemed vacant. Marching forward, Jenny unlocked a second door which led into another windowless room.

Overhead lights blinked on. Abigail whirled back towards the darkness in time to see Sigrid close the door behind them. The agent confirmed it had relocked.

Evie pulled on Abigail's arm. They went forward into a room furnished with desks and chairs. Jenny left through another door. The group entered a labyrinth of smaller rooms connected by narrow hallways. Their footsteps echoed in the silence.

Jenny paused outside a door with faded lettering. She pushed it open to reveal a pristine washroom, complete with a wall of mirrors.

"You can scream all you like in here," Jenny said. "No-one will hear you."

Abigail shrank closer to Evie, who trembled beside her. Sigrid stood in front of the only way out.

Jenny studied Abigail. "Sigrid, go and get a couple of chairs. It looks like this is going to take longer than I thought. And leave the door open. Abby needs convincing she can trust us."

"What are you talking about?" Evie asked.

"I've brought some wigs for Abby to try, but first that hair has to go," Jenny said, as she opened her bag. "It's too thick and tangled for a wig to sit naturally. Here are the clippers. If I show you how to use them, Evie, do you think you could shave her head? I don't think she trusts anyone else."

Sigrid was back with the chairs. Jenny pushed Abigail onto one and wheeled it in front of the mirrors. Evie closed her eyes for a moment. Her smile returned, and then she dragged another chair over. Evie's lips were moving, but Abigail couldn't hear anything. Was Evie praying? Abigail looked in the mirror. Jenny's stony reflection held her gaze.

Evie picked up the clippers and tested the operating mechanism.

"Just do it," Abigail whispered, closing her eyes. Then she felt the metal implement vibrating across her scalp.

Something fluttered against her cheek, and a scream awoke deep within her. Her hand swatted at the falling hair.

An answering cry came from Evie. The buzzing ceased. The clippers hit the floor. Abigail's eyes flew open as Jenny grabbed her flailing hands. Evie was holding the side of her face with tears streaming down her cheeks.

"Show me," Xanda said. Evie pulled her hand away. The red mark stood out against Evie's pale skin. Xanda passed Evie a water-soaked wad of paper towel before turning back to Jenny. "I don't envy you having to explain that black eye to Piper."

"I'm sorry! So very, very sorry!" Abigail cried, pulling away from Jenny. "Evie, I never meant to hurt you."

"What just happened?" Jenny demanded.

"I-I'm s-s-sorry," sobbed Abigail. "I c-can't s-s-stand anything tou-touching m-my f-face. N-not s-since..."

"It's okay," Evie said, and she gently patted Abigail's hand. "Why don't we try again? Do you think you could use the clippers?"

Xanda passed Abigail some paper towel to blow her nose. Abigail's reflection frowned as her shaking hand accepted the clippers. The sliding switch activated the blades. Buzzzzz. The vibrations ran up her arm. Abigail yelped. Evie caught the clippers before they fell.

Abigail tried again. In the mirror, she saw the metal teeth come closer to her scalp. A high-pitched keening filled the air. Her reflection was wailing. Abigail closed her eyes.

"I can't do it."

No-one said anything. Evie removed the clippers from Abigail's hand. Jenny stormed out, with Sigrid and Xanda in her wake. Evie wrapped her arms around Abigail, rocking her until the sobbing ceased.

"I haven't always been like this," Abigail told Evie. "I used to be strong and brave. My foster parents told me my boldness would get me into trouble one day, but I didn't believe them.

"I thought I could stand up to anything and anyone because God had my back. But then I discovered sometimes God allows bad things to happen for a greater purpose."

Evie was silent for a long time. Finally, she asked, "Do you know what that greater purpose is?"

"I have a gift," Abigail whispered, gesturing with her hands in the air. "A photographic memory and the ability to draw what I remember to perfection. I could draw you a realistic portrait of the men who hurt me. God helped me stay alive, so I could share my story. I have to make sure they never hurt anyone ever again.

"It took me a while to realise God had a plan. I knew He could have stepped in and rescued me, and yet He didn't. I was frightened and confused. But then I met the man giving the orders, and everything became clear. God helped me remember."

"What did you remember?" Evie asked.

"This was not the first time I had been his prisoner. Until I saw him again, I had convinced myself it was a dream, a childhood nightmare. When I saw that man, I knew everything was real. He was older, but his eyes were the same. He didn't like the look of me – then or now – the colour of my skin and my dark hair. He said it would be easier to sell me if I was blonde. When I heard those words, something unlocked in my mind.

"I screamed at him. I asked what he'd done with my sister – I didn't even know I had a sister until then. What had happened to Ruthie? I remembered, but so did he. He told the others I was the little black girl who got away twenty years earlier.

"And he could see that I was putting the puzzle pieces together and understood how powerful he was. He laughed. He said he'd show me what he'd done to my sister, but he would have to cover my face. He tried to put a bag over my head.

"He said he would kill me this time, but not before he made me pay for my meddling. He said my sister had saved me all those years ago when she told me to run.

"I couldn't shut out the memory of Ruthie's screams. I know I kept running until I couldn't hear her screaming anymore. I was little, and I didn't know what was happening to her. But now I do."

Evie was crying.

Abigail sniffed and blew her nose again. She scrunched up the paper towel and tossed it onto the counter.

"How did you get away from them this time?" Jenny asked from the doorway. Abigail glanced at the mirror. The three female warriors stared back at her. Abigail looked away, turning her thoughts inward. She sighed.

"I pleaded with them to kill me, and they laughed. They took me out into the bush. The old man told me to run. We all knew I wasn't little anymore, and it would be easy to catch me. He promised I would discover his fun had only just begun.

"So I ran as I did before, and when I couldn't go any further, I hid. I waited for them to find me. It was going to be easy for them. They'd ruined my face, and I was making too much noise as I struggled to breathe. The waiting was even worse than the pain. Every little noise terrified me, but I was too exhausted to move. At first, I begged God to kill me. I wanted my life to end. Why was He allowing this horror? I prayed until I had nothing left.

"I don't know why they didn't find me. It was getting dark, and a storm came. I thought God must be angry with me, shouting at me in the thunder and lightning. The pounding rain shook the ground. Now I was afraid of dying too. It rained and rained. My hiding place filled with water, and I crawled out. The whole area flooded. Streams of water merged to become a river wild and mighty. The river washed everything away…"

"This happened six months ago?" Jenny asked. "In northern New South Wales? You were pulled from the swollen river by a rescue helicopter? I saw that on the news, but I thought nothing more about it. They made it sound as if you were some stupid hiker who ignored the weather forecast and got caught by the floodwaters."

Abigail's sobs echoed from the bathroom walls.

Evie reached over and hugged Abigail, before turning to Jenny. "Do you have any scissors? Abby can't stand the vibrations. If we work together, we should be able to keep the hair from falling on her face. But you'll have to be quick."

Jenny produced a pair of scissors from nowhere. Evie turned Abigail's chair away from the mirror and reached for both of her hands. She nodded to the others.

"Sigrid, please wrap your arms around Abby, so she can't hit anyone. Xanda, your job is to catch the loose hair. Are you ready, Abby? Jenny, wait until the timing is right, and then don't stop until it's done."

The gentle woman leaned closer to Abigail and smiled. Then Evie opened her mouth and began to sing.

"Father in heaven, listen to our plea. We need Your help for Abby to be free. Please take the chains of fear that bind her and replace them with Your peace. Surround her with Your love and be her strength.

"The walls of pain and sorrow that imprison her, we dedicate to You. Write Your name over every curse and every threat, and bring her justice.

"Take these unforgettable memories. Wash them in the healing river that flows from Your throne.

"Bring Your forgiveness and redeem this child. Renew her courage and restore her favour. Grant her blessings and bestow on her the faith she needs to stay on the path You've set before her. Please come and surround us with Your presence, and make Abby safe. Come fill her with Your Spirit..."

Abigail stared into Evie's eyes. She had heard singing like this before. In her daydream, the princess beside the waterfall sang the same song. A new vision awoke before her inner eyes.

The princess was standing in a turbulent river. The wild water bubbled and churned around her. The singer showed no fear and stood her ground. The words of the song were echoing from the rocky cliffs, growing in strength. They caught in the rainbow spray from a mighty waterfall before launching into the sky. Now the princess held her hand towards Abigail, calling her to wade into the water.

Abigail took a step forward...

Snip. Snip. Snip.

ଔ ✿ ଓ

"What are you going to tell Piper?" Evie asked.

"I'll wait and hear his questions before I tell him anything."

Jenny glanced over her shoulder. Abigail was still asleep, curled up on the floor. It was not a natural sleep, for no-one could rouse her. The broken woman had slipped gently from the chair when Sigrid released her.

A smile illuminated her ruined face.

Jenny shook her head. "If I hadn't been here, I wouldn't believe her story. What was that song, and how did you know you could sing her to sleep? She was so wound up, I thought she'd never let us work on her hair, but she didn't even blink when I started snipping."

"As soon as she mentioned the river, God told me what to do," Evie smiled dreamily. "Sometimes, it is easy to forget that God works in mysterious ways."

"I'll leave you to explain that to Piper. He's not been the same since he came back from Thailand. Having to rescue your sister Sofia from a river only compounded the problem. You know how annoyed he gets about your constant reference to God as your protector and guide."

"He can't deny the way Romano has changed since he met you," Jenny continued, "but that doesn't mean Piper's ready to admit God is real."

"What about you?" Evie asked. "Are you ready to admit God is real?"

Jenny turned away. "It's time for us to go. Sigrid, carry Abby to the van. I don't think she's going to wake anytime soon, but be prepared for anything. Come on, Evie. Romano's impatient for your return. He's sent me ten messages already."

"What about Evie's face?" Xanda asked. "Shouldn't you try to hide the bruise?"

Jenny turned Evie around to face Xanda. The swelling and developing bruise which had been obvious had vanished.

"What happened...?"

"That was a powerful song," Sigrid remarked as she stood there with her heavy burden. "If I'd realised what was happening, I would have asked Evie to sing away my shoulder pain. It hasn't been the same since I tore all the ligaments in Jenny's last challenge."

Distance - Leave Behind

ॐ ✵ ॐ

Ephesians 2:17 (WEB)
He came and preached peace to you who were far off
and to those who were near.

ॐ ✵ ॐ

"What do you think you're doing?" a voice asked from behind him.

Freddie spun around. His "long-lost cousin" stepped out of the shadows. The tall woman folded her arms across her chest.

"I couldn't sleep," he said. "I'm going for a walk."

"At the train station." Sigrid snorted.

"I'm taking the train, and then walking home from wherever it takes me. I didn't want to risk walking somewhere, only to find I didn't have the strength to get back."

"Ever heard of taking a taxi?"

"I've tried that. When I walk away from here, every passing taxi stops and offers me a ride. For some reason, if I'm coming from the other direction, they leave me alone."

A train whistled to a halt in front of them. Sigrid shoved Freddie onboard. "Don't bother sitting down. We're only going to the next station. Tomorrow we'll get you a treadmill. You might not need any sleep, but I have to go to school with Butch in a few hours."

"Explain that to me again."

"The Principal has agreed to have Butch back if he has a responsible adult with him. That would be me, as you're clearly not in your right mind. I get to hang around the school, and no-one will know I'm really there to protect Abby."

"I don't understand why she has to go back. She needs more time to recover from the accident."

"Hiding her in the apartment isn't going to help us catch the people who are after her. She'll be fine. You haven't seen Abby since Evie Romano sang over her. That woman has some kind of mystical powers. The swelling has gone, and Abby says she's pain-free; ready to go back to work."

Freddie stewed over Sigrid's comments. It wasn't his fault he hadn't seen Abigail. He'd tried, but this woman had stopped him. They both knew she was strong enough to keep it that way.

"How did you know I was at the train station?" he grumbled.

"When the night crew realised you were on the move, they woke me."

"Are you telling me Romano has me watched?"

"No need to have you watched. Piper just put a mobility alert on your phone. If you go anywhere that's not on your schedule the computer raises a red flag. I've seen your file, a few pages of the same boring routine. This is the most excitement you've had in years."

"What if I'd left my phone behind?"

"There might be a sensor on your door. And a facial recognition filter scanning the security cameras in the area, but I won't confirm or deny that. I wouldn't advise you to try sneaking out. You'd only have more explaining to do when your boss finds out."

The train pulled to a halt at the next station. The platform was empty. Freddie stomped forward into the semi-darkness.

"Which way?"

"Don't ask me," Sigrid snorted. "This is your plan. I'm just here to make sure you don't compromise my mission by getting into any more trouble."

Freddie checked his phone, waiting for his navigation app to open.

"I didn't ask for any of this," he muttered as he headed down the dimly lit street. "I want my old life back."

"Your girlfriend would be disappointed to hear you say that."

Freddie gritted his teeth and accelerated his pace. "She's. Not. My. Girlfriend."

"Tell yourself that if it makes you feel better," Sigrid taunted him, and then trotted past him to the next corner. When he reached her, she held out her phone. "Look at this."

"What?" he snapped, moving straight past her.

"You're not the only one who can't sleep," Sigrid informed him, as she jogged backwards in front of him. She flashed her phone at him. He stopped, unable to understand what he was seeing. A black and white image of his face shone out of the digital screen. There was something heroic about the angle of his head and the light in his eyes. He snatched the phone from her. "Where did you get this?"

"Did you know Abby's a gifted artist? She drew that from memory. It was a pity to watch her destroy it afterwards."

"D-destroy it?"

"Her handlers have forbidden her to draw because her style is unique. Someone shared one of her drawings online a few weeks ago, and her enemies traced her. Jenny convinced Abby that as long as the drawings are destroyed when she's finished, there won't be any problems. Abby doesn't know Jenny ordered Xanda to take photos."

"What else has she drawn?" he asked.

Sigrid swiped through the photo album. Among the drawings of the new people in her life, there were four portraits of Freddie. The final one showed him in profile, holding a woman close to his chest. The woman was hiding her face, but it was obvious this was Abigail. His facial expression in this drawing brought him to a halt.

Freddie opened his mouth to protest that this wasn't real. This never happened. But the words went unspoken. He looked up in confusion. How did Abigail know? Until that moment, even he hadn't been certain.

The Freddie Kidman in this drawing was in love.

Disavow - Deny Any Association

ॐ ☼ ॐ

*Luke 9:24 Try to save your own life, and you will lose it.
But if you are ready to lose your life for Me, you will save it.*

ॐ ☼ ॐ

"How did Freddie react when you showed him the drawings?" Jenny asked.

Sigrid sipped her coffee and frowned. Why had Jenny summoned her? They were seated in the van, two blocks from Freddie and Abigail's apartment building. "He took off like a rocket and didn't say anything all the way home. Why was it so important for him to know about the drawings?"

"I'm a hopeless romantic."

Sigrid rolled her eyes. "What's the real reason?"

Jenny shrugged. "Piper thinks Abby will run. He doesn't want to lose her. By pushing Freddie to declare his interest, Piper's giving her a reason to return."

"She's that important?"

"Piper thinks so, and he's rarely wrong. Of course, he won't stop digging for information until he's sure."

Sigrid was puzzled. "Why are we keeping Freddie and Abby apart?"

"Sometimes, the fantasy of being in love is more powerful than reality. You've met Freddie. He doesn't know anything about passion or romance. That should change once his frustration over Romano's constraints gets strong enough."

"What do you want me to do?"

"About Freddie?" Jenny shook her head. "Nothing. How are you getting on with the nephew?

"Butch is tough on the outside, but that kid's traumatised. I finally got him to tell me what the fight was about. The other kid, Tyler Kelly, was selling pictures of his own sister. The kind that would get an older man thrown into jail. Butch said Kelly didn't see the harm, because his sister was okay with making some extra pocket money. Butch told him that was the first step to selling his sister into prostitution. Kelly accused Butch of being jealous because he didn't have a sister people would pay to look at. That was when Butch hit him."

"Kelly? That's the same surname as the *Romano* employee who was selling information about Evie. I'll let Piper know so he can follow it up."

"Kelly's a common surname. Surely there won't be a connection?"

"This is Evie we're talking about. Nothing happens by accident where she is concerned."

Sigrid lifted the plastic lid to check how much coffee was left. "I have to go soon. Butch mustn't be late for his re-entry appointment with Principal Melrose. I want enough time to remind him again that he can't let anyone know Abby is his neighbour."

"You still have half an hour before the train leaves. Don't worry about Butch. He's not going to talk to anyone without your permission. The school is expecting some backlash from the other students. Kelly's a popular student, and Butch is new. A second fight would ruin your cover story. To help you, Piper's had Butch transferred into some of Marco's classes—"

"I'd forgotten about Marco. Aren't they in different grades?"

"Yes, but Piper persuaded the Principal that Marco would be a good influence. He also suggested Romano would like Butch to catch up. He's so far behind the other boys."

"Marco is Evie's nephew?"

"That's why I'm here," Jenny said. "To make sure you don't forget to keep an eye on him as well. Marco's involvement in the fight on Monday is one complication too many. If anything happens to Marco, we'll all answer to Romano. I've seen that giant when he's angry and don't want to repeat the experience. Piper would agree with Romano, so I would have two powerful men to pacify.

"When Marco isn't in the same room as Abby, you'll be with Butch in the library. That's next to Marco's homeroom and across the hall from Abby's maths classroom. I'll send you this map."

Sigrid waited as Jenny clicked buttons. Her phone buzzed, and she opened the file. Her superior pointed to the relevant rooms.

"The only time you won't be close to Abby," Jenny said, "is when she's in the science lab, which is why Xanda is working in there."

Sigrid looked up again. "How did Piper convince the lab tech to step aside for Xanda?"

"The man had an unexpected family situation. He's enjoying a visit with his parents in Queensland."

"And the school?" Sigrid asked. "How did Piper get them to agree to all this?"

"What Piper's connections can't achieve, Romano's money usually delivers." Jenny rubbed her fingers together and smiled as her subordinate considered this reality. "Romano is a school patron, as his father was before him. Money talks. The implied threat of cutting the annual donation achieved a lot. Of course, Principal Melrose will deny that, so don't mention it. You're not supposed to know."

Sigrid nodded.

"I want you watching the apartment from across the street before Abby's taxi arrives to pick her up." Jenny waved her hand in that direction. "It's imperative to know if anyone else is watching the apartment. No-one is supposed to know she's returning to school today. Xanda and I are going to tail Abby, so wait five minutes before you go inside to get Butch."

Jenny's phone beeped. "That will be Xanda telling me she's coming through the garden now."

Sigrid had her hand on the door lever, ready to exit the van.

Jenny wasn't finished. "Abby didn't give the school this address, but we can't be too careful."

That was a repeated reminder. Sigrid frowned and scanned the area again.

Jenny went on, "When the taxi nears the school, the driver is going to keep Abby in the car. Long enough for Xanda to jump out of the van and get inside the building ahead of her. Once Abby and Xanda officially meet at school, they can arrive and leave together."

Sigrid opened the door and stepped out. Jenny was still talking, so she held the door in her hand. She could see Xanda walking along the footpath towards them.

"Is there anything else you want to clarify?" Jenny asked.

Sigrid frowned and hesitated. "I've been puzzling over why Xanda was chosen? Piper already knew what Freddie looked like, so I was an obvious choice for a stand-in relative. But did you choose Xanda because we make a good team? Or because she's of similar height to Abby and her skin is dark? Are you planning to use her as a body-double for Abby when trouble arrives?"

Jenny's stare didn't waver. "Piper chose you both before we knew any details."

She held up her hand when Sigrid opened her mouth to respond. "We built the cover stories around you. In a way, each of your unique qualities has dictated how the mission will proceed. We know you're good with unpredictable situations, which is why you're tagged with Butch."

Sigrid nodded, and Jenny continued, "Xanda's scientific background has come in handy. I'm certain there'll be other useful parallels as this situation unfolds. Rely on your training and be prepared to adapt to whatever happens."

A shiver ran through Sigrid. The last time Jenny had delivered that advice, she had learned the hard way to be more vigilant. What kind of trouble was Jenny expecting?

Jenny checked her mirror again. "It's time for you to go."

₧☯ℳ

"It is good to see you have recovered from your misadventure," Principal Melrose said, as he ushered Abigail into his office.

The nervous teacher patted the wavy brown wig. She couldn't believe this simple change made such a difference. She still wore a pair of dark glasses. Jenny had swapped them for a larger frame that concealed more of the damage.

Butch and Sigrid were already seated before his desk. The teenager jumped up in surprise at her changed appearance. Abigail stopped short. Sigrid dragged him back to his chair and gave him a silent reminder to keep quiet.

"Now there's no reason for alarm," the principal continued. "Butch has promised to be on his best behaviour. This is his guardian, Ms Ericson. She will be with him at all times, to ensure there is no further trouble."

"Call me Sigrid, Ms Golding," 'Ms Ericson' said, leaning forward to shake Abigail's hand. "I can assure you my cousin will be the perfect gentleman. He's about to apologise to you for all the trouble he's caused."

"Sorry," Butch muttered. "Won't 'appen again."

Sigrid nudged him with her elbow. "Sorry, Ms Golding. And sit up straight. You've embarrassed yourself enough already. There's no need to remind everyone you're an uneducated, uncouth country boy."

"Sorry, Miss Gold-ding," Butch said, piercing Abigail with his stare. He looked down his nose and in a snobbish voice went on. "My behaviour was unacceptable, and I can assure you that it will never happen again. I most certainly would not want you to think that I am 'an uneducated, uncouth country boy'. To have you hold such a low opinion of me would bring shame to both my family and to this honourable school. Please accept my humble apology."

Then he ruined the performance by winking at her. Abigail mumbled a reply.

"Very good," Principal Melrose told Butch. "Please wait here, Ms Golding. I need to give Butch his revised timetable." He ushered the boy and his cousin from the room.

Abigail sat looking at her hands as she waited for the principal's return. Butch had surprised her with his acting ability. She hadn't been allowed to talk to him. Or to Freddie, since that confrontation with Piper Maxwell at the service station.

How many times had she arisen, intending to visit the apartment next door? But then she would glance towards Xanda, her constant companion, and change her mind. How was she to explain the way her thoughts kept returning to her first meeting with Freddie?

He was only a kind stranger who had taken pity on her. Here she was, daydreaming about him as if she were a smitten schoolgirl.

∞❂∞

Freddie was stirring a tin of pink acrylic paint. John Edwards came through the garden gate to the private courtyard.

"Thanks for letting me visit," John said. "I can see you're busy, but Romano said I should check on you. How are the renovations going?"

"The plumber's coming to finish installing the new bathroom this afternoon. That only leaves the kitchen. I'm painting all three bedrooms while I wait for the tradesmen to finish." Freddie's shoulders were slumped, and his movements lethargic. "Romano's holding off on the new floor coverings until I finish with the paint, in case I mess that up too." He turned sorrowful eyes towards John.

"Is there anything I can do?"

"Did you bring your car?" Freddie asked with more enthusiasm. "I still have boxes of Constance's belongings to get rid of. Evie's checked there's nothing Romano should keep, and sorted what can be recycled. I've thrown the rest in the skip."

"When did Constance die?" John asked as they carried the boxes out to his car.

"At the end of May, about five weeks before Evie turned up and changed everything. If the old woman was still here, Evie wouldn't have stood a chance at catching Romano's attention."

And neither of us would be here, Freddie thought, as he returned to his paint preparations. No Evie, no wedding, no adventure for Sofia. Nobody to speak on Freddie's behalf, no transferring Butch to Marco's school. No new school, no fight. Abigail would be just another neighbour. Definitely not someone who filled his every waking moment.

She even haunted his dreams.

"Hey," John said, pointing at the mess Freddie had made. Pink paint was splattered all over the pavement. Freddie swore and grabbed some rags.

"Who picked the colour?" John asked. "That shade of pink is hideous."

"It's special ceiling paint. It goes on pink and then the colour changes to white as it dries. It's supposed to make it easier to see where I've missed, to make sure I do the job right."

"So when Romano comes to visit, his courtyard won't be pink?" John asked as he stepped back from the spreading paint. "That's a relief. I can think of a lot of things that would be easier if the colour changed when it was 'right'."

"Let's talk about something else."

John nodded. "Was the aunt as difficult as Romano describes her?"

Freddie laughed. "Difficult is an understatement. That woman found fault with everything and made sure everyone knew about it. She warned us about Romano before he arrived. Some of the men quit rather than risk working with the dangerous criminal she described."

"You weren't tempted to go?"

Freddie frowned. No-one had ever asked him that question. The words ricocheted inside him. What had made him stay? Was it the same reason he was still here?

"I didn't have anywhere to go. I'd already moved states to be here, and I didn't want to start again. I couldn't go home either. My dad's still mad at me, and it's been ten years.

"Anyway, when Romano arrived, it was a relief to find he wasn't a monster. It took time to get used to him double-checking our work as if he was the only one who knew anything about working here."

"So how did you end up managing the service station?"

"I don't know," Freddie said, as he finished mopping the spill. He began stirring the paint again, more careful this time. "He said he'd been watching me and knew I was reliable. He didn't discuss his plans for the servo, the car park, or modernising the workshop with anyone, not even Dave."

Freddie shook his head. He checked that John understood the significance of that omission. "No-one dared ask him what he was doing. Constance made a bigger deal than usual about him wasting his father's money." He grimaced at the memory. "She insisted no good was going to come of it. We watched to see how she would react. It was obvious the servo was a money-making scheme that might surpass the workshop, but she refused to admit she was wrong. Instead, she looked for something else to complain about." He put aside the paint stirrer and stood.

"That was when Piper Maxwell turned up. Constance was outraged by the new security measures. She was angry that Romano's presence drew the wrong kind of attention. But she was even angrier that he was making enough money to cover the extra costs."

He paused, reflecting on the changes Romano's success had brought to everyone. "About then she started goading him about not being married."

"Why did she remain if she was so unhappy?" John seemed genuinely concerned for the bitter old woman.

"He offered to pay for her to go home to Italy, but she refused." Freddie surprised himself by how accurately he could remember how she spoke. "Who did she have in Italy, she wanted to know? What was the point? She had wasted the best years of her life taking care of her brother. All because he had to deal with the disgrace of having a criminal – a murderer – for a son."

He spat out those recriminations, surprising himself that he recalled that bitter woman's tone so well. And then he straightened his shoulders with pride. "Romano kept silent. Not once did he tell her what he thought of her vicious tongue. Most of the time, it was impossible to tell what he was thinking. He acted as if he didn't care."

He lowered his voice, "But sometimes he came over to the servo, and I could hear him smashing things out back. I learned the warning signs and knew when to steer clear. After his rages, he would come in as if nothing had happened."

"I wonder what it would be like to have his self-control?" John asked. "It might be useful to pretend nothing happened."

"It would have its advantages," Freddie conceded, carrying the paint inside. He poured paint into a tray and loaded the roller, before climbing up the ladder. Deep in thought, he watched the old creamy surface disappear under pink streaks.

"Can I ask your advice?" he finally asked.

John's eyes narrowed. "What do you want advice about?"

"My phone's on the kitchen counter? Bring it over here, and I'll show you."

John retrieved the phone. With a few clicks, Freddie opened the drawing Sigrid had forwarded to him. He stared at the image, frowning again at the way he held Abigail, and the foolish look on his face. He handed the phone to John and turned back to the ceiling.

"I didn't ask Sigrid to send it," Freddie admitted, "and I wish I'd never seen it. Abigail is a talented artist, and that's one of her drawings. What am I supposed to make of that?"

"Tell me why you wish you'd never seen it."

"How did she know? I haven't seen her since Tuesday morning, but I can't stop thinking about her. She's drawn me with that foolish longing on my face. If I hadn't seen that drawing, I could pretend she'd forgotten all about me."

"Clearly, she hasn't forgotten you." A smile lit up John's face. "Have you considered that she doesn't know how you feel, and this drawing is about her longing for you?"

Freddie cried out as he lost his footing. The ladder fell sideways with a clatter. What a mess. Thank God he'd put down the extra drop sheets. He stepped around the pink spill, picked up the ladder and retrieved the dropped roller. He couldn't look at John, who must have paint on his suit.

Freddie tightened his jaw to keep silent. He climbed the ladder and resumed painting, pretending nothing had happened. John watched without saying anything for about ten minutes.

"What is more interesting is why Sigrid let you see this drawing," John said. "She wouldn't have done that without Jenny's permission, no matter how independent she seems. The *Maximum Security* agents obey Jenny's commands, and she answers to no-one but Piper."

Freddie froze. "Why would Piper want me to see Abigail's drawings?"

"What was your reaction when you first saw it?"

"You mean, after I denied I had any feelings for Abigail, and stormed off?" Freddie said. "When I calmed down, I wanted to go to her apartment. I imagined knocking on her door to find out what would happen if I did try to hold her like that."

"Why didn't you?"

Freddie knew John was only getting him to speak his thoughts out loud, but his temper was rising. He slopped paint on the ceiling and settled into a rhythm.

Slap. Swish. Swoosh. Slap. Swish. Swoosh.

"Sigrid is stronger than me," Freddie confessed. "I tried to see Abigail on Tuesday afternoon. Sigrid nearly dislocated my shoulder when she dragged me away from the door. She made it clear that Piper's instructions were not to be disobeyed."

"Did Piper forbid all forms of communication? Abigail is using her drawing to express her feelings. Why don't you find another way to let her know you're thinking about her?"

"Huh?"

"You could write her a note or buy her a present." John held up his fingers and counted off the options. "Get some flowers. Cook a meal. I'm sure you will think of something while you're finishing this ceiling."

John noticed the paint spatters on his hands. He looked down at his clothes. His smile wavered. "I'm going to the drycleaners while this colour-changing paint on my suit is still pink. You have my number. Let me know what you come up with and how it works. I'll see myself out."

"What about you?" Freddie called out. "Are you taking your own advice with Sofia?"

"I don't need to," John shook his head. "I have Evie to pass messages for me. When the time is right, Sofia will send a message back."

"How long are you going to wait?"

"Sofia's not going anywhere. I have all the time I need. But you don't. Abigail could be gone tomorrow."

"That might be the best for everyone," Freddie muttered to himself, but he knew it was a lie.

Distract - Divert Attention

ಬಿ ☼ ಆ

*Genesis 2:3 God blessed the seventh day, making it holy
when he rested from all his work.*

ಬಿ ☼ ಆ

It had been a long day. Abigail was eager to hide in her apartment. Xanda led the way upstairs. They arrived at her floor to discover the ceiling lights had been repaired. But what was that large parcel leaning against the end wall? Xanda raised her hand. Abigail halted while the agent went to investigate.

Yesterday, they had arrived home to find Freddie had left two presents outside her door. A single red rose in a protective tube and a new ceramic mug in a box. His phone number was written on a slip of paper hidden inside the box, but she hadn't been brave enough to call him.

"Are you expecting a delivery from an art supply store?" Xanda asked as she pulled out her phone. Abby couldn't hear what was said, but her hands twitched with excitement. Her mind was busy assessing the size of the parcel. The dimensions suggested this could be her favourite A1 paper.

Xanda turned to her and smiled, beckoning her closer.

"Let's get this inside."

Only after Xanda picked up the large parcel did they discover the smaller one hiding behind it. Abigail opened the larger parcel first. To her delight, her guess was correct. She closed her eyes and ran her hand over the surface of the white paper. Dozens of creative ideas flooded her mind.

"Aren't you going to open this other one?" Xanda asked.

Abby pulled the box onto her lap. Her hands struggled with the tape. Xanda produced a blade to cut it open. Abby stared at the knife. She closed her eyes and reached into the box. Her hands encountered a plastic tube with a sealed top – a spray can of some kind and a long narrow box. Her eyes flew open. Her hands held a box of artist-grade pastels and a can of fixative. She looked from the box to the paper in wonder. Now she could indulge her love of colour.

Abigail jumped up with the pastels clutched to her chest and danced around the room.

"Aren't you going to read the note?" Xanda asked in amusement. "Don't you want to know who gave you such a delightful gift?"

Abigail went still. "There's a note?"

"Will I read it to you? 'Hi Abigail, I hope these art supplies are useful, Freddie'."

∞

(Sunday 5th November)

Xanda stood in the doorway and surveyed the chaos. Abby was snoring, face down where she had collapsed on the floor beside her artwork. At intervals, the snorting and snuffling stopped. Then Xanda would rush in, fearing her charge had smothered herself.

The bedroom furniture had been shoved out of the way so the artist could access the longest wall. This made it awkward to enter the room because the gap was so narrow. Sheets of paper had been taped to cover this windowless wall from floor to ceiling. Abby had needed to balance on a chair to reach the upper section.

Xanda considered the wall in amazement. Abby had created this masterpiece in a single weekend.

What a pity that it would have to be destroyed.

With a shake of her head, Xanda started taking photos with her phone. She was taking close-up shots of the individual panels when the phone in her hand began to vibrate.

Xanda squeezed through the gap and went into the living room. As a precaution, she pulled the bedroom door closed behind her.

"Xanda!" a male voice said. Who was on duty tonight? It was either Vincent or Trey. A surge of adrenalin hit her. The voice continued, "Get the target to a safe location and prepare for visitors. Sigrid will be with you in a few minutes. She's making sure the kid is locked in."

"What about the uncle?"

Xanda heard the voice talking to someone else, and then the words were loud in her ear again. "Sigrid says he's downstairs using the treadmill. He should be safe there. We've alerted Piper. Reinforcements are on their way."

There was a noise at the door. With a bound, Xanda slapped the light switch. The living room and kitchen instantly darkened. She waited for her eyes to adjust to the dark as she scanned the room. A crack of light in the hallway behind her outlined the closed bedroom door. There wasn't time to fix that now. The apartment door swung open. Xanda held her breath, crouching low.

"Xanda, it's me," Sigrid hissed. Her tall form slipped into the room, backlit by the bright lights in the hall. The agent's shadow leaned against the door and darkness reigned again. Click. Rattle. Snap. "Secure."

"Sigrid's here now," Xanda said into her phone. The call ended.

The two women waited in the darkness. Footsteps sounded in the hallway, stopping outside the door.

Knock, knock, knock.

Xanda and Sigrid froze, holding their breath.

Knock, knock, knock.

"Who is it?" Xanda called out, a perfect imitation of Abby's nasally voice.

"Ms Golding, you don't know me. Please open the door. Your location has been compromised, and we have to move you."

"Who are you?"

"Open the door, and I'll show you my ID."

"Why didn't someone phone me?"

"Your phone has been tapped. We couldn't contact you without letting them know. Please open the door. There isn't much time before they get here."

"Wait there while I make a phone call," Xanda said, stepping away from the door. Moments later, the door burst inwards with a loud bang. It takes a lot of force to break a door like that, Xanda thought, as she crouched down into a defensive position.

For a few moments, the darkness would give her an advantage. A dark shape pushed into the room, followed by more. How many men had they sent to grab Abby?

A cry rang out as Sigrid launched an offensive. One of the intruders went down, and the others turned to face their unknown protagonist. Xanda launched her attack. She whirled and kicked, knocking another one down. In the dark, the struggle could have gone their way, but someone found the light switch. Their advantage was gone. Xanda lost herself to the battle, refusing to acknowledge that they were outnumbered.

She was thrown into the wall and staggered. The room spun. Xanda gasped for air.

"Give up, or we kill your friend," the first man said.

Sigrid was slumped on the floor, debris from a wooden chair surrounding her. She was bleeding from her nose and mouth. One of the men kicked the unconscious form. Sigrid made no sound. Two men seized Xanda's arms, before pulling her head back by the hair.

"Are you sure this is the right woman?" one of the men asked. "I thought we were told she was fat and her face was scarred."

The leader walked across and looked at Xanda. "Are you Louise Silverton?"

"Who else would I be?"

৪০ ✿ ୬

A buzzing sound and a strange vibration woke Abigail. She rolled onto her side, wrestling her phone from under her as she leaned against the wall. The buzzing and vibrating stopped, but what was that louder noise?

Banging and shouting were coming from the next room. Abigail rubbed her eyes. The phone vibrated again; a single buzz then it was still. She looked at the display. The screen was filled with messages: Three missed calls from an unknown number and a text message.

HIDE

The shock brought her fully awake. From her low position, all she could see of the door was a narrow section under the bed. As quietly as she could, Abigail crawled towards the bed. She prayed that the space beneath it was large enough to take her bulk. Where was Xanda, and what was happening in the next room?

With a final wriggle, Abigail squeezed under the bed. She tugged on the edge of the quilt. Swoosh. Fold after fold of fabric tumbled onto the floor, blocking her view of the door.

The noises in the other room ceased. Abigail strained to hear what was happening. Footsteps sounded in the hall outside her room. She prayed that she could stay silent. The bedroom door opened as far as it would go. With a thud, it banged against the dresser she had shoved there. Xanda had complained about having to squeeze through such a small gap.

The wooden door shuddered, as someone pushed against it. The dresser banged into the bed and then the whole lot budged a few centimetres. "Hmmph."

The intruder was in the room. A pair of dark-trousered legs and feet shod in shiny black leather appeared beside her. The unknown man faced her artwork. Then he turned and scanned the rest of the room. He strode over to the wardrobe. The doors slid open with a bang. He turned towards the door again, lifted the quilt and dropped it back on the bed. He didn't bend down to check under it. "There's no-one else here, Rick," he bellowed, "so it must be her. You said she was an artist, and she's drawn all over the wall."

The bedroom door shook as the intruder went back through the narrow gap. The footsteps moved away. Abigail bit her lip trying not to cry. A woman's voice cried out in the other room. Xanda was still there.

"You'll never get away with this. Piper Maxwell will find you and make you pay."

A man laughed – was it the man named Rick? "Piper Maxwell will be too late. He's such a disappointment to his grandfather, always choosing the wrong side. He should have learned his lesson when he failed to save his cousin. He didn't stop to question why someone asked him for a list of safe houses. I look forward to seeing Piper discover he's been out-played."

Abigail bit her fist to keep from crying out.

"Piper's involvement was my idea," the same voice said, "my private joke at his expense. He dishonoured me in Sydney, and now I, Ricardo Barononi, have my revenge."

So it was Rick! He had given his full name, and Abigail vowed to remember.

The cruel voice continued: "He can take the blame when they find you dead. You were never going to live long enough to testify. My organisation could have dealt with you months ago. But Clayton Wolfe didn't want his cover blown. That's why you've been moved around so much. He wanted you out of New South Wales so that your death couldn't be traced back to him."

Tears came to Abigail's eyes. She struggled to breathe, fighting the panic.

"What a pity the Victorians weren't able to find you in time," Ricardo Barononi sneered. "Piper's meddling will be investigated. We did what we could to add to the confusion. Wolfe changed your identity again and forgot to tell them. When Louise Silverton wasn't at any of Piper's addresses, Wolfe pretended to be embarrassed. Especially as you hadn't been in touch like you said you would. But how could you? The number he gave you forwards calls directly to me."

No! The horror of her situation crushed her spirit. Yet she mustn't stop listening as the evil man continued to gloat.

"You were such a good girl, doing exactly what Wolfe said and keeping me up to date. The Vic team would be surprised – your file describes you as an uncooperative whinger with an agenda. You deliberately put your protection team at risk on numerous occasions. Your actions forced them to move you from one location to another. The file also includes credible doubts about the value of your testimony. Only Piper has been trying to protect you. What a shame you're the only eyewitness."

"I'm not going quietly," Xanda cried. Loud banging and shouts indicated she was fighting desperately for her survival.

Anger flared in Abigail, and she used the external noise to cover the sound of her movement. She wriggled out from under the bed. She picked up a pastel. In bright red script, she scrawled "Clayton Wolfe is a traitor" on the back of the door. Underneath she wrote "Ricardo Barononi framed Piper Maxwell". Turning to the closest wall, she sketched the faces of the men she had to identify in court. Clayton had all her original sketches. Abigail blinked away the tears. The sound of Xanda's struggle ceased.

"Grab her arms and legs," Barononi commanded.

"How are we going to get her down the stairs?"

Barononi laughed. "She's not going down the stairs. Take her to the banister and toss her over. Even if she survives the fall, she'll bleed out before anyone finds her."

Xanda screamed, and then the room went quiet.

Distort – Alter the Account

ᘒ ☼ ᘓ

*Joshua 2:11 Hearts melt and spirits fail,
because God is Lord of heaven and earth.*

ᘒ ☼ ᘓ

With all her might, Abigail threw herself at the narrow gap. She tried to squeeze through, but now she was stuck between the door and the frame. She pushed and wriggled, gasping as pain ripped through her abdomen and lower back.

At last, she was free. Making her way past the broken furniture, Abigail dropped to her knees beside Sigrid. The wounded woman was taking shallow and irregular breaths, but she should be okay for a while. Abigail was reluctant to abandon her, but she had to find out where the intruders had taken Xanda. She rolled Sigrid onto her side, checked her breathing again. Next, Abigail crawled to the wall to drag herself upright, fighting another spasm of pain.

A trail of blood led out the door and along the hallway. Abigail was careful not to step in it. She leaned against the wall as she followed the trail. When she came to Freddie's apartment door, she could hear Butch shouting for someone to let him out. She closed her eyes. Where was Freddie? Then she remembered her task and went on. The blood trail ended at the banister rail.

She peered over the edge.

An unmoving heap lay far below.

ᘒ ☼ ᘓ

Go. Go now.

Freddie grabbed his phone to check the hour. It was almost midnight; time to return to his apartment. From the treadmill, he glanced around the renovated ground-floor apartment. His tasks were almost done. He frowned. His eye was drawn to the side door that opened onto the private courtyard.

He shrugged. What did it matter which exit he used? The same technology that safeguarded the *Romano* workshop operated here. As soon as he opened an external door, the watchers at *Maximum Security* would notify Sigrid. What would the security agent think if he changed his routine? Well, it was she who had challenged him to "be adventurous for a change".

Flash. How had he forgotten the motion-sensitive security floodlights? As his eyes adjusted, he considered his next move. Would he go out the security gate to the street, and give Sigrid something else to think about? Or should he take a walk within the compound's community garden?
The garden.

Freddie shook his head. Romano was wrong. Physical exhaustion was not a good remedy for his troubled mind. The hour he had spent on the treadmill tonight had made things worse. Now he was hearing voices.
One Voice.

He took the path leading towards the pool. Solar-powered lights marked the way through the darkness. Freddie rested his hand on the gate. He knew better than to open it. If he did that, powerful floodlights would come on, waking the nearest tenants. Butch had found out the hard way, sneaking out to take a moonlight swim. Freddie was in enough trouble with the Residents' Committee already – his nocturnal wanderings had been noted.

What was that noise? He dropped down behind the only shrub. He heard a screen door open, then the security lights covering the rear entrance of the apartment building burst into life. The four-storey building loomed out of the darkness.

Bang!

One of the lights blinked out.

A string of muffled curses was followed by a muttered exclamation. "Idiot! Use the silencer."

Pop! Pop! Pop!

The other lights went out one by one. But not before Freddie caught a glimpse of a group of men. Big men with guns. They were coming straight towards him. There was nothing but open space between him and the safety of the building.

Hide.

He squeezed behind the large shrub beside the pool fence. Thank God he was small enough. Now what?

He could hear Sigrid's critical voice in his mind. What kind of man was he? Why was he hiding? Only a coward would hide in the shadows!

Now is the time to be silent.

Thanks for the advice, he muttered but felt better as the words echoed inside him. What if he wasn't talking to himself? Comforted by this thought, he crouched lower.

"Here is the place to leave the knife," a voice said in the darkness. "Right under Piper's nose."

Heavy footsteps paused in front of Freddie.

"I don't understand, Rick. Why did you use one of Valentino's signature blades? Everyone knows he died in Thailand. What if Piper makes the connection with you?"

"By the time Piper works out I'm involved, his career will be ruined. The death of a crown witness under his protection is only the beginning. He's not going to understand the message this knife is delivering until it's too late."

Freddie's hiding place began to rustle. He froze. The branches flopped back into place. A cruel laugh echoed across the pool. Freddie waited. The heavy footsteps faded. The intruders must be heading towards the security gate in the side fence. Did they know a silent alarm would sound if they opened it?

He nudged the ground in front of him with his shoe and encountered resistance. It wasn't his imagination – there really was a knife sticking into the ground there. What were the chances the murderers would hide their weapon right next to him? Was this another of Evie Romano's famous coincidences? Or was there something more powerful than a coincidence at work here?

He wondered whether it was safe yet. Had the murderers gone?

Murderers?

Freddie leapt up and ran to the main rear entrance. He flung it open, no longer caring if anyone heard him. It was imperative that he know Abigail was safe. He raced through the visitors' lounge, heading towards the closest set of stairs. Something made him pause. He spun around and cried out in alarm. There was someone lying in a pool of blood in the middle of the foyer.

"Abigail!"

Freddie rushed forward, turning the body over. No. Not Abigail. He closed his eyes.

Thank God!

Who was this?

Before he could gather his thoughts, Freddie heard sounds coming from above. Someone was on the stairs.

‮ஐ‬ ✿ ೞ

"No! No! Noooo," Abigail wailed, rushing onto the winding stairs. She stumbled halfway and tumbled to the first corner. Abigail moaned. Seizing the banister, she dragged herself upright. She must keep moving. Was there no end to the going down?

Her back ached. Spasms of pain ripped through her body.

With one arm wrapped around her abdomen, each step became a new challenge.

Rounding the final corner, she halted. There on the polished floor lay Xanda's twisted body. Someone was kneeling beside her.

ಙ☼ಬ
(Monday 6th November)

Freddie gasped as someone tumbled down the stairs. The woman looked at him as she crawled towards the dead body. The real Abigail. Why hadn't Sigrid stopped her from leaving the safety of her apartment? It could mean only one thing – the bodyguard was also dead. Freddie rushed to meet Abigail.

"Freddie?" Abigail whispered as he pulled her to her feet. "Is she dead? They thought Xanda was me!"

"You're safe now," he whispered as she clung to him. Abigail buried her face in his shirt. He cautiously put his arms around her. This was not how he expected her prophetic drawing to be fulfilled. He kissed the top of her head, staring towards the dead woman.

> *There is a time to be born and a time to die.*
> I know.
>
> *There is a time to keep and a time to let go.*
>
> No. I'm not ready.
> *A seed has to die before there is new life. Trust me. There will be a time when she returns renewed.*

The door to the street opened. The room filled with people and noise. Freddie accepted their coming without a thought. It seemed natural that Piper Maxwell would arrive only minutes after midnight. Freddie met the security operative's stare with sorrowful eyes. Piper stepped aside. Romano entered the foyer. Piper nodded to Romano, and the giant approached Freddie.

Romano was careful to avoid the sticky red mess.

Freddie looked down at his bloody footprints on the floor.

"You did well to keep her away from the body," Piper said quietly as he appeared beside Freddie. "No-one can know there were two women here."

Romano removed Abigail from Freddie's embrace. The heartbroken young man's arms had lost their strength.

She turned frightened eyes towards Freddie. He smiled sadly. "You have to go with Romano. Your enemies think you're dead. Now you're free. Go!"

Freddie heard Piper's voice from a great distance. "Did you see them?"

Freddie's eyes followed Romano's retreating figure. Abigail would be safe in the ground floor apartment. It was not too late. He could follow them...

Piper shook Freddie, turning him towards the body. "Did you see the people who did this?"

Freddie watched as three men ran their hands over the crumpled body. They removed the dead woman's phone and emptied her pockets. That didn't seem right, but he didn't have the energy to ask. Piper shook him again.

Freddie blinked and recovered his voice. "I found this woman here. I knew something bad had happened. There were strangers in the garden. I hid – they didn't know I was there. There was a man – Rick, his name was Rick. Rick said he wanted revenge. He said he was going to ruin you. Then he hid the murder weapon right next to me."

"Did you touch it?" Piper hissed.

"Only with my foot."

"Tell me where it is, and then forget any of it happened."

Freddie nodded. It was easy to give the location. There was only one bush beside the pool gate. He watched Piper relay the information to others, who hurried off to investigate. He blinked.

Piper glared at him. "You have blood on your clothes. Why did you touch the body?"

"I thought it was Abigail. I rushed to see if I could help her. Then I realised she was dead, and she wasn't—"

"Stop right there. You're mistaken. This is Abigail, your neighbour and your girlfriend. You're upset because someone has killed her. Where had you been that you were here in the foyer at midnight?"

"You already know that. You have me watched. You know I was in Romano's apartment—"

"Wrong again. You went for a walk, and you were just returning home when you found her here. Get your story straight. You're about to be suspect number one. Women are usually murdered by someone they know."

As if to reinforce that point, Butch appeared at the top of the stairs. "Freddie! Why did yer lock me in my room!" One of Piper's men rushed to prevent the teenager from stepping onto the floor. But not before the boy shouted, "And what have you done to Abigail?"

"I didn't—" Freddie began, and Piper silenced him. The owner of *Maximum Security* signalled to one of the others to stay with Freddie. The man stood close and prevented him from following. A strange stillness overwhelmed Freddie. His senses were heightened. He had always wanted superpowers, but now he wished to be blind and deaf.

Piper stalked across to where his man struggled with Butch on the stairs. The security consultant reached out and grabbed Butch by the shirtfront. He hoisted the tall boy off his feet and shoved him against the banister. The boy turned frightened eyes towards his uncle, who was unable to move.

"Where's Sigrid?" Piper asked.

Butch looked around in confusion. Then alarm registered on his face. Piper dropped the fifteen-year-old to his feet. The boy turned and ran back up the stairs. Piper was close behind him.

Freddie stood transfixed, listening to the pounding footsteps overhead. Then there was a closer sound.

The caretaker pulled open his door. "I have called the police."

Jenny materialised beside the caretaker. She was wearing a security guard uniform. Freddie had never seen her in uniform before. There was something strange in the way she stood before the caretaker. First, she tentatively offered the old man a business card.

"Thank you," she said. Her voice had none of the usual harshness. "I'm Jennifer Prescott from *Maximum Security*. Our firm has taken over the contract for this building. There was an alarm raised at," she paused to look at her clipboard, "eleven-fifty-five. There may be intruders on the premises.

"As you can see," Jenny continued, pointing to the body on the floor, "someone's been injured. I'm not sure yet if it's one of your tenants. For your own safety, I must advise you to stay in your apartment. My team are still checking the building."

The caretaker took a step back into his apartment. Jenny rewarded him with a smile. "Thank you for calling the police. I was about to do that. I'll wait here for them to arrive. Did you also call for an ambulance? You did? Good."

The old man was eager to retreat. When the door closed, Jenny turned around. Her quick eyes scanned the scene. Freddie took comfort in the familiar glare she directed at him. Another of the *Maximum Security* operatives appeared beside Freddie.

Ten minutes later, the front door opened again. Two uniformed police officers entered the foyer. Jenny was ready for them with her clipboard. "My team have secured the scene. Identify yourself for my report." She partially blocked their view of the body, with her back towards Freddie.

"I'm Officer McCormick, and this is my partner Officer Vitali," one of the policemen said. His companion stood a few steps behind him, scanning the room. "Someone phoned to report an intruder. We also received a call about possible gunfire, just before midnight. What are you doing here?"

After she formally introduced herself, she asked to see their warrant cards. This information was carefully transcribed onto her clipboard. "My team were conducting a routine patrol. One of the security sensors on the perimeter of this property was tripped. We arrived to find a woman lying on the floor. Unfortunately, the casualty was already deceased. She has a single stab wound, and extensive trauma consistent with a fall from above. There's no indication a gun was involved."

The officers looked up. They noted the number of security operatives present. Finally, one of them noticed Freddie. "Who's this?" Officer McCormick asked.

Jenny checked her notes. "When we arrived, we found this man in a state of shock. You can see that he's staggered around the crime scene. We stopped him before he went up the stairs. My men searched him. He isn't carrying a weapon."

"Did he see what happened?" Officer Vitali approached Freddie and noted his blood-stained clothing and the footprints.

"He claims to be the victim's boyfriend," Jenny explained. "He said he found her here. He isn't making much sense, and my men had to restrain him. His bloody footprints have messed up the scene."

Officer McCormick went through the front door, talking into his mobile phone. Officer Vitali crouched beside the body. He looked towards Jenny. "This is a large team for a 'routine patrol'."

"*Maximum Security* has important clients in this area." Jenny stood taller and straightened her jacket. "We must be ready to respond appropriately to any threat."

"Important clients? Or *one* important client? Would you be referring to that big black building opposite the shopping centre? The mechanics' workshop? The last time we attended a suspicious death in this area, the body was there."

"Do you think there's some connection?" Jenny asked, looking up from writing on her clipboard. Freddie couldn't understand her behaviour. The blonde beauty was fluttering her eyelids. Was she flirting with this policeman?

"Our witness says he's the manager of the *Romano* service station," Jenny said, "He said the owner – let me check my notes – oh that's right, Sebastian Romano. He said Mr Romano could confirm his relationship with the deceased."

"Yes, to the *Romano* building," Officer Vitali said. "But that victim wasn't stabbed, and she didn't stay dead..."

"What do you mean, 'she didn't stay dead'?" Jenny asked.

Officer McCormick interrupted the conversation. "Bringing up that story again? The logical explanation is that woman wasn't dead but in a deep coma. She played her cards well. Poor Romano didn't stand a chance. He felt obliged to marry her – something about Italian family honour. Of course, Vitali's an expert on Italian families. He has more family connections than anyone I know."

"Does he know anyone famous?" wide-eyed Jenny asked.

Freddie waited, sensing the importance of the question. Officer Vitali never answered. The arriving paramedics distracted them all.

Discard - Throw Away

❧ ☼ ☙

*Isaiah 5:20a Trouble awaits those who call evil good, and good evil;
who exchange darkness for light and describe bitterness as sweet.*

❧ ☼ ☙

Butch had a head start on the stairs. But his youthful enthusiasm was no match for Piper's strength and determination. The security consultant caught him at the top of the first-floor landing. The teenager frowned but stayed silent.

"Listen carefully," Piper said, neither slowing nor attempting to halt Butch's progress. "Promise to obey my instructions. If you don't, there's a good chance the police will arrest your uncle Freddie for murder. Then you'll be thrown back into foster care."

Together they reached the second-floor landing. "What did you see?" Piper asked.

"Nothin'." Butch wouldn't look at him.

They continued up to the third-floor landing. "Not even this?" Piper pointed to the blood trail leading to the banister outside his apartment door.

"Nuh. I was followin' someone – I heard 'em hurrying downstairs, but never saw who it was. There was screaming 'n' banging coming from Abby's place like there was a fight. I wanted to check it out, but Freddie locked me in."

Piper blocked the hallway. "Does Freddie lock you in every night?"

"I dunno. I'm asleep. All I know is I wanted out, and the door wouldn't budge. I had to kick a hole in it."

"Is there anyone else who could have locked you in?"

"Only Sigrid, but why would she?"

"Hopefully, she's alive to answer that. Stay here."

Piper walked to the last doorway. He photographed the ruptured door frame to Abigail's apartment, and the broken deadlock. The security chain dangling where the timber around the metal screws had ripped away.

"What did that?" Butch asked. The teenager dashed past Piper into the room.

"I told you to stay out there," Piper growled. They both moved towards Sigrid's prone form. Piper held Butch back and shoved him out of the way.

"This room's trashed," Butch declared as he walked around.

"Don't touch anything!" Piper hissed.

Butch glared at him. "What kind of idiot do yer think I am? I'm not leavin' my fingerprints anywhere. Look, I've pulled my sleeves over my hands."

"You go and check the other rooms," Piper told Butch. He watched the teenager move towards the hallway before activating his phone.

"Jenny," Piper said when she answered his phone call, "send the paramedics up here to the third floor. There's a second victim, and this one's still alive. Battered not stabbed, and the apartment's been turned over."

"Hey! Yer gotta see this!" Butch yelled from along the hall. Piper stretched carefully and went to find him. The first bedroom door was ajar. The light was on. Piper was already wearing his leather gloves. He forced his way through the narrow gap. Had Abby barricaded herself in? She didn't seem strong enough. He stopped inside the room, staring at the colourful artwork on the longest wall.

"Not that!" Butch said. Piper turned to see what the boy was pointing at.

He stared at the red markings on the painted wall for a few seconds. Piper pulled out his phone and captured the rough sketches. These line drawings were hastily done. He glanced at the heroic beauty Abby had revealed in the larger drawings. In contrast, the red drawings were ugly sketches – four men with cruel eyes. Abby had invested them with evil intent.

Only when he turned to scan the room did Piper see the message scrawled across the back of the door. He froze for a moment, recognising his name, allowing the messages to sink in.

His chest tightened. It had only been a few weeks since he last crossed swords with Ricardo Baرononi. That day was seared into his memory. It was the 24th of October, the day Piper's team returned from Thailand with his cousin Valentino's body. The security operative understood the need to proceed with care. He glared at the boy who was watching his reaction.

"You haven't seen this," Piper told Butch. The teenager shrugged and turned his back.

Piper shoved the furniture away from the door. He stepped into the hall and made a quick call. Immediately afterwards, he sent an SMS message to Jenny.

Paramedics only.

Delay police.

Cleaner coming.

The sound of falling paper caught Piper's attention. He looked back into the room. Butch balanced on a chair, removing tape from the top corner sheet of the drawing attached to the wall.

"What are you doing?" Piper demanded. He stood next to the chair.

"I heard yer on the phone," Butch muttered, without pausing. "Yer gunna make this disappear. I know you been destroyin' Abby's drawings. You're not gettin' this one."

"And where do you think you can hide it?"

"Under my bed till the police is gone. If I put the unfinished pages on top, be nuthin' but a kid scribbling. I'll take the blank paper an' art stuff too. They dunno Abby drawed 'em 'less you tell, an' you're not gonna do that 'cos – I – know – stuff."

Piper looked at the drawings again. Each sheet of paper was secured independently of the others. It was going to take time. Was he going to help?

The kid was right. This wall-sized drawing was too good to destroy. He rubbed at the closest drawing, and looked at his fingers. Good, she'd used fixative. He considered the composition. Abby had drawn Evie wearing flowing robes. A princess with a white rose crown, like the one she wore at her wedding. She stood in the middle of a raging river. Romano was there too, standing behind her, his tattooed arms crossed over his broad chest as he guarded his wife.

Sigrid was kneeling near the water, a sword and shield beside her. Her attention was focused on the princess in the river. There was Xanda, too, eyes closed in slumber, under a tree. She was dressed in ornamental armour, but her weapons rested on the ground. The now-dead woman seemed at peace. She had tried to keep her history a secret, and he considered what her response would have been when she saw this. Had it made the end easier?

Piper shook himself. He stepped to the wall and began removing tape from the lower sheets of paper. Here was Jenny, clad in black leather. Abby had captured her fierce determination. That wilful stubbornness was portrayed in the tilt of her jaw. But why had Abby drawn Piper standing back to back with Jenny? They were both looking sideways, away from the other figures. Towards where Piper stood now. He examined his representation. He considered the way Abby had captured the essence of the others. He stepped back and pulled out his phone to snap a few photos. What was the artist attempting to convey, and why did it elude him?

Butch was almost finished with his row of sheets. Piper began work on the two sheets that held images of Freddie and Abby. They stood facing each other. She had her hands on his chest, and his hands rested on her waist. There was none of that shy man's awkwardness in the way he was gazing at his beloved. Abby was slender. She had drawn herself with long flowing locks which concealed her broken features...

The final section of the drawing was incomplete. Simple lines and shapes to suggest what the artist intended to add. That figure might be Butch, Piper decided, and there was Marco...

₧✿₨

The doctor came secretly to the ground-floor apartment. Romano admitted the white-haired man via the private entrance through the courtyard. Piper had assured Romano the doctor was trustworthy. He was kept on the *Maximum Security* payroll for occasions such as this. Romano knew his kind. There had been men like him in prison who would suture a wound without reporting the incident to the guards.

Romano was mindful of a previous occasion when Piper had called this doctor. Following Evie's abduction, Piper had insisted she have a full medical examination. He wanted to confirm she had returned unharmed – untouched by Romano's enemies. The doctor did not acknowledge the earlier meeting. Nor did he ask any questions, despite the nature of the emergency.

Abby was lying on the floor in a dimly lit, unfurnished room. There was a bloodstained plastic drop-sheet beneath her. Romano remained in the room, because Piper wanted a full report on everything Abby said. Romano faced the shuttered window, burdened by his intrusion on the woman's privacy.

The doctor began his examination. "The pain started before you fell down the stairs?"

"Yes." Abby's voice was faint.

"But after the fall it intensified to a series of painful spasms.'

"Yes."

"Was this pregnancy planned?"

Her snuffling suggested she was weeping now. She must have shaken her head.

"No?" the doctor surmised. "And you weren't a willing participant? Is this man responsible for your situation?"

Romano spun around. He had been accused of many violent acts, but not this.

"No!" Abby cried out.

"Were you offered a termination? There was no need for this pregnancy to proceed."

"Those men ruined my life, but that didn't mean I had to kill this innocent baby. I thought God had given me something to live for, a glimmer of hope."

"Hmmm. I remember another young woman who talked about God. This man," the doctor glanced at Romano, "was also present when I examined her. How can you believe in God after all the evil things that have happened to you?"

As if to emphasise the finality, he spoke bluntly. "Your baby is dead."

Romano clenched his fists. He stayed silent, watching the heartbroken woman wrestle with the news. He sensed what she said and did next was important.

This man's comments were not dissimilar to the kind of testing that went on in prison. There, emotional vulnerability meant death, or worse, slavery to the dominant few. Would Abby be able to pass the test?

"How can I not? If God hadn't been with me, to give me strength, I would have died. It was His presence that sustained me."

"Some would suggest death was the better option. Do you have the strength to go on, now that your hope has died?"

Abby gasped.

The doctor continued, "How can you expect anyone to love you, once they learn what has happened to you? It will be difficult for you to tolerate intimacy with a man. What happiness will you find with the kind of man who can ignore your ugliness—"

"It's time for you to go," Romano growled, taking a step closer. He would have to talk with Piper about this man.

The doctor shook off Romano's guiding hand. He took his time rising. He turned at the door to address the angry giant as if Abby were no longer present.

"She should be in a hospital, but with proper care her condition isn't life-threatening. She must have complete bed rest. The bleeding and discomfort should settle in a few days.

"The psychological and emotional recovery will take much longer. That is the greater danger. She claims that staying alive is her preference, but I would advise you to watch her closely.

"The injuries from the fall are superficial. She is no stranger to that kind of pain. And she is young. She may become pregnant again."

The doctor moved towards the door through which he had entered, with Romano close behind. The older man turned and looked up at him. Had Romano been wrong? Perhaps it was not Abby who was being tested?

"You think me heartless. You, who are no stranger to the ways of evil men like those who destroyed her life. But something about you is different. You are not the same as them. As long as there are strong men like you and Piper Maxwell, there is hope for the world. I don't know what you intend to do with her, but here is a strong sedative."

He produced a small bottle from his pocket and offered it to Romano. "The instructions are on the label."

Romano closed his fingers around the bottle.

As Romano reached out to close the door behind the departing doctor, the man spoke again. "I was undecided whether I should leave that sedative with you. Piper insisted this would be necessary – she has to be moved secretly, and soon. But I didn't know if I should trust you. I had to be sure you weren't going to abuse her."

Romano stood thinking about what the doctor said, long after his departure. Finally, he stirred and walked back to where Abby lay.

She was pale and still. An occasional tear rolled down her cheek. He thought about his own wife and her pregnancy. He pushed away the emotions that rose at the possibility Evie may face something like this.

He shook his head. His children were a precious answer to a promise God had given them.

But isn't that what Abby had thought? Yet God had allowed her baby to die.

Then he thought about Abby's situation and the words she had used to describe her hope. He had no experience with grieving women. What reference did he have for the heartbreak she was experiencing? He used this weakness and inadequacy to frame his prayers.

> God, give me the right words to give her new hope. I can't accept the harsh verdict the doctor delivered. You are bigger and better than that. You took my brokenness and made me strong again. Please do the same with her.

She stirred. Romano moved to stand where she could look at him. "Abby," he said aloud. "You already know God is bigger and more powerful than the evil that has come after you. Piper is going to move you somewhere safe. Your enemies must think they were successful in getting rid of you. When it is time, I'm going to give you some medicine to put you to sleep. I don't want you to be afraid."

Romano could see she was trying not to cry. "Abby Golding is dead, and I don't know who you are going to become. But of one thing I'm certain: God didn't put you in the apartment next to Freddie by accident. That man loves you. He would walk away from everything for you, but he can't. He has to play his part in convincing the world you are dead."

Romano went to the door and turned again. "Freddie loves you as you are, with your broken heart and your wounded spirit. He sees the hidden beauty within you. He loves you enough to set you free.

"And he will be waiting for you when it's safe for you to return. That's a promise for you to hold on to. He can't come and deliver that promise himself, so I hope I am a convincing messenger.

"Evie and I will be praying for you."

Distress – Increase Sadness

ஐ ☼ ೞ

Ephesians 1:16
I haven't stopped thanking God for you,
remembering you in my prayers.

ஐ ☼ ೞ

The paramedics strapped Sigrid onto the stretcher. Piper turned to Butch and pushed him forward. "You have to go with her."

"What?" Butch protested. One of the paramedics looked up. The teenager dropped his voice to a whisper. "Freddie can go. Why do I hafta go?"

"The police are going to take Freddie. If you're still here, they'll ship you off into emergency care."

"I can take care of myself."

Piper looked him in the eye. "I'm sure you can. But Sigrid did what she could to keep you out of trouble. The least you can do is stay with her until I send someone else."

"Alright. Hang on – why are the police takin' Freddie? You know this ain't down to him. Sigrid could pick 'im up and throw 'im with one hand. Besides, yer already know who di— oomph! Whadya hit me for?"

"I told you to forget what you saw. A police cell may be the safest place for Freddie. It would be convenient for the real killers if he turned up dead. The police would think he took his own life in remorse after murdering his girlfriend. End of story."

"You hafta warn 'im!"

Piper ignored his plea.

He called out to the paramedics as they moved the stretcher towards the door. "Her cousin is going with her."

ಙಿ✿ಲ

Freddie was still where Piper had left him. A whisper passed through the room. Slowly everyone stood. They watched as the paramedics came down the stairs. Butch and Piper came behind them. Sigrid was wearing an oxygen mask. The paramedics carried her stretcher out to the ambulance.

Freddie's shoulders slumped with relief. Sigrid was still alive, and Piper had included Butch in whatever he had planned.

"See ya, Uncle Freddie," Butch called as he passed. "I'm gonna be with Sigrid. Come an' get me when yer finished – I'll wait there. Everything's sorted, so don' worry."

Jenny hurried to intercept Piper at the door. She was still pretending to be in charge. Piper said something. Jenny looked as if she was going to argue with him, and then she shook her head. When she turned, Freddie shivered with dread. Jenny moved towards the two police officers and spoke quietly to them.

Officer Vitali went in the direction of the garden and returned a few minutes later. He was with Piper's men who had investigated Freddie's account of the murder weapon. Freddie had thought Piper might make the knife disappear. But from the eager way Vitali was talking into his phone, those plans had changed.

Jenny and Officer McCormick walked towards him. Freddie waited. He knew he was in deep trouble.

"Now, Mr Kidman," Jenny began, "Understandably, you're upset by recent events. It can't have been easy for you to come back from your walk, and find your girlfriend lying in a pool of blood. This officer is going to send you to the police station so you can make a formal statement."

One of the security guards seized his arm. Freddie tried to shake himself free.

"I can see," she said, "that you're not happy, but it's the best place for you." Jenny turned back to the police. "You can see that he's a little confused. If you're lucky, he might say something incriminating before he realises he needs a lawyer."

�✿�

"How long will they keep me here?" Freddie asked the young man who introduced himself as his lawyer. Grant Messinger didn't look old enough to be a lawyer. He wore his blonde hair in a trendy hipster bun. Instead of a suit, he was wearing blue jeans and a white tee-shirt under his red tartan vest.

"That depends on what the police decide to do next."

"When can I have my clothes back?"

"You had blood on your clothes and your shoes. You won't see them again before the trial."

"You seem certain there'll be a trial."

"The police are building a strong case against you. You need to prepare yourself to be charged. But as soon as they do, we'll make an application for bail. You have good character references and a clean record. Getting you out on bail should only be a formality. You already have a financial guarantor."

"Who did you say hired you?"

"Evie Romano. She asked me to pass on a message." The lawyer looked down at his notes: "She's praying for you. 'Be certain that Abby is in a better place. Remember to keep your story simple. Let your yes be yes and your no be no' – she said you'd know what that meant. Something about you 'going through a difficult interrogation before'. Then Evie finished with 'Butch and Sigrid are safe, so don't worry'."

�✿�

Piper flashed his ID at the front desk of the private hospital, and stormed into the emergency department. He had phoned ahead to prepare them for his coming. Patrick Sims pulled himself upright from where he leaned against the wall.

"What are you doing here?" Piper demanded, keeping his voice low. He looked the young man over thoughtfully. "You're supposed to be on sick leave. Didn't that knife attack in Thailand teach you anything?"

"I'd do the same again, and you know it," Patrick said, running his hands through his blonde hair. "I saved Sofia. That's what you paid me to do."

"You've lost weight. Has the doctor cleared you for work?"

"I'm scheduled to return next Monday. A week isn't going to make much difference. Anyway, Jenny called me because she only needed someone to watch this kid until you got here."

"I'm not a kid!" Butch protested. He emerged from behind the blue curtain that hid the patient from view.

Before Piper could tell the teenager to be quiet, footsteps signalled an approach. A young nurse in a navy uniform hurried towards them. Butch ducked back out of sight. Patrick Sims smiled in her direction and stepped forward to meet her. Jenny Prescott had personally recruited the operative because of his charm.

"I'm sorry, Nancy," the younger man said. "The kid didn't mean to make so much noise. But you have to concede it can't be easy for him, having to wait for his cousin to go off to theatre. Is there any news about when the surgery is likely to happen?"

"The orderlies are on their way now, Patrick. I was coming to tell you," Nancy said with a smile before she focused her attention on Piper. "Is this your employer? Hello, Mr Maxwell. I've been waiting for you to arrive."

She held up her clipboard. "Your office forwarded the medical power of attorney documents. The doctor has confirmed everything is in order. He still needs to talk to you about the surgery. I'll go and tell him you're here. While you wait, here are the forms you have to sign."

After flashing Patrick another smile, Nancy hurried away.

"Why do you hafta sign?" Butch asked, reappearing again. "Youse not a relative."

"Piper has medical power of attorney for all his employees," Patrick said quietly. "It makes managing an emergency easier."

"Sigrid works for *you*?" Butch squawked.

Patrick looked from the boy to his employer in alarm. He took a step further away. "I thought he knew."

Butch didn't notice. He muttered to himself. "Does Uncle Freddie know?" The boy shook his head. "Course he knows. Everybody knows. He probably works for Piper too. That's why Abby come knockin' at our door. Nobody tells me nothin'."

"Because you don't know when to keep your mouth shut," Piper growled.

The boy squinted at Piper. He straightened his posture. Butch stepped closer until he looked the security consultant in the eye. One day, this teenager would be a match for Piper, in strength and stature, but not yet. He was too undisciplined.

As if he could read Piper's thoughts, Butch mimed zipping his mouth closed. He clicked his heels together, raising his hand in a mock military salute. After whirling around, he returned to his chair within the cubicle.

🐲☉˜⊃

Jenny frowned when she saw Marco Fontana on the footpath across the road from the apartment building.

"Why aren't you in school?" she hissed.

"No school today – I'm too sick," Evie's nephew said with a wink. "I've got a terrible cold." The lanky thirteen-year-old grinned. Then he surprised Jenny as he handed her a large takeaway coffee. "Strong and black, just the way you like it." He leaned closer and whispered, "My aunt sent me. Evie said to tell you she'll need more food if she has to feed *two* teenagers."

Jenny nodded. She opened her mouth to tell Marco to go home when there was a buzz of activity at the corner intersection. A delivery truck advanced towards her. Who had authorised that vehicle through the barricade? She thrust the coffee cup back into Marco's hands.

The truck crawled past all the emergency response team vehicles. It had the *Romano* logo emblazoned across the side. As it approached, Jenny could see the driver and his passenger clearly.

Why were Nelson Felmingham and Oliver Johnston pretending to be delivery men? These *Maximum Security* operatives had extensive military training. And why had Piper Maxwell failed to let her know? With her hands on her hips, Jenny frowned. The truck went to the end of the street and executed a precise three-point turn. It stopped outside the security entrance leading to Romano's ground-floor apartment. Romano appeared on the footpath. The two men disembarked and went to meet him. They were wearing the distinctive black overalls with the red *Romano* insignia.

Glancing around, Jenny saw two policemen turn in their direction. She wondered why Officers McCormick and Vitali were still on the scene. She hurried to intercept them, but they were too close. Jenny checked Romano for any sign that he recognised them from Evie's accident last year.

"You can't park here," McCormick said.

Romano gave them no more than a glance. "That's not what your Police Superintendent said." He threw open the truck's heavy steel doors. "I've been inconvenienced enough. I won't wait any longer." He dragged out the ramp, nodding to Nelson and Oliver. "Start unloading."

His "employees" went into the back of the van. They wrestled with a large object swathed in grey blankets and protective bubble-wrap.

"Where are you taking that?" McCormick asked, while Vitali talked into his phone. "You can't go through the foyer. It's a crime scene."

Romano turned towards his corner of the apartment block. "I have my own access. Do you want to come and inspect my aunt's apartment, in case I'm hiding something there? Or do you think I've already been here and come back to clean up? Do you want this *Maximum Security* guard to pull up the security camera footage?" He pointed at Jenny. "You have authorisation for that?"

"Of course," Jenny murmured, pulling out her phone. "One moment, Mr Romano, while I send for someone—"

"That won't be necessary," Officer Vitali said, returning from making his call. "Just let us check this van. Then you can go ahead with the unloading." Nelson and Oliver came back to the pavement. The two police officers took their time making their inspection. Occasionally they glanced towards the glowering giant.

As soon as the policemen stepped down, Romano sprang into the back of the van. With little effort, he seized the plastic-wrapped bundle and carried it out to the footpath. Nelson and Oliver followed his lead, struggling to carry an identically wrapped item. It was shaped like a couch. About the size of the furniture Romano had up the road. Two steps from the gate, Romano stopped and turned towards the policemen again. He balanced his burden against his hip, pointing to the rubbish skip beside the footpath.

"You have my rubbish skip taped off. What for? I need it to dispose of this plastic wrap. Then the skip is going to be collected."

"That isn't going to happen. The forensic team have already slapped a warrant on your skip. Any extra rubbish will have to go back in the van."

Romano grunted, glaring at them. The two officers moved backwards, bumping into Jenny.

"Make yourself useful," Officer McCormick muttered at her. "Keep an eye on him. Once a criminal, always a criminal."

Jenny gasped at the insult, spinning towards Romano. His granite-like glare didn't falter. He nodded towards the gate. "You heard them. Make yourself useful."

She placed her hand on the security panel, waiting for the gate to unlock. Romano seemed impatient, standing too close. The heat of his breath hit her neck. His deep voice whispered near her ear. "As soon as the van has cleared the barricade, find some excuse to get out of here. Take your team with you."

"What's going on?"

"Later," he said. "Keep those officers away. And get rid of Marco."

Jenny blinked. She had forgotten about the curious teenager.

"Your coffee's getting cold," Marco said with a smile, appearing beside her. He peered into the delivery van. There were still more wrapped bundles. "I don't know why Romano needed anyone to help. Did you see how he picked up that couch?"

"Thanks for the coffee," Jenny replied. "Get yourself home and tell Evie not to let you leave the compound again."

Marco looked at all the activity. He shrugged and smiled broadly, before running off towards the main street. Jenny used her phone to instruct someone to make sure he arrived home.

She finished her coffee while she waited for the men to take the second load of furniture away. It wasn't long before they returned. Nelson and Oliver carried a massive roll of bubble-wrap between them. Romano followed with a mound of grey blankets. He paused as the two lighter men struggled to carry their load up the ramp. Oliver tripped, and his end of the roll smacked the ground. Jenny held her breath. Nelson stood at the top of the ramp, his arms still wrapped around the roll. He was in danger of falling.

Romano put down his load to grab Oliver's end as if the rolled object were only an oversized newspaper. He nodded to Nelson, before launching the fallen end into the van. The impatient giant didn't linger. As soon as his hands were free, he turned to retrieve his bundle.

The momentum took Nelson by surprise. He fell back against the inside of the truck. Bang!

With a groan, Nelson emerged from under the roll. Oliver scrambled to help him move the bubble-wrap further from the door.

Officer McCormick's voice came from nowhere. "There's more than bubble-wrap there."

Romano glared at Jenny. The uniformed officer peered into the truck.

"Help yourself to another inspection, Officer," Romano said. He stepped to the open door. "I can't use my skip, so I bundled the drop sheets in with this lot. My painter was clumsy, but he used lots of plastic. Perhaps you want to check out these blankets too?"

As he spoke, Romano launched his burden into the back of the truck.

Whoomph! Even Romano looked surprised as the bundle of grey fabric partially unfurled. It spread out to cover everything in the truck. Nelson bore the brunt. Oliver dragged him from under it. They both descended to the footpath.

The police officer mounted the ramp, tossing a blanket out of the way. He crouched next to the bubble-wrap roll, peeling back the layers at Nelson's end. He picked up another blanket and tossed it behind him. Then he stood, viciously kicking at the roll further along. McCormick turned to see how Romano responded to his actions. He stomped on the roll.

"Satisfied?" Romano asked. "If you've finished your inspection, I have work to do."

Romano reached for the ramp and picked it up. Officer McCormick had to jump out of the way as the angry giant tossed the ramp onboard. The heavy doors slammed shut.

"What are you waiting for?" Romano demanded of his "employees".

Nelson and Oliver leapt into action. They each ran to their side of the cab and climbed up. The doors banged shut. The engine roared. In a smooth motion, the truck headed back the way it had come. Romano didn't linger, striding off towards the main street without a backward glance.

Jenny watched them leave before signalling her team. She told the Crime Scene Supervisor her intentions before strolling to her waiting van.

"Where to?" the man in the driver's seat asked, uncomfortable with this unexpected responsibility.

"Just drive," Jenny snapped. "I need time to think…"

Dissent – Differ in Opinion

ॐ ☼ ॐ

Hebrews 6:10 God will not forget the love you invested
when you served His people.

ॐ ☼ ॐ

When Jenny arrived at the private airport, she parked beside the *Maximum Security* vehicles already there, and hurried across the tarmac towards the waiting helicopter.

"What took you so long?" Piper asked as he appeared from the shadows of the hangar.

"It would have helped if you told me where to meet you," Jenny snapped.

Piper opened the door and Jenny clambered aboard as the rotors began to spin. Oliver Johnston nodded from the pilot's seat.

Jenny listened to Piper's reply, as he buckled himself into the co-pilot's position. "You're here, so stop complaining. You're the only one who understands where I'm taking Abby. She's going to need you when she wakes."

Jenny looked away from her infuriating employer. Only then did she acknowledge the other passengers. She stomped on her feelings, annoyed that she had allowed Piper to distract her.

"Take over from Nelson," Piper said to her.

Nelson Felmingham, one of Piper's more experienced field operatives, was squeezing a bag attached to a mask over Abigail's mouth and nose. The broken woman was unconscious, lying on a stretcher.

Nelson moved aside, allowing Jenny to take over the procedure. A surge of adrenalin hit Jenny. Did Piper realise the panic that would erupt when Abby awoke? In this confined space, the consequences could be catastrophic. Jenny checked the patient's arms were securely strapped into place.

"Why does Abby need the bag valve mask?" she asked.

Nelson shoved a pair of headphones on her head, before climbing over her to exit the compartment. The door slammed behind him.

"You were there." Piper's voice was hard to hear over the engine's roar as the helicopter rose into the air. "That policeman stomped on her, and then he smothered her with blankets. Romano knew what he was doing with the bubble wrap, or she might not have survived. She wasn't breathing when Nelson unwrapped her – inside the *Romano* workshop, no more than a few minutes later. From the blood on her face, her nose is smashed again. Nelson revived her, but with the sedative in her system, she needs help to breathe."

"You're taking her to the Institute? Did you tell her what you planned, or is she going to wake up as I did and discover what you've done?"

Piper's laugh was infuriating. "I've heard no complaints about your new face."

"You acted without my consent. I could have sued you!"

"But you didn't."

Jenny looked at her patient. *Stay focused. Keep Abby ventilated and alive.* Her hands remembered their training, but her mind retreated to those dark days. That terrible awakening, the sterile place of bandages and constant pain. Piper had been waiting for her when she opened her eyes. She had hardly known him then, this mercenary captain who had taken charge of her life.

Piper had leaned closer so she could see him through the bandages that swathed her head. After finding her broken body when the battle was over, he had carried her to the Institute. He listed her injuries as if they were nothing of any importance. But then he finished with the unforgivable revelation. She had undergone extensive facial reconstruction. The surgeon was world-renowned. Piper had granted him permission to go beyond repair to remodel her appearance.

The face that looked at Jenny in the mirror each day was undeniably beautiful. But it was not her own. She had hated him then. This proud man who thought he was doing her a favour.

Only later did someone show her the before-surgery photos. He was right – her old face was gone. This new one was a blank canvas. One he had taught her to camouflage with makeup as each case required her to become someone new. He was the only one who truly knew her...

Piper's autocratic decision had erased the physical scars he said would have inspired pity and self-loathing. But the recovery had been painful – more than physical. The trauma had ripped apart her emotional and spiritual equilibrium. In remaking her face, he had undone her connection with her identity. It had been a bitter fight – finding herself again, recovering the will to live.

Piper had shown her no sympathy. He had refused to leave her wallowing in self-pity. His actions had driven her from that dark place. He had made himself the target for her anger, goading her to prove she was more than a broken soldier. He had insisted that she fight harder, to convince him she was worthy of his time.

Only when she'd been fit enough to leave the hospital had he revealed his plans. He said the decision was hers to make. She could walk out the door and never see him again. Or she could pledge herself to his cause. But they both knew which she would choose. Had he known, when he had taken her from the battlefield, that he could bind her to him with invisible cords?

Jenny closed her eyes. She knew Piper was watching her. He had never stopped testing and challenging her. One day, he would push her too far, and she would leave. As her hands squeezed the bag, she registered the whoosh of life-giving air delivered to Abby. Unexpected empathy awoke within her. This broken woman was unprepared for the journey ahead.

"You will have to keep her sedated," Jenny said. "It will be months before the bandages finally come off, and she's not strong enough to survive."

"Someone said the same about you."

She looked at him then. "You never told me that."

"I've been waiting for the right time. What would Evie say if she knew what it cost you to become who you are?"

"Evie would say God has a plan."

"And what would you say?"

"Evie says God has a time for everything. I'll reserve my answer until I'm sure the time is right."

Piper laughed and turned back towards the windscreen. The helicopter flew on.

ଊ ✧ ଋ

The uniformed custody sergeant marched Freddie to an interview room. The door closed behind him. He was wary. It had been hours since his arrest and removal from the murder scene. The chair where his young lawyer should be sitting was empty. Why had he been summoned?

There were two unfamiliar men already seated at the small table. They were not part of the murder investigation team, so what did they want? The silence lengthened.

"Where's my lawyer?"

"We want to have a little informal conversation," one of the men said with a smile. He had perfect teeth. His jacket

124

looked expensive. "Just the three of us. There's no need to trouble your lawyer over this trivial matter."

Freddie remained standing. The confident man continued, "My name is Clayton Wolfe, and this is Brian Grovener."

The second man stood. He gestured towards an empty chair on the opposite side of the table. "Please take a seat, Mr Kidman."

Freddie sat, with his arms folded across his body. He glanced up at the video camera in the corner. Clayton Wolfe leaned forward. "This conversation isn't being recorded, so feel free to say whatever you want."

"You have nothing to fear from us," Brian Grovener added. "We're with the Federal Police Witness Protection Agency. I'm based here in Melbourne, and Clayton has flown in from Sydney. We have a few questions to ask you about the woman who was killed."

Freddie nodded.

"Did you know Louise was in the Witness Protection Program?" Brian asked.

Freddie took his time answering. He frowned as he glanced from one man to the other. "Louise who?"

Brian's face showed confusion. "Louise Silverton."

This grey-haired man was the elder of the pair, closer to retirement with a weary look about him. But the younger dark-haired man didn't seem surprised at Freddie's reply.

"Perhaps you knew her by another name," Clayton suggested. "Abigail Golding?"

Freddie unfolded his arms and placed both hands on the table. He stared at his hands, forming the words carefully. What game was Clayton Wolfe playing? "I know – knew – Abigail."

"Did Abigail tell you she was in the Witness Protection Program?" Clayton asked.

Freddie looked straight at him. "No." *She* hadn't told him.

"Did Piper Maxwell tell you not to cooperate with us?"

Something was definitely wrong. The detectives investigating the woman's death made no mention of Piper. "No."

"No? Are you sure Piper Maxwell didn't apply pressure to you?" Clayton asked.

"I told you, no. You don't seem to be listening. Before I answer any more questions, I want my lawyer."

"Has Piper Maxwell been communicating with you through your lawyer?" Clayton asked.

"No."

Clayton didn't let up. "What did Piper Maxwell promise you for your compliance?"

Freddie turned towards Brian. "I answered his question. If you have nothing more to ask me, I want to go back to my cell."

"You're going to regret your decision not to cooperate," Clayton told him. "In the next hour, the murder team are going to formally charge you with Louise Silverton's murder. Then you will find out your loyalty to Piper Maxwell is useless. You're going to jail for a very long time."

Freddie rose to his feet. "I didn't murder Louise Silverton, or Abigail Golding, or whatever her name was. If she was in Witness Protection, she didn't tell me. Trusting you obviously didn't work for her, and I don't intend to make the same mistake."

"You've made yourself an enemy," Clayton snarled. Freddie remained silent. Eventually, they called for the sergeant to take him away.

Dispute –
Call into Question

ଽଠ ✹ ଔ

2 Corinthians 5:19
God reconciles the world to Himself
through Christ,
and we carry His reconciliation message.

ଽଠ ✹ ଔ

Beep, beep, beep-whoosh. Beep, beep, beep-whoosh.

That sound was beginning to annoy Jenny. Her patient had stabilised, and remained sedated. Her breathing was assisted by the machine as she awaited surgery. Every footfall in the hallway had the security agent ready to leap up. It had been ten years since Jenny's last visit to the Institute. Yet the interval had not diminished the potency of her memories.

She returned her attention to the unconscious woman, studying her ruined face. Jenny's gaze landed on the handwritten name above the bed. The words troubled her: Xanda Jadaran.

Jenny had been too involved with Abby's medical care to realise what Piper had done. Afterwards, he had dismissed her protests, silencing her with one of his looks. He expected her to trust him, as she had done a thousand times before. They both knew he was seldom wrong, but that did nothing to appease the gnawing doubts.

It made perfect sense. Swapping the identity of the deceased *Maximum Security* agent with their fugitive.

Abby would have a passport, employment record, health insurance and a bank account. This should make it impossible for her enemies to find her.

It had also proven convenient for organising her surgery. Even here, at the secretive Institute, protocols had changed in ten years. There were permission forms to be correctly authorised and approved. As one of Piper's employees, Xanda had already signed over to him medical power of attorney. Piper intended to make full use of those provisions.

With an almost imperceptible noise, the door swung open. A nurse in a crisp white uniform stepped inside, followed by two young men in doctor's coats. The next person to enter was an older, silver-haired man, dressed in an elegant suit. Jenny stood, ran her hands through her blonde hair, and unconsciously approached her patient. The final man to enter was Piper. He closed the door behind him.

"Jennifer," the older man said, striding across the room. He studied her silently for several minutes before taking hold of her chin. He tilted her face into the full glare of the light. "I never expected to see you again, and certainly not under these circumstances."

He turned to the younger doctors and waved them forward. The surgeon pointed out the almost invisible scars. He discussed the extensive work he had done in his reconstruction. Jenny felt sick as he dispassionately described the injuries. He extolled the multiple operations required before he was satisfied with his work. She kept her eyes focused on a spot on the ceiling, falling back into old habits.

"You have taken good care of your new face," he concluded. "You have aged well and retained your beauty. There is no need for me to do any repair work."

Jenny gasped and lost focus. This surgeon still knew how to cut through her defences. For a moment, she looked directly into the doctor's eyes.

He smiled. "You are relieved about that. And now you have brought me another young woman in need of a miracle."

"It was Piper who brought her," Jenny muttered.

"It is always Piper," the doctor said, patting her on the shoulder as if she were a small child. "But he has decided you should make the final decision."

Piper leaned against the wall. Jenny couldn't read his expression. Why was he putting this decision in her hands? He knew she disapproved.

"What do you intend to do to 'Xanda'?" Jenny asked.

The surgeon approached the unconscious woman and detailed the work. "Repair her nose so she can breathe again. Make it a little narrower, and enhance the shape. Remove the scarring from these older injuries; re-sculpt her eyebrows; adjust her cheekbones and soften the shape of her jaw.

"Her own mother won't recognise her when I'm done," he concluded. "But you have firsthand experience of that. Only you can truly appreciate the miracle. Walking out into the world, free from the danger that your enemies might recognise you."

Those words hit her hard. She glanced at Piper.

He smiled.

He knew he had won.

৪০✿৪

(Wednesday 15th November)

It was ten-thirty. Freddie stood on the footpath outside the remand centre. He had been rudely awakened after lights out and informed he was free to go. All the charges had been dropped.

129

A uniformed officer had delivered him to the front entrance without ceremony. Before he could gather his thoughts, he was expelled into the darkness.

He had no money and no idea where he was. His phone had been returned, but the battery was dead. Freddie looked both ways before crossing the street. The few passing cars paid him no attention. Perhaps he had become invisible?

Heavy rain began to fall.

Perfect!

Freddie started walking but found no comfort from the activity. He fell into a familiar rhythm. The distant city landmarks came steadily closer, yet he experienced no relief. He had longed for freedom, but the reality left a bitter taste in his mouth. He should be thankful, but with each step, it became harder to remember why.

His mind picked up the well-known monologue of despair.

While in detention, he had been kept in isolation, segregated "for his own protection". It had been a week since he'd had any contact with anyone from the outside. Not even his lawyer had visited him. Alone with his thoughts, he had waited in vain for the voice in his head to return. The longer the silence, the more determined he became in asking for assistance. Surely his untimely release was affirmation that he had not been abandoned?

Okay, God. I asked You to get me out. Now what?

Blinding headlights came around the corner. Freddie raised his arm to shield his eyes. He heard the powerful roar of a sports car approaching, then a rapid deceleration.

Screech. Swoo-oo-shhh. A spray of cold water from the gutter washed over him as the vehicle executed a daring one-eighty-degree turn. The sports car stopped beside him, and the passenger door swung open.

"Get in," a familiar voice said from the red Maserati.

Freddie obeyed.

Romano sped away. "I almost drove past you – I wasn't expecting you to have walked ten kilometres in this rain."

"A little rain never hurt anyone." Freddie suddenly felt much better. He hadn't been forgotten. "Your timing is perfect. How did you know where I was?"

"Evie told me you'd been released. It took her a while to convince me she was serious. I waited for Piper to confirm she was right. I should have known better. Then Evie told me I had to hurry or you'd think God had abandoned you. That's why I was taking a short-cut, and there you were."

ॐ ✿ ॐ

(Thursday 16th November)

"Stop arguing and eat your soup," Freddie told Sigrid. He was standing beside the injured woman's hospital bed, holding a spoon to her lips. She had her jaws clamped shut. The intimidating woman was helpless, with both arms in plaster and one of her legs in traction. This made her stubbornness more admirable.

Butch was watching the exchange from a comfortable chair beside the window. The private room had a great view of the city, but this unfolding drama was more entertaining. "Now yer see what I've had to put up with," he chuckled. "Worse than a little kid, our couz."

Freddie turned towards his nephew. "You do know she isn't a relative?"

"Sure! She tol' me again and again when she started talkin'. But with you in the nick, I needed a rellie. An almost-dead pretend one's better than nothin'."

"Freddie's out now," Sigrid muttered. The red-haired man pounced, thrusting the spoon into her mouth. She spluttered

131

and spat. Soupy liquid dribbled down her chin. "Urgh! I hate this hospital muck. If you're going to insist on feeding me, send the kid out to get me some real food."

"Italian?" Butch asked. "Marco just sent a pic of what he's having. His grandfather's restaurant's only a tram ride away. If Freddie hands over some cash, I'm off."

A quick negotiation followed, and Butch was on his way.

"It would be wonderful if all our problems could be so easily sorted," Freddie remarked as he cleaned up the mess. "Now that we're rid of Butch, tell me the real reason you don't want to come and live with us when you get out of here."

"You said yourself I'm not a relative."

"I can't see anyone else lining up to offer you somewhere to live."

"I like being on my own."

"Do your family even know what's happened?" Freddie asked.

Sigrid gazed out the window. She took a long time to answer. Freddie was comfortable with her silence. Finally, she turned dull eyes towards him. "Not everyone has a family that cares. But you know that already. I've seen your file. Apart from your half-brother, you haven't had any contact with your family in years. Your father's an abusive alcoholic, and your mother has dementia. She forgot who you were years ago. I bet you didn't even let your brother know you were arrested."

Freddie frowned at her. "Your point is?"

"Why would you want me? We have nothing in common. Everything about your boring little life infuriates me."

The insult bounced off him. He smiled. He'd heard worse in recent days. He settled back in his chair. "It's going to be a long time before you're fit enough to return to work. Keeping an eye on Butch and tormenting me will give you something to do."

Sigrid grunted. "Those stairs make it impossible. There's no way I could manage them on crutches."

"Already sorted while I was locked up." Freddie laughed. "Butch and Marco moved most of our belongings into Romano's ground-floor apartment. They recruited Romano to deal with the heavy stuff. You get a room to yourself. I have to share with Butch so his sister Nikki can move in when we get the all-clear."

He pulled out his phone and brought up some pictures.

Sigrid leaned closer. "Show me the rest of the apartment."

Freddie flicked through the album. Sigrid caught her breath when he reached the photo of the lounge room. Abigail's unfinished drawing dominated the view.

"Piper let you keep it?"

"Butch insisted. He reckons he has a hold over Piper because he 'knows stuff'. I haven't worked out what, but I'm not going to say anything. I don't want to risk Piper changing his mind."

Sigrid leaned back against the pillows, frowning at him. "She's not coming back."

Freddie met her stare with a smile. "You don't know that for certain. I'm going to hang onto the hope she will find a way."

"She won't be the same. She won't be Abby."

"I know," he said quietly. "Abigail was buried when they had the funeral for your friend. No-one told me her name."

"Xanda," Sigrid whispered. "We made a good team. We understood each other. She was the sister I never had."

Silence followed. Freddie wondered if she had said all she was going to reveal.

"We both understood the risk," Sigrid said with a faraway look in her eyes. "The enemy took us by surprise."

He watched her face harden. The warrior mask was back in place. "But I can assure you Piper will make them pay. This isn't over yet."

Disown - Refuse to Acknowledge

❧ ✿ ❧

*John 3:36a Only those who believe
and do not reject the Son will receive eternal life.*

❧ ✿ ❧

"Do you know where you are?"

Abigail spun around. The warrior princess she knew as Xanda stood there, beside a giant tree. This woman wore the same armour and held the ceremonial weapons she had imagined. But they were brighter and more extravagant than her drawing. There were other subtle differences. Xanda's eyes sparkled, the hint of amusement softening her expression. Her dark hair was longer, and her helmet decorated with jewels. Abigail looked around, but they were alone in the meadow.

"I'm in my drawing," she said, "but this is much better than I could ever have created."

"What else do you remember?"

Abigail searched for answers. Pictures flashed in her mind. Scene by scene, she experienced again the fear and the despair. "You're dead!"

With a bound, the warrior sprang into the air. She executed an amazing sequence of spins and turns before she landed. Xanda continued to twirl and dance beside her.

"As you can see, I am very much alive." The warrior held out her hand, inviting Abigail to dance with her among the wildflowers. They jumped and whirled across the grassy meadow. The joy continued until they were near the river of her imagination. The waterfall thundered and roared. Abigail stood transfixed beside the mighty cascade. Feeling the wetness on her skin, she plunged her fingers into the rainbow spray.

"It's so beautiful," Abigail whispered. "I could stay here forever."

A shadow passed across Xanda's face. "We both know that is impossible. This is but a dream. Soon you will awaken. Open your heart and soak up the memories. They will sustain you until you are out of danger."

"Xanda, why am I here?"

"You call me Xanda, for that is the form I have taken in your vision. But that is not my name."

"So, who are you?"

"I have had many names, as I have worn many faces. You may call me Wisdom."

Abigail nodded. A new idea sprang into her mind. She asked eagerly, "Do you know what my name is? I've had so many names I no longer know who I am. I don't remember the name I was born with. I forgot it when I lost my sister."

"I cannot tell you your true name. But I can tell you what you are to call yourself when you wake. The woman who died in your place has passed on her name to you. They buried her broken body with your name. You are to live with hers."

Abigail stepped back in shock. "I can't steal her name!"

"It's not stealing if it's gifted to you."

"But her friends – every time they hear my name, they'll know I'm not the real Xanda."

Wisdom smiled and reached out her hand. Abigail extended her own. As soon as the warrior's fingers took hold, she was drawn right to the edge of the river.

"Then use her full name, the one on her passport. Call yourself Alixanda Jadaranata. Live her life."

Abigail looked at the waves. Her fear began to stir. "I couldn't take her place. I'm nothing like her."

"You only have to be yourself."

"What if I don't want to be me?" she asked, directing her eyes away from the river. "Wisdom, can't I stay here with you? I have nothing and nobody to live for."

Wisdom pointed across the river. There, shimmering and transparent on the farther side, stood Freddie Kidman. He carried a small child on his hip, and an older boy held his hand. They watched her from across the water. As she stared, the children began to fade. Now he stood alone. He waited. His figure aged with the passing years. Finally, the old man lay down beside the river.

With a cry, Abigail threw herself into the river. The roar of the waterfall grew louder, and a strong wind whipped the waves. The sky darkened, turning day to night. Now the heavens filled with brilliant flashes. The stars tumbled, falling towards her. She screamed. Water flooded her open mouth as she plunged out of her depth. The velvety blue waters were warm, and sweet like honey. Her head bobbed back to the surface as she gasped for breath.

While struggling to keep her head above the water, she searched in vain for the riverbank. There was nothing but raging water in every direction. Exhausted, her body sank beneath the waves.

The river wild and mighty swept her away.

଼ ☼ ଼

Jenny had fallen asleep. She awoke to the sound of strident alarms. The familiar beep, beep, beep from Abby's monitor had been replaced by a single note.

"No!" Jenny screamed, leaping to the bedside. "Don't you die on me!"

She shook the unresponsive body, dimly aware she was no longer alone. Someone shouted for her to get out of the way. Pushed aside, Jenny stumbled and caught herself as she was about to fall. The medical team ignored Jenny as they attempted to resuscitate the patient.

"No! No! No! This isn't supposed to happen!" Jenny paced in the background. "God! You can't let her die. This can't be your plan."

My plans never fail.

What? Jenny froze. Where had that voice come from? As she looked around, the air in front of her shimmered. The hospital room faded from view. Strange blue darkness surrounded her, so dense she could feel it soft and warm on her skin like a thick blanket. Behind her, there came a mighty roar. Even as she turned, she knew what she would see: Evie's river. Jenny stood transfixed.

It was more beautiful than she had imagined – and wilder. The din was deafening. She marvelled as the velvety-blue waves fluoresced in the darkness.

"Why is it so dark? Evie said this place was filled with light."

A warm breeze ruffled her hair, then suddenly the sky was ablaze. Jenny shielded her eyes.

Now, she was standing on the grassy verge at the river's edge. From somewhere to her right, the figure of a small woman stepped forward. Jenny squinted to see her more clearly.

The woman was wearing some kind of ancient armour. Recognition made her gasp. It looked like Xanda, dressed as Abby had drawn her in that final artwork.

Horrified, Jenny called out, but the warrior did not pause.

Xanda stepped into the raging river. In heavy armour, Xanda wouldn't stand a chance. Jenny rushed forward, launching herself feet first out over the waves. She refused to lose another life.

Whoosh! Water shot high into the air as Jenny landed in waist-deep water. Xanda turned then, a few metres beyond her would-be-rescuer's reach. The water was already up to the shorter woman's chin. The warrior saluted her before disappearing beneath the surface.

Jenny called Xanda's name as she pushed through the water. When she reached the spot, the woman floated just below the surface. Plunging her arms under the waves, Jenny grabbed hold of the unresisting body. She heaved Xanda out of the water. She was much lighter than Jenny expected, flying high into the air.

What had happened to the ceremonial armour? Xanda now wore a long clinging gown. Then Jenny realised her mistake: gravity still worked in this place. The body plummeted towards the water. The rescuer leapt to retrieve her. With a sigh, the woman in the water rolled over onto her back. Jenny stared at an unfamiliar face. She puzzled over a sense of recognition. There was something about the wide brown eyes...

The revelation hit Jenny like a wrecking ball. Those eyes belonged to Abby.

Jenny touched the new face. "What will I call you?"

As her fingers grazed the smooth skin, a blue light flashed. Every part of Jenny's body felt the shock. Darkness clouded her senses, but she thought she heard a whispered reply...

୫ ☼ ୧

With a groan, Jenny pulled herself upright. Her head hurt. She tried to move, but her right arm was tethered by something. Her eyes flew open. Why was she lying in a hospital bed, attached to one of those monitors? She yanked the sensor from her finger. Another strident alarm sounded.

She swore, swinging her legs over the side of the bed. The floor loomed to meet her. A nurse saved her from pitching face-forward onto the floor. Shaken, Jenny allowed herself to be shoved back onto the bed.

"You've finally come round," Piper said, from the doorway. "It's been three hours since you fainted."

"I never faint," Jenny snapped. She glanced at the nurse, as Piper stepped closer.

"If I hadn't seen it happen, I'd agree with you." He waved the attendant away. The nurse closed the door as she left. Piper drew a chair closer to Jenny's bed. He leaned over and stared into her eyes. She battled the desire to hide from his inspection.

"What did you see?" she asked. "Wait – what are you doing here?"

"Today was scheduled for removing some of the stitches," Piper said. He leaned back, folding his arms across his broad chest. "I wanted to be here in case anything went wrong. I walked in to find the crash team in her room using the defibrillator. You were standing out of the way, staring into space. I've never seen you that shade of grey. Then you keeled over. Looked like a faint to me."

She raised her hand to her temple, patting the dressing. "What have they done to me?"

"Your favourite surgeon wanted to make your new scar disappear. I told him you wouldn't appreciate his handiwork. They used glue to close the wound. I'm more interested in finding out why you fainted. I got them to run a barrage of tests. They couldn't find anything wrong with you. They even did a tox screen in case you'd been self-medicating."

"What happened to A-a-alixanda?"

He frowned. "Why are you using that name?"

"She told me to."

Piper recoiled. "When?"

"After—" Jenny hesitated. He wasn't going to like what she said. "After I pulled her out of Evie's river."

Piper stormed from the room. He was back a few minutes later, to resume his seat. Jenny had never seen him so angry. He glared at her. "She confirmed your story."

"What? She's awake? Oh, God!" Jenny tried to get off the bed. "Tell me they didn't attempt to remove the bandages with her awake?"

His muscular arms restrained her. They regularly sparred in the gym, and she knew he was stronger. He held her on the bed. For a moment, she forgot he was someone she could trust. Her heart threatened to explode within her chest. He stared into her eyes, acknowledging her panic. Jenny stilled; and he released her.

"Get a grip, woman. Nothing happened to warrant this hysteria. They had to bring her round after they got her heart going again.

"The doctors asked her if she knew who she was - I was ready with some excuse.

"But she looked straight at me. She said her name was Alixanda Jadaranata. Then she asked for you. She made me promise no-one would touch her until she'd seen you."

"Thank God!" Jenny breathed a sigh of relief.

I told you My plans never fail.

Dismiss - Refuse to Consider

৪ ☼ ৫

*Isaiah 8:15 Many will stumble, fall and be broken,
becoming ensnared and captured.*

৪ ☼ ৫

Freddie yawned and stretched. He had chosen to spend New Year's Eve in Sigrid's hospital room rather than attend Evie's celebration at her family restaurant.

"Happy New Year!" Butch shouted, raising his bottle of soft drink. He looked from Freddie to Sigrid. Their response was lacklustre.

Sigrid grabbed the television remote. "You've seen the fireworks. Now go home."

Butch opened his mouth, uttering something uncomplimentary. Sigrid poked him with one of her crutches. "Enough of that language, boy," she scolded him. "One of my goals for the New Year is to teach you to watch your mouth."

"Ya have to catch me first," the teenager said, ducking out of her way.

Sigrid was on her feet in an instant. She pinned Butch against the private hospital room wall with a crutch, then hobbled from her armchair until she stood nose to nose with the cheeky teenager. "My second goal is to teach you how to stay out of trouble. That looks like a long-term challenge."

"I'd rather yer teached me how to use those sticks as weapons," Butch retaliated, as she released him. He rubbed his chest, careful to take a step further away. "For a cripple, yer move fast."

Sigrid whirled, on her way back to the armchair. Freddie stepped between them. "Take it easy, you two. If you can't stop bickering, I'll tell the doctors Sigrid's release on Tuesday won't work. She'll have to stay here for rehab, instead of being a day patient. That will ruin both your plans."

"Just havin' fun," Butch complained. "You know my sister Nikki's comin' ta visit, to see how she likes it. Yer can't cancel now."

"I'd like to see you try and stop me leaving, Kidman," Sigrid snorted.

Freddie stood his ground, a smile lighting his face. "Sigrid, I forgot to give you your New Year's present from Piper." He activated his phone. "Take a look at this."

She glared at the screen.

Orders for Sigrid Ericson.
Welcome back to active duty.
Placing you under direct command of Freddie Kidman.
Obey all reasonable directives.
This order is in force until you are medically fit.
PS Don't kill him.
Don't make me come. Piper.

Sigrid shrugged and turned away. "Round one to you, Kidman. Thanks for giving me the extra incentive to pass rehab as fast as I can. Now get out of here. I need my rest."

❧ ✿ ☙

"Where are we going?" Jenny asked as she climbed into the helicopter. From the pilot's seat, Piper tossed her the second headset as he completed his pre-flight check. The rotors roared. She buckled her harness as the machine lifted into the air. Jenny considered the post-midnight traffic on the multi-lane highways below. New Year's Eve revellers were making their way home.

144

"What's so urgent that you hauled me out of the party before the clock struck midnight?" Jenny asked. "And why weren't you there? Evie kept asking me if everything was alright. You said you were going."

"Something came up."

"What kind of something?"

"I've tracked down a lead on one of the men from Alixanda's red sketches. I know where he's going to be later today, and everything is set. All I need now is the bait."

"So I'm the bait?" she asked. "Is that why you told me to change out of my party dress?"

"You're too old for this mission. Our target prefers his victims much younger. He haunts bus depots looking for runaways. I need you to coach Alixanda—"

"You what? Are you crazy? She's not one of your minions—"

"She's on the payroll."

Jenny snorted. "That's a technicality, and you know it. She's not trained. She won't be able to defend herself."

"We'll be close by. As soon as she has the incriminating evidence, you can leap out and rescue her..."

Again. Rescue her again. The unspoken word filled the silence between them. When had he started holding back? Jenny frowned, staring into the darkness outside. Things had changed between them.

It had started when his now-dead cousin, Valentino, went missing. Piper excluded her from briefings and ordered everyone to keep information from her. There were secret phone calls and clandestine meetings. He sidelined her from daily operations by assigning her unimportant jobs.

Like being nursemaid to John Edwards during the original Sofia-Valentino mission. Piper had insisted she remain available to shadow Evie Romano. He had held back his reasons for granting that woman Priority One status.

Wait. That was when it really started: after Evie's kidnapping. Jenny had been instrumental in her miraculous rescue. The security expert's instincts had always been good, but what were the odds Jenny's hunch about the *White Rose Café* would deliver the kidnappers to them? It had been fun watching Piper arc up over the implications that Evie's God had told Jenny where to look.

There was her mistake.

Now her harmless banter had become a wall between them.

A stumbling block.

Piper's voice cut through her reverie. "You've changed."

"What?" She glared at him.

"You're different since you fainted at the Institute."

"No I'm not."

"Tell me you're not hearing voices or dreaming about Evie's river, and I'll believe you."

Jenny blinked. The words formed, but she shook her head. He would know she was lying. She looked away. "I'm not the only one."

"Not the only one dreaming about the river, or not the only one who's changed?"

"Both. You already know about Alixanda. I've seen the psych evaluation. She's not the timid little mouse she was when we first met her."

"Which brings me back to my original point. She's ready for action."

"What about her bruises. You know she's still recovering from the latest round of surgery on her face."

"That's the perfect cover story. With the right clothes, people will believe she's a battered kid on the run."

"What if they recognise her?"

Piper snorted. "Would you?"

"What if they recognise her voice?"

"You can teach her how to say what's necessary in fewer words. She's already perfected helpless and terrified."

"I still think this is a big risk."

Piper shut down the discussion: "She's already agreed."

֎ ✿ ֍

Jenny ran through the technology checks a final time. The tracker bracelet's signal was clear. Being able to monitor that on a smartphone map simplified everything. Jenny checked the new operative's vital-sign readings on her wristband. It was important to watch her stress levels. The hidden microphone Alixanda wore in the neckline of her T-shirt worked well.

Across the concrete concourse, the young woman waited in line for the next bus to the Gold Coast.

Piper was correct. To the uninformed eye, Alixanda fit the profile. She was short enough to be a younger teen. Her hunched shoulders made it seem as if she were trying to make herself invisible. She wore a pink backpack, and her tattered blue jeans were ripped at the knees. The concealing hood of the oversized top completed the picture.

Alixanda no longer bore any likeness to the disfigured, overweight witness. The weeks in hospital had contributed to her weight loss. As had the intensive fitness regime Piper had asked Jenny to prescribe. Would Jenny have cooperated if she'd known what he had in mind?

The crowded depot was loud. Hundreds of shouted conversations competed with the roar of the engines. Buses came and went every few minutes. The bus next to Alixanda slammed its doors. It vroomed out, replaced a few minutes later by another arrival. A man wearing the Transport Authority uniform stepped to the head of Alixanda's line. He began reading names from the clipboard. His voice rang clearly in the earpiece Jenny was wearing.

He called the cover name. Alixanda approached him with her ticket, keeping her eyes downcast. He checked her name on his clipboard, directing her to board the bus. The small figure mounted the steps. The girl took a seat near the front. Excellent; the driver would have a good view of her in the mirror. Only when the doors had closed, and the bus drove out the exit, did Jenny move. She sent Piper a message.

The bus has left.

Pick up in five.

Distend - Stretch Out

ॐ ☼ ℘

*Proverbs 27:6 Hard words from a friend can be trusted,
but an enemy multiplies kisses.*

ॐ ☼ ℘

Jenny pretended to doze. She still wore the earpiece, listening to the bus conversations flowing around Alixanda. After sixteen hours, the bus was nearing its destination. Piper drove the hire car in the evening traffic. He trailed the lights on the back of the bus from the furthest lane. There were no more scheduled stops. Soon, he would overtake the bus so they would be waiting at the depot.

It must have been a tedious journey. Alixanda had ignored a few attempts at conversation from her fellow passengers. The only break in the monotony came when she left the bus at the rest stops to use the bathroom. Unlike the other passengers, she hadn't gone into the shops. Jenny knew she had used all the cash Piper had given her for the ticket. She must be hungry and thirsty by now.

Twice, the bus driver had spoken to her as Alixanda mounted the steps. Both times, he advised her she had plenty of time if she wanted to buy something to eat. She had mumbled a reply. Alixanda's heart rate and blood pressure had spiked then, but she'd recovered quickly. At no time did she sleep. Jenny wondered what thoughts kept her company on the road.

An hour ago, Piper had made the necessary phone calls to confirm his arrangements. Jenny read an incoming message on the dashboard screen.

Confirming Target arrived at your destination.
Location 2 secure.
Standing by.

In response, Piper flicked the indicator and changed lanes. The well-lit bus flashed past. She kept her eyes on the reflected image in the side mirror until it was no longer visible. She rechecked her equipment and sat upright in her seat. The waiting was harder than she expected. Her senses were heightened. She glanced at Alixanda's increased pulse and blood pressure readings. They suggested the young woman was aware the dangerous phase was about to begin.

Piper stopped to allow Jenny to step onto the footpath. He rolled forward as she slammed the door. Despite the late hour, the bus terminal buzzed with activity.

After entering the building, Jenny checked the arrival and departure boards. Next, she strolled towards a drinks dispenser. With a cold drink in her hand, Jenny stationed herself at her chosen vantage point. She selected the Target file on her phone and surveyed the crowd for anyone matching his description. The photograph was grainy - Constantino (Barbie) Barbara was a difficult man to pin down.

The bus arrived, and people disembarked. Alixanda was one of the last passengers to appear.

The bus driver spoke to her as she moved towards the exit. "Is anyone meeting you here?"

The young woman made no reply. She stepped onto the concrete, dodging other pedestrians who hurried around her. It was warm, but she had her hood over her head, which made her stand out in the crowd.

As instructed, Alixanda disappeared into the restroom. Jenny watched closely. No-one followed the young woman. Neither did anyone try to intercept her when she re-emerged five minutes later.

Alixanda shoved her hands in her pockets.

Jenny watched for any sign that Constantino Barbara had tagged the potential victim. The operative tarried until Alixanda stepped from the building onto the busy footpath. For a few seconds, the young woman would be out of view, but with the tracker and microphone, the risk was minimal.

"Excuse me, miss, but you dropped this," a voice said in her earpiece. Jenny reached the corner. Under the streetlight, a man held something towards Alixanda. Her vital signs spiked. Jenny increased her pace. This man didn't match Barbara's description. He was much taller, and bigger all over. There was no correlation – this was a different man.

Piper had dismissed this improbable scenario. His orders were clear – she was to allow the situation to unfold without her interference. Jenny was a "highly-trained operative". She'd do what she always did – adapt.

"That's not mine." Alixanda's voice wobbled.

"Are you sure?" the man said. "I thought I saw you drop it. I knew you wouldn't want to lose fifty bucks."

"It's not mine." Alixanda turned away.

The man took hold of her arm. Alixanda squawked in alarm. He let go, holding up both open hands. "Look, I'm sorry. I didn't mean to scare you." He leaned down and peered under the hood at her face. "I can see you've had a hard time. My name's Earl. What's yours?"

She hesitated. "Allie."

"Nice to meet you, Allie." He offered his hand as if expecting her to shake it. Alixanda looked at it. He dropped it again. The smile didn't leave his face. Friendly, confident, trustworthy. "How about I buy you some coffee to make up for your fright?" He pointed towards a crowded café.

"There's no need," Alixanda murmured.

Earl persisted, moving in front of her to keep her from leaving. She wasn't making this easy for him. Jenny smiled.

"I have a kid sister your age," he said. "If she was in trouble, I'd want someone to help her. You look hungry. Let me buy you a burger. We can sit inside. There are plenty of people about, so you're perfectly safe."

Alixanda's vital signs spiked even more. She looked around and then back towards the café. With her arms wrapped around her body, she nodded.

"Good girl," Earl said encouragingly. He let her go ahead of him. Jenny slipped into the café a few minutes later, choosing a seat at a window table. The agent picked up the Specials menu off the table, checking her surroundings. She saw no sign of Piper, but he shouldn't be too far away. Alixanda stood at the counter, looking at the hot food on display. She tentatively pointed to a small burger.

"That one, please?"

The girl behind the counter reached for the item. "Eat in or takeaway?"

"Eat in," Earl said. "We'll have two cappuccinos and a large fries to go with that. And a piece of chocolate cake."

"I'll just get you a tray," the girl said.

"Allie, you go and save us a table," the man said to Alixanda, "and I'll bring the tray."

The young woman looked around the room. Her glance lingered on Jenny for a few seconds, before she walked to an empty table not far away. Alixanda sat with her back to the wall, providing Jenny with a clear view of her face. There were only two chairs at this table, arranged at right angles to each other. Provided Earl didn't move the other one, all the action would be visible.

Perfect. Jenny set her phone to record video and laid it upright against the salt and pepper shakers. She checked that it was recording, before covering the screen with the menu. After depositing her voluminous handbag on the table, Jenny walked to the counter. She passed Earl, who carried the tray. Jenny made a show of watching him go.

"I'll have a slice of that cake," Jenny said to the girl, still turned in Earl's direction. "And a short black double-shot espresso."

When Earl arrived with the food, Alixanda's eyes locked on the burger. Her small hand reached for it. She caught herself and withdrew her hand.

Earl laughed. "I knew you were hungry." He sat down.

Jenny returned to her table, smiling because his face was in profile for the camera.

"Thank you," Alixanda murmured when he passed her the burger. She took a big bite. Earl watched her with interest. She closed her eyes, stuffing her mouth with food. Within minutes, the burger was gone. He passed her the fries, which she ate at a slower pace.

"It's nice to see someone appreciate good food," Earl laughed, offering one of the cups. "Sugar – one sachet or two?"

Alixanda glanced up. Jenny had been watching. His hand hadn't gone near the sugar bowl, yet Earl had a sachet in his hand. The young woman held up two fingers. He ripped off the top of the sugar sachet and poured it into her cup. He selected a second sachet from the bowl on the table, and tipped it in. He stirred her coffee. Earl slid the drink across the table, then offered the chocolate cake.

"You'd better slow down, or you'll make yourself sick," he advised. Alixanda picked up her cup. She took one sip, and then another, before glancing up at him.

"Thanks for being so kind," she whispered.

"Anytime." Then Earl brought out the fifty dollar note again. "Surfers Paradise can be a dangerous place for a kid."

Alixanda's eyes widened. Earl placed the money in her hand. He folded her fingers over it. "Take it. Consider it a loan. When you're settled, you can pay me back." Alixanda stuffed the money in her jeans pocket. "Smart girl, Allie. I knew when I saw you that you were clever. All you need is someone to take care of you, and everything will be alright."

Earl appeared in no hurry. He watched her finish the coffee and demolish the cake. "All finished?"

Alixanda rose to her feet, but then she grabbed hold of the table.

"I told you not to eat so fast," he laughed. "Let's get you outside for some fresh air."

Alixanda's vital signs on Jenny's wristband declared it was time to move. Whatever Earl had slipped into that cappuccino had worked fast. Jenny swallowed the last of her espresso, grabbed her bag and snatched up her phone.

Alixanda made no protest when Earl slipped his arm around her waist. By the time they reached the footpath outside, she was leaning on him for support.

A taxi pulled up beside the pair on the pavement. "Right on time," Earl said. He opened the door, pushing Alixanda inside. He climbed in beside her. The taxi sped off into the traffic.

"Where are you?" Jenny screamed into her phone.

"Turning the corner now." Piper's car stopped beside her.

"Why didn't the police grab him as soon as he came out of the café?" Jenny demanded. "They're getting away."

Her eyes followed the flashing beacon on her screen.

"Stop worrying," Piper said. "We follow Alixanda's tracker. Then we confirm the exact location of the rendezvous for the police. No point catching one guy when we can take out the whole operation."

"Does she know this was part of the plan?"

Dissipate – Scatter and Gradually Vanish

ॐ ☼ ॐ

Psalm 18:30
God's word is perfect, shielding everyone who takes refuge in Him.

ॐ ☼ ॐ

Open your eyes. Use your gift. Remember everything you see.

Alixanda struggled to obey. A dense fog clouded her thinking. She tried to pray, but all she could manage was a sigh. The mist lifted. From the way her body jostled, she must be lying in a moving vehicle. Someone was taking her somewhere? This was important. She had to remember...

Open your eyes.

The desire to obey that voice consumed her.

Finally, her eyelids fluttered. In front of her, a glowing panel displayed a series of numbers increasing with speed – she was in a taxi? A white shape, a rectangular object swung in her limited field of vision. A coloured image filled most of the shape, a man's face. Under the photo, there was a name and a series of numbers.

The driver swore, and the vehicle came to a stop. "Another red light," he muttered. Then he leaned sideways, blocking her view. He turned towards her – the same man in the photo, except his hair was different. He swore again. "She's looking at me!"

Another voice spoke. "Allie, are you awake?"

There was pressure on her arm, and someone shook her body. She groaned. From a great distance, she heard the voice say, "She's still out of it. Even if she saw you, she won't remem..."

I have to remember. Her eyelids flew open, but nothing made sense. The darkened world was upside down. She looked up. There was the ground, and a pair of legs with feet attached. The feet were moving. She looked down. There was the night sky. And the back of the big man who carried her over his shoulder.

What else could she see? A circle of light, a street sign, and a light-coloured car. The car had an illuminated sign on the roof and writing on the door.

Another circle of light, another car, another pair of legs.

A white number plate stood out against this car's dark paintwork.

The door was open. The inside of the car was lit by a small glow.

She was flying – no, she was falling. Her body hit a padded surface.

A door slammed. She was inside another car. Hands rolled her body over. Now a glimpse of a different man looking at her from the front seat. The light went out.

્☼૎

"Drive faster," Jenny shouted. She relayed information received from Alixanda's hidden microphone. "They've swapped cars. Two men are arguing. The driver took an off-ramp. They're heading back toward Surfers Paradise."

Piper swapped lanes. He found a place to turn around before he made a phone call. "There's been a change in plans. Leave one car there, and send the rest of the team back towards Surfers. I'll let you know when I have the new location."

The tracker icon flashed on the digital map. The distance between their receiver and the unidentified vehicle narrowed. "They're still shouting. The new man says there's an important customer in town. Something about a special opportunity. The driver insists Alixanda has to be there."

Piper revved the engine as he switched lanes again.

Jenny sucked in air. "They're one short on their quota, and she will have to do. He says the customer is willing to pay a bonus for the right girl. Earl's percentage would be four figures if she's chosen. Earl says she isn't ready, but the new man says Nadia is meeting them at the resort."

"Which resort?" Piper banged the steering wheel. He was stuck in this lane with a large truck beside him, matching his speed. The tracker beacon went past them, heading in the same direction. In the dark, it was impossible to determine which vehicle the signal came from.

ଛୁ ✿ ଓ

Someone was shaking Alixanda. "Wakey, wakey!" It was a woman's voice.

"Uuhh." Her heavy eyelids momentarily opened, and slammed shut again. She repeated the process. This brought her brief glimpses of a hotel room. A bed, a television, a large mirror – a limp body lay on the bed – her reflection. Her legs disappeared towards the floor. Her face was half-hidden by her open backpack.

"Come on, little miss. Let's get you out of those old clothes and into the shower." The woman removed each article of

157

clothing, starting with her shoes. Alixanda snatched glimpses of the process in the mirror. Her body offered no resistance, remaining floppy and unhelpful. A rustling sound reported each discarded item stuffed into her backpack. Then the woman turned her over. Now Alixanda could see flashes of Nadia's face. Big hair, dark eyes, bright red lipstick.

"Good," Nadia said. "The bruises are only on your face. That makes my job easier. Let me look at your arms – hmm. That's a pretty piece of silver, a little souvenir for me."

Nadia unclipped Alixanda's silver bracelet and snapped it onto her own arm. She jiggled it. "Nice." The woman resumed the examination. "Excellent – no track marks, and you don't look like you've been using. A healthy amount of puppy fat – customers no longer like starved waifs."

Nadia pulled her upright by her arms, half carrying her towards an open doorway. There were cold tiles under Alixanda's bare feet. She stumbled on a small step. Her legs folded. Now the smooth tiles were under her, and beside her. Nadia's hands massaged something smooth and fragrantly fruity over her body. The same product went onto her hair. Whoosh. Icy needles of water hit her. Every nerve in her body screamed during the cold shower. She was unable to move a muscle, or make a sound. Finally, the torture was over.

Alixanda opened her eyes. The woman leaned over her. "I thought that would wake you up a bit."

After her icy shower, Alixanda's body shivered. Nadia wrapped her in a thick towel. Hot wind ruffled her damp hair: a hairdryer.

"Now to get you dressed," Nadia said. Whipping the towel away, she dragged the helpless victim back to the bed. "It's taking too long for that drug to wear off." She wrestled Alixanda's uncooperative body into a tight, knee-length satin negligee. "Earl is going to have to carry you to the party."

Alixanda could see again. She stared at her reflection from the bed. Shiny white fabric – contrasting with a face dominated by frightened eyes. This time her eyelids closed at her command.

Nadia's voice was close to her ear. "Be a good girl, and keep still while Nadia covers those nasty bruises on your face. You want to look your best for our important guests."

Delicate feathery strokes caressed her face, surprising Alixanda with Nadia's soft touch. "There, bruises away. Now, just enough mascara to accentuate those eyes. Perfect – I'm done. Let's drag you over here so I can fix your hair."

Tugged upright, Alixanda then fell back into an armchair's embrace. Nadia ran a wide toothed comb through her hair. "I'm not going to straighten your curls, or try to put your hair up. The aim tonight is to make you look younger. Open your eyes. Let me look at you."

Alixanda struggled to obey, sighing when she was successful. The woman studied her for a few seconds, then nodded. Nadia rose to stow her cosmetics in a case.

Knock, knock, knock.

Alixanda looked past Nadia. There was the doorway to the bathroom and beyond that another door.

"Hey, Nadia," a voice called out through the door. "Are you done yet? They've sent a message to tell me to hurry up with the new girl."

"Perfect timing," Nadia said happily. "Let's see if you can walk."

Nadia pulled Alixanda upright, but her legs refused to bear her weight.

"Earl, you'll have to carry her," Nadia called out, leaving her lying on the floor with her eyes closed. The door opened, and heavy footsteps approached. The big man grabbed

Alixanda by the arm, hoisting her into his embrace. Her body shivered.

"Where are her shoes?" he growled.

"No point giving her any," Nadia retorted, "if she can't stand."

"If the boss complains," Earl warned Nadia, "it's coming out of your cut."

He headed into the hallway. For a few seconds, Alixanda opened her eyes and looked into his face. He grinned at her. "Come on Allie, time for your curtain call. Tonight could be our lucky night."

Disobey – Fail to Obey

ജ ✸ ങ

*Romans 3:12 They have all turned away;
not even one remains who does good.*

ജ ✸ ങ

"I'm not sitting here." Jenny pulled her handbag onto her lap as she reached for the car door release.

Piper grabbed her arm. "You're not going anywhere."

Jenny half-turned to him. "I was angry that I had to leave Evie's party early, but now I'm glad." With her free hand, she withdrew her rumpled party dress from her oversized bag. "I have the perfect outfit to fit right in with the resort crowd."

She waved it in his face. "All I have to do is find somewhere to get changed."

Piper let go of her arm. She looked at the marks he had left on her skin while he turned his attention to the street. There were plenty of pedestrians about. "There's a toilet block around the corner," he said. The warm night pressed in as Piper stepped from the car.

Jenny slammed her door after joining him on the pavement. "You don't have to come. I can take care of myself."

"If I don't come, I won't get to hear the rest of your plan."

She wanted to smack the smug expression from his face. "Suit yourself, but don't think you can stop me."

ജ ✸ ങ

"Hey, Earl. You took long enough."

Where did that voice come from? Alixanda's eyes opened. A man with a very firm grip carried her, but she couldn't see his face. Earl – did she remember that name? She was cold.

His heartbeat pounded in his chest. He paused and turned towards the wall.

The movement changed her view. Now she could see two pairs of shiny black shoes, attached to two sets of trouser legs. Behind the legs, she could make out the lower half of a white painted door. "It doesn't pay to keep the Big Boss waiting."

Where was she? That voice sounded familiar. Her mind wrestled with the puzzle, while her eyes searched for the top of the door.

Finally, she found the shiny brass numbers: 1-4-4-6. The shapes floated on a glossy white sea.

Earl jostled her again. The features of two men came into focus beside the door. The guards wore dark suits. One man leaned closer. "Rick's not going to be happy, when he finds out you're manhandling the merchandise."

Earl jerked her body out of his reach. "Hands off, Barbie."

"Barbie" was one of the names Piper had told her to remember!

"Barbie" growled, "You need to remember your place, Earl. There'll be trouble for you when this party is over."

Flashes of memory thrashed her and a new terror awoke. Not only was the voice familiar, but this man wore a pungent aftershave. Those evil hands had touched her on another occasion, delivering pain. The mask of her drug-induced stupor kept her secret, but Alixanda's mind screamed. Barbie was one of the men who had tortured her.

Fearing betrayal, her eyelids slammed shut.

𝖘𝖔 ✿ 𝖈𝖘

Jenny kept silent until Piper delivered her to the toilet block. He ignored her protest and entered the shadowy building at her side. She banged one of the inner cubicle doors, shutting him out. As she changed clothes, Jenny muttered to herself.

She took out a makeup bag. Using her smartphone torch for illumination, she worked on her face to match the dress. Next, she fished jewellery out of her party handbag. After stuffing her sensible shirt and jeans into her larger bag, Jenny seized her flat shoes.

Transformed, she stepped barefoot from the cubicle. She paused long enough to thrust both the heavy bag and her shoes into his hands.

Piper didn't miss a beat, matching her long strides.

࠰✿࠱

With her eyes shut, Alixanda waited for the nothingness to return. She longed to forget, but with each second, her awakened senses became more insistent.

She heard the door open.

An obscene chuckle from her old enemy followed her. "You owe me, Earl. Sweetheart, I'll look for you in the morning."

The door closed behind them.

Earl entered a noisy room. Suddenly, the fear of not knowing won over the need to escape her past. Her eyes opened.

Earl carried her across a crowded room. Her attention fluttered from person to person.

Conversations stopped.

Men stared.

Earl's grip tightened. The throng parted as he carried her towards a set of steps at the end of the room. In a few strides, he delivered Alixanda onto a raised stage.

A group of girls came into view. They watched her approach with varying interest. More than one girl stared vacantly into space. Others glared at her. A few turned their backs.

A wail erupted from the corner.

Earl turned in that direction. Another cluster of girls cowered next to the heavy curtains flanking the stage. Each of them wore a similar white dress. They wept and clung to each other.

He dumped Alixanda across three chairs, part of a row along the stage.

"Be quiet," Earl growled at those girls. "I don't want to have to teach you some manners in front of these important guests."

The horrible wailing ceased, replaced by the occasional choked sob.

"Why don't you ask Rick to give them something," a high-pitched voice snapped. "Where have you been? How long do I have to put up with these babies?"

Earl turned to face a blonde girl. She wore too much makeup, a red cocktail dress and high heels. She was one of the few teenagers who appeared comfortable with this situation. The confident girl sashayed towards Earl, wrapping her arms around him. He fended off her embrace.

An immediate outcry erupted further along the stage. Other girls hurried towards him, demanding their share of attention.

"Is there a problem here, Earl?" a new voice asked.

Alixanda's heart almost stopped.

This voice belonged to the man who had killed Xanda.

Every part of her wanted to flee, but she remained motionless.

A tear escaped the corner of her eye, as the memory of a broken body at the foot of the stairs crowded out the present scene.

"No, Rick," Earl muttered. "The regulars are wondering why they're here with the newbies. They're asking why you haven't handed out their favourite treats?"

The girl in the red dress draped herself over Rick's arm. She sneaked her hand into his jacket pocket. "Don't you have a little something to make this girl happy?"

Rick slapped her hand and pushed her away. "There will be nothing for you until you remember your place."

Then Rick turned to Alixanda. He peered at her, a frown on his face. "What's wrong with this one?" He was tall with black hair, and eyes like lumps of coal.

Earl approached, wrapping his arms around her prone form. "This is the girl I picked up from the nine-forty-five Sydney bus." He hoisted Alixanda to her feet. "The one you told me to expect. I was taking her to the usual place when the driver said you wanted her brought here to make up the numbers."

Rick gripped her jaw, forcing her to look into his eyes.

Earl continued, "I told the idiot driver she wouldn't be presentable in time, but he insisted."

"No-one's touched her since you picked her up?"

Earl squirmed. "Nadia did her best to make her look nice."

"You didn't have a little fun with her on the way?"

"No!"

"No? You wouldn't be the first."

"I saw what you did to my predecessor. Your orders today were specific. You wanted this new girl left alone until you'd seen her. I'm not going to risk a good gig because I can't keep my hands to myself."

"What did you give her?" Rick asked. "She should be coming round by now."

"Just the sachet of the special sugar you gave me today," Earl assured Rick. His worried look belied his confidence. "You know I'm all out. You promised me new supplies tonight. She was fine when she finished her coffee. I walked her out of the café to the taxi. She went out cold right on schedule." Earl lifted Alixanda's floppy arm. "This is the longest she's been able to keep her eyes open, so maybe it's wearing off."

"Hmmm," Rick said. "Not quick enough. Earl, go and get some strong black coffee. A little caffeine works miracles."

Earl's clammy hands laid her back on the row of chairs.

Rick dragged a chair out of line to sit beside her. He was handsome, but his eyes were cruel. He slipped one hand into an inner pocket of his jacket, then prized her jaws open with his other hand. A bitter pill landed on her tongue. He used his finger to poke it towards the back of her throat. With a quick movement, he lifted her head and applied light pressure to her neck. Unexpectedly, her swallow reflex kicked in.

Spit it out, her mind screamed, but she couldn't.

Her eyes filled with tears, and he smiled.

Her already racing heart began to gallop. Beads of perspiration clouded her vision as they dripped down her face. Her body felt too hot. Then just as suddenly, an icy chill struck her. She thought she was cold before, but now her body was violently shaking. When the shaking stopped, every nerve in her body was on increased alert.

Rick stayed close, his eyes looking into hers. "I can see that you're awake," his cold voice said. "If only your employer could see you now, unable to defend yourself."

He stroked her face. "You're a pretty little thing. Piper took a risk sending you undercover."

Her tormentor stood. "He's lost an agent and earned himself a whole heap of trouble."

He arranged her across the chairs, like an artist carefully preparing his model.

"You lie there," Rick said. "Think about that information while my pill works its magic."

"Mr Barononi," a voice called. "It's almost midnight."

"When are you announcing the successful bidders."

Rick Barononi turned away. "I'll be back for you soon," he called over his shoulder.

Alixanda's eyes followed him as he left the stage. For a few moments, she had a clear view of the whole room.

Then another girl appeared in front of her. This one had curly bleached hair. She wore a strapless green dress covered in shimmering tassels. She looked as if she was fourteen, but her expression was shrewd. She knelt, shaking Alixanda by the shoulders.

"You really can't move, can you?" the new girl remarked. "Otherwise you would have spat that pill right in his face. You wouldn't be the first to try the 'I'm still asleep' trick on Rick." The girl in the green dress glanced over her shoulder. "Look, I'm going to convince Earl you need to go to the bathroom. Earl's new, but he's easy to manage. Here he comes with your coffee. I'm going to tip it down your throat, and afterwards, you're going to want to vomit. Go ahead, but try not to get any on me. Ready?"

The girl went towards Earl. Alixanda couldn't hear the conversation. He nodded and left the stage.

Now the green tassels swayed as the girl returned, sipping from the cup. "Not too hot," she said cheerfully, kneeling beside Alixanda with her back to the room. The girl's hand slipped into a pocket hidden among the tassels. "Shh. My secret." The girl pulled out a flat vial. The contents spilled into the coffee, and she stirred it with a finger. The vial disappeared again. "Hey, Scarlet. Come over here and make yourself useful."

The red-dress-girl turned. With a few brisk steps, Scarlet was there with a scornful smile. "What do you want, Kitty?"

"Take hold of her head," Kitty said. "Rick wants her awake *real* fast. I'm going to pour this coffee down her throat. I need you to make sure she doesn't spit any of it out. I know Rick has taught you his tricks..."

Scarlet's cruel smile inspired new terror in their victim.

Alixanda's mouth filled with the hot bitter liquid. Scarlet clamped her jaws closed, then tilted the victim's head back and applied pressure. Again, she couldn't stop the swallowing reflex. Scarlet prized her jaws open again, and Kitty continued with her plan.

Alixanda lay helpless.

"Go and tell Earl the new girl's sick," Kitty told Scarlet. "I'm taking her to the bathroom, so she doesn't mess up the ceremony."

"What are you up to, Kitty?" Scarlet asked.

"Taking out the competition to get you more attention."

The two girls glared at each other.

"Hurry and do what I say," Kitty hissed. "In a few minutes, she's going to be sick – real sick. You don't want to be standing there when she starts."

Scarlet took a step back.

Kitty continued. "I saw Rick give her one of his special pills – one of the red ones..."

Scarlet went rigid, her eyes wide with understanding.

Kitty pressed on. "We both know he has something extra in mind for her. She's not going to be any use to him now. Believe me, I'm doing us all a favour. He'll think twice before he risks another valuable asset."

Scarlet put her hands on her hips but said nothing.

"I don't know how you can handle the cocktails he serves," Kitty concluded. "But I do know Rick's wasting his time with this new girl – she's already half dead."

Disable - Render Unworkable

ॐ ☼ ॐ

*Hebrews 11:15 If they longed for the country they had left behind,
they would have returned.*

ॐ ☼ ॐ

Alixanda's stomach roiled in revolt. Whatever was in the coffee worked fast. Kitty dragged her uncooperative body behind the curtains to a hidden bathroom.

"I'm sorry," Kitty said, wrapping Alixanda's arms around the toilet bowl and shoving her head forward. "I can't stay to help you."

The words echoed in Alixanda's head as her body surrendered to the spasms. Moments later, she expelled the coffee with the contents of her stomach. As the stench filled her nostrils, her body rolled sideways.

Alixanda lay still.

ॐ ☼ ॐ

"You have the dress," Piper said. He tossed Jenny's bag and shoes into the boot of the car, "but you left your party shoes in Melbourne. They won't let you in with bare feet."

Jenny turned her attention to the street. The sound of laughter carried over the traffic. There were plenty of clubs and bars filled with the buzz of happy holidaymakers. "Hand over some cash, and I'll remedy that."

Piper pulled out his wallet and counted three hundred dollars in fifties. Jenny snatched his money.

She could feel his intense gaze on her back as she dodged the traffic to reach the other side. A group of giggling women exited one of the nightclubs. Here came the answer to her unspoken prayer. "Hi," Jenny began. "You look like you're having a great time. How would you like some extra cash to make it a better one?"

The women looked at her with interest.

"I have a really hot date..." She threw a glance towards Piper. "And we've just come from the beach." Their suggestive remarks assured Jenny she had their full attention. "Now he wants to go clubbing, and I've lost my shoes..."

The spokeswoman looked at her. Jenny straightened the hem of her dress. They giggled. "What size are your feet?"

"Nine."

"That's your size, Vera."

One woman bent down and began to slip off her shoes.

"Hold on, Vee. We have to sort out the price first."

"Would a hundred be enough?" Jenny asked, opening her clutch bag. She peeled off two notes.

The spokeswoman's hand darted forward. "Make it everything you have, and it's a deal."

Jenny closed her fingers, snagging the woman's greedy hand. "I want the shoes first," she said. Her captive waved to Vera. Once the shoes landed in her free hand, Jenny smiled and released her. She let the woman keep the cash.

"Enjoy the rest of your evening, ladies," Jenny quipped as she turned. She could hear the women laughing, making plans to celebrate their easy victory.

⳩ ✿ ⳨

Alixanda opened her eyes to the familiar meadow – the scene from her drawing. She lifted her head.

Wisdom sat beneath the same tree. "You're back again."

"Am I dead this time?" Alixanda asked.

The warrior princess shook her head. "You have a special calling. Those girls need you to be their witness. Someone has to ensure justice catches up to these evil men."

Alixanda sighed. She could hear the roar of the waterfall.

"Come with me to the river," her companion said. "See what you will see. Then remember."

⁊☼ℭ

When Jenny returned with the shoes, Piper leaned against the car. "Okay," he said, "you look the part. What are you going to do? The team aren't ready yet. I know you're good, but not even you can pull off a one-woman rescue."

"At least I'll be doing something," Jenny muttered. "I refuse to wait here while Alixanda's in danger. You heard them talking about the side-effects of those drugs. Now she's lost both the microphone and the tracker. She's defenceless and alone."

"What do you think you can achieve? We know Alixanda's in the resort, but not which floor. She could be anywhere from floors four to forty. You can't start knocking on doors..."

"I'm not planning to. All I have to do is find Nadia. She's wearing the tracker – I'm getting her vitals now. If I get close enough, I only need a few minutes alone with her. She'll tell me everything I need to know."

⁊☼ℭ

In the meadow, the sky was clear. Wisdom led Alixanda to the riverbank. The water glistened in the bright sunshine. Her eyes went to the opposite bank. She thought she could see Freddie Kidman waiting for her in the distance.

"What do I need to do?" Alixanda asked.

"Lie down and look in the water."

Alixanda lay down with Wisdom beside her. The lush grass was soft. They both peered into the shimmering blue water. The sun was warm on her back.

The waves stilled to become a flat mirror.

A white shape appeared on the reflective surface. Alixanda looked up, but there was no corresponding cloud in the sky. Understanding awoke in her. She refocused. Instead of a cloud, she was looking at a small figure, dressed in white. This girl lay on a tiled floor. Alixanda gasped in recognition.

She raised her head, but Wisdom redirected her. "Watch."

The image shifted, becoming clearer as if she was looking through a window. Two people appeared beside the still body. When they spoke, their voices were easy to hear.

"Are you crazy?" Earl asked, bending down beside the body. He shook the still form, then stood. "You've killed her."

"Better she died here," Kitty retaliated. "She was paralysed, but fully awake. If you'd looked in her eyes, you would have known."

"Rick's going to kill me," Earl muttered, pacing back and forth. "Perhaps she's not dead?"

He rolled the body onto its back, then recoiled in horror. "She's cold to touch, and her lips are blue. Oh no, no, no."

"Sit her on that chair. Clean her up, and make it look like she's sleeping. Then get out of here, and keep going."

His hands busied themselves, complying with Kitty's instructions. "Why did you do this?" Earl slipped off his jacket, wrapping it around the body. "Maybe I can convince Rick she's sick – get her out of here before he finds out..."

Kitty stood in his way. "You have to listen to me! Rick likes to play a little game. This isn't the first girl who hasn't woken up. Sometimes, he spikes his 'special sugar' with an extra ingredient. Then a girl arrives for processing and won't wake up, and they give him a call. That girl gets *individual attention* from Rick, and then no-one ever sees her again."

"This has happened before? I don't believe you."

"While you were getting coffee," Kitty said, "Rick checked her out. He spoke to her like he knew her, like he wanted to be sure she understood what was happening. Then he popped her one of his red pills. He said she was powerless to stop him. I had to do something. She faced a worse death with him."

"He talked to her like he knew her?" Earl asked. "Wait – that means Rick planned this! My orders were to meet the Sydney bus and grab *this* girl – not to let anyone else distract me. I didn't think anything of it. You know, I ran out of the sugar sachets. Rick said he could only give me *one* today..."

He looked towards Kitty, but she had stopped paying him any attention. Instead, she stared at the mirror. She raised her arm and pointed.

"What happened to our reflections," Kitty squeaked.

Earl whirled towards the mirror.

"I can see two women watching us," the terrified girl said.

Alixanda looked at Wisdom. "They can see us?"

Her companion removed her sword from the scabbard.

"There's one who looks like this dead girl," Kitty said, "and a scary one wearing armour. The scary one has a big sword."

The warrior plunged the blade into the water, disrupting the image. Wisdom leapt into the river and vanished. Alixanda tried to follow, but her feet only sank into the mud on the river bottom. She clambered back onto the riverbank to wait for the ripples to subside.

Wisdom appeared on the other side, in the bathroom with Kitty and Earl. She was huge. Earl's bulk was insignificant by comparison.

Kitty squealed and ran for the exit.

Earl stared. "Are you an angel? My Gran told me God would send an angel to deal with my wickedness."

"I've not come to deal with you," Wisdom said. "I'm here to help you deliver Alixanda from her enemies."

He attempted to speak, but no words came. Earl blinked. He tried again. "Alixanda? Is that her ghost in the mirror?"

"There's no ghost," Wisdom said. "Alixanda's not dead." The words echoed in the room, building in power.

As if in reply, a low groan came from the body.

Earl swore, lost his grip, and the not-dead girl tumbled to the floor. His hands flew upward in horror.

His eyes went to the vision in the mirror. “I'm sorry!”

A long silence followed. Wisdom lifted Alixanda's body as if it had no weight. The angel passed her to Earl.

“She looks dead,” he said. “She's not dead?” Now he cradled the body gently in his arms. “But she will be if Kitty's telling the truth. I have to get her out of here.”

Wisdom wrapped Alixanda's body in Earl's jacket.

ꙮ

Jenny slipped her feet into the recently acquired heels.

“Why are you wasting time?” Piper asked. “Off you go. I'll confirm the team's status, then follow you in.”

She mounted the stairs to the resort entrance. Her fury made her reckless. At the top, she paused under the floodlit canopy.

She removed her mirror compact and a lipstick wand from her party bag. With her back to the entrance, she applied the lipstick. Her mirror confirmed the uniformed doorman was watching her.

“That man makes me so mad,” Jenny told the doorman, using an American accent. She gestured towards Piper, across the street. Her employer waved, continuing to speak into the phone.

“He said we were going clubbing,” she whined, “and now he's on the phone to his mother.” Jenny put one hand on her hip, then tossed her head. “Who takes their mother on a holiday? I told him he'd better choose between his mother and his girlfriend if he wants to have any more fun tonight.”

The doorman smiled. “I need a drink.” Jenny said. The guard winked and Jenny flashed him a smile as she entered.

Dislike - Develop an Aversion

❀

Romans 12:9 Love with sincerity.
Hate what is evil, and cling to what is good.

❀

Alixanda watched the scene from the meadow.

Earl carried the not-dead girl in his arms, with his large jacket draped over her body. The warrior princess led the way from the bathroom onto the stage.

"Where's Kitty?" he muttered.

Alixanda scanned the room. A few of the more confident girls circulated among the guests seated at the tables. She located Kitty talking with the man in charge of the bar.

The barman said something to the girl. She turned her head quickly and stared at Earl. Kitty's face went pale. She drained her drink, then held out her glass for a refill.

Earl's eyes darted left and right as he walked stiffly across the stage and down the stairs.

When he turned in the direction of the door, Ricardo Barononi materialised beside him. That powerful man steered Earl into a space at the centre of the room.

Alixanda, in her meadow, leaned closer to hear Rick's quiet words. She was not the only one who wanted to know what was happening. Her portal into this room made it easy to follow the scene as it unfolded.

Nearby guests moved closer, as a whisper wafted across the room. Eyes turned. Conversations ceased. Men arose from their tables. The atmosphere intensified.

"I was coming to see you," Rick said. "Kitty told me the new girl is sick."

Alixanda's enemy flipped the jacket away from her motionless form. It fell to the floor. "The coffee didn't agree with her? Or did you slip her something else?" Rick clicked his fingers.

Someone appeared with a swathe of crimson fabric to replace the jacket. There were golden dragons embroidered on the luxurious silk sheet. Rick repositioned one limp, dangling arm.

"She's a valuable asset," Rick said. "I'd hate to think you would do *anything* to jeopardise my arrangements."

"You know this isn't my fault," Earl muttered, fixing his eyes on the red silk. His fingers tugged the fabric closer to her chin. "Let me take her back to her room so she can sleep off whatever she's taken."

"I can't allow that. I'm about to make the announcement." The evil man clapped his hands to attract attention. "I advertised twenty products, and twenty products is what I intend to deliver."

As he waited for everyone to assemble, Rick frowned. "Earl, you look as if you could do with a drink." He clicked his fingers again, and the lackey reappeared. "Get Earl a drink. Make it a double. He's done valuable work tonight." Rick raised his arms to encourage the spectators to respond. "We owe Earl a vote of gratitude."

Earl's name arose in a chant from the crowd. Someone clapped, and everyone joined in.

Her reluctant defender drew Alixanda's body closer to his chest. "Can't you see that she's unconscious?" he whispered to Rick. "I don't think she'll be alive in the morning. A dead girl's not good for business."

Wisdom moved closer to Earl. No-one else gave any sign that they could see the giant warrior.

Rick slapped his arm across Earl's shoulders, holding him in a firm embrace. Now the body in his arms was close enough for Rick to stroke Alixanda's face. Her eyes remained closed, her body made no response.

Rick frowned, then shrugged. "My customers are willing to take their chances."

⁔✿⁖

The foyer was bright. Jenny paused to assess her situation. To the left was reception, the manager's office… and there was the bank of lifts. To her right, a resort directory listed the shops and restaurants available.

Alongside the directory was the entrance to one of the bars. Jenny went straight there. The security guards were watching her with interest. She purchased a drink and activated her phone.

In the time it had taken to get here, the tracker location had changed. While it still flashed for this address, the proximity reading was getting closer. She picked up her drink, drained her glass, and headed for the foyer to wait at the lifts.

There were four lifts, two pairs facing each other across a well-lit corridor. Only one of the lifts was coming down.

⁔✿⁖

Swish. Wisdom unsheathed her sword.

Whoosh. The blade flashed upward, and the warrior brought it down to touch the floor.

Blue bolts of light flashed from the sword to swirl around Earl. His arms were tightly bound to the silk-wrapped burden, and his legs immobilised. He looked to the guardian.

"Wait," Wisdom commanded. "I will tell you when it's time to move." Her voice echoed across the room.

Only Earl reacted. No-one else heard.

Rick raised his hands above his head to ask for silence. With a loud voice, he proclaimed: "Gentlemen! It gives me great pleasure to announce that nineteen of the twenty lots offered this evening have reached a favourable conclusion."

A circle of interested faces waited for Rick to continue.

"When I finish my speech, the Keeper of the Bedrooms will confirm the successful bidders. Then he will allocate rooms."

A man wearing a red jacket appeared on the stage. The Keeper placed a leather-bound book on the podium. Next, he laid a bundle of electronic key-cards beside the book.

The crowd erupted in loud cheers of celebration.

"Gentlemen!" Rick exclaimed. "Your enthusiasm is heartwarming."

The crowd waited for Ricardo Barononi to continue.

"The Keeper has spaced appointments to allow customers to take refreshments. And rest, if they have been successful with more than one bid. Of course, the bar will remain open."

Again the crowd were loud in their approval.

"I am pleased to announce four outright purchasing contracts. Those fortunate customers will enjoy an exclusive appointment with their new acquisition."

There was another round of applause.

"One of the new girls will be flying to Europe in the morning."

Alixanda watched a man raise his arms in victory. His companions congratulated him. She looked towards the stage where the group of sorrowful girls still huddled in the corner.

Which one of them did he buy? And what terrible fate awaited the others?

Was there anything she could do to save them?

"Scarlet is going to Hong Kong..." Rick continued.

"Lucky man," someone shouted.

Eyes turned in Scarlet's direction. The girl was clearly well-known. The girl in the red dress staggered. Her companions threw their arms around her. Yet they turned towards Rick.

The crowd hushed.

"And Kitty, sweet Kitty," Rick said, moving from the circle to stand beside the girl at the bar. "Kitty will be leaving us for a South American coffee baron. I hope she learns a better appreciation for good coffee."

The girl laid her head on the counter and wept.

"You said there were four?" a voice called out. "Is Sleeping Beauty the remaining one?"

Laughter was the answer. Rick rotated, his arms raised so that all could see his smile. He re-entered the spectator circle that surrounded Earl. The crowd pressed closer.

The master of this ceremony tilted the unconscious Alixanda's chin to reveal her face. "Sleeping Beauty is an apt description. Her present condition moves her into a very *special* category."

The unseen watcher in the faraway meadow memorised each face. She clenched her small fists. Alixanda wanted Wisdom to take her sword and strike them all. "See," Wisdom had said. "Remember."

Alixanda vowed to do that and do it well.

"This little lady presents someone with the unique opportunity for revenge. She works for the man we know by the codename 'Phoenix'. There is no need to ruin the atmosphere by using his other name. Her enhanced value is because our group's nemesis has lost her, even though he's in this city."

This news came as a shock. Some in the crowd looked over their shoulders as if seeking an escape route. Rick addressed their concerns, "Do not fear. I can assure you that no matter how earnestly he seeks her, he is powerless to retrieve her."

Earl stared at Rick as the room fell silent.

"The current bidding has reached one million dollars."

A ripple of excitement went through the room:

"Did I hear someone say they wished they had bid?" Rick exclaimed. "The question you must ask is what price is too high for this unique opportunity for revenge. How much would you pay to destroy your enemy?"

The room erupted in excited cheers, forcing Rick to pause. "If you are unable to raise the capital on your own, the Keeper will be able to connect you with others who are in a similar situation."

Rick had their full attention. "Sleeping Beauty will go to the Emperor's Bedchamber. An exclusive, limited edition video is available afterwards for our members. A fifty thousand dollar payment will secure your copy.

"Anyone wishing to make a bid will find me in my study." The circle of men parted as Rick strode towards a door near the bar. Two of his dark-suited lieutenants came from among the crowd to fall in step behind him.

The gathering waited until the door closed. A few rushed immediately to the stage to consult with the Keeper.

Earl stood in the centre of the room. The electrified storm holding him there sizzled and flared. One of Rick's lieutenants offered him a drink. Earl shook his head. The man drank it himself, and then tucked a crimson silk-wrapped parcel into Earl's pocket.

Her confused protector looked down at his shirt. A bright tassel hung from his pocket. It swung above the face of the woman he was holding.

"You get all the breaks," the small lieutenant told Earl. "Here's the room key. Rick says you are to stay with Sleeping Beauty until the party is over." The lieutenant patted the tasselled pocket. "And remember to wear one of the masks. You don't want your face on a video that's going viral."

"Move!" Wisdom said.

Earl took a faltering step forward. The lieutenant pointed him in the direction of an open door opposite the main exit.

Alixanda was sure this door hadn't been visible before. The water shimmered, and now she was gazing through the doorway. She caught a glimpse of an internal hallway with multiple doors. Each of these doors bore a brass nameplate.

One of Rick's dark-suited men escorted an unhappy girl in a white dress towards the doorway. Alixanda recoiled.

ಏ ✿ ಐ

Ping. The lift door flew open, and a crowd of people stepped out. They headed in different directions. Jenny watched them pass, ignoring the men. There were four women – only one of them carried a pink backpack. Gotcha!

"Hey, Nadia!" Jenny shouted, pushing towards the older woman with big hair. Her target wore a too-tight black dress and killer stilettos.

Nadia turned towards her. "Do I know you?"

"Sure, you do! It's Jen. You know, Jen. Earl's friend? He said there's a party here and I should drop in."

A sneer appeared on Nadia's face. "You're too old," she snorted. "The guests at that party have very special tastes."

"Earl said there'd be other punters after the main event. Men who'd appreciate a woman with more experience." Jenny winked and wiggled her hips.

"He didn't say nothing to me..."

"Look, Nadia, Earl knows I'm desperate," Jenny said, dropping the smile. "My life is over if I don't make some big money tonight. Earl said he could help me out, but I can't remember which room the party's in. I've been hanging around here, hoping to see someone I knew."

Jenny smiled. "You're an answer to my prayers."

"You said Earl sent for you?" She looked Jenny up and down. "Tomorrow you'll discover you've sold yourself to the devil." Nadia laughed bitterly. "The action's happening on the fourteenth floor. I can't tell you the room number but look for two men in suits guarding the hallway to keep out uninvited guests. If you find them, they'll expect a free sample of what you have to offer. If you make it past them, your money troubles will be over."

The look in Nadia's eyes said more. Jenny pretended not to notice.

"Thank you, thank you, thank you." She bounced with delight and threw her arms around a startled Nadia.

Over the older woman's shoulder, Jenny watched Piper enter the foyer. He was with another man. Piper's eyes locked on Jenny.

"Wish me luck," Jenny said to Nadia, then ran for one of the lifts, shouting, "Wait for me!"

The doors were closing, but she made it with seconds to spare. She leaned past the other resort guests to punch the button for the fourteenth floor. No-one paid her any attention.

Jenny shuffled to the back corner to send Piper a message:

14th floor.

No room number.

2 sentries.

ݣ ☯ ݣ

Alixanda relaxed – the mirage flashed back to the man who carried her body.

Blue lightning sparked and swirled around Earl. He took another step towards that dreadful door. Instead of moving out of his way, some of the men pushed closer. Alixanda cringed. Earl slowly turned. The only open space was behind him, a clear path directly to the external door.

Wisdom stood with her sword pointed towards the exit. The lightning grew more violent, flashing and streaming across the space.

"Take her the long way," the lieutenant hissed. "Out into the main hallway, then around the corner. You'll find the alternate entry. I'll call ahead and tell them to let you in."

The lieutenant hurried towards the man on duty inside the door. "Earl is going to have to make a quick escape," he whispered, beckoning Earl to hurry.

Wisdom stood like a statue until Earl stepped through the doorway. Then with a mighty leap, the warrior landed in the hallway beside him.

As the door closed, Alixanda realised two things. Her portal was still focused on the room, and the wall-mounted phone was chirping.

Alixanda watched the lieutenant reach for the phone. The smile on his face changed to a frown. He replaced the handset, then tapped his ear to activate his Bluetooth earpiece. "Boss," he said abruptly. "Code Red. I repeat, Code Red."

The man listened to a reply. He walked to the security panel beside the door. He pressed buttons, and the room lights dimmed. Other lights flickered on, bathing everything with a reddish tint.

Rick appeared in the doorway of his office. "Gentlemen."

Everyone turned towards him.

"We are expecting unwelcome guests. I apologise for the inconvenience. Please follow the emergency protocols and make a quick exit. My men will sanitise the room, so please take any essentials with you. I will send the details for rescheduling our activities by the usual channels."

As the guests rushed to the secret door that led into the bedroom wing, Alixanda's watery view began to stretch. Now she could see the whole room in a single glance.

The Keeper of the Bedrooms picked up his leather-bound book and the unclaimed keys. He shepherded the girls to the rear of the stage. With a snap, he wrenched apart the curtains, revealing another door. A few passed through the door without hesitation, but others tarried.

The sentries came in from the hallway, locking the door behind them. They moved purposefully to the stage. The one who called himself Barbie seized the closest girl - the other girls fled. That hidden door closed behind them, and the curtain dropped back into place.

The activity in the wider room puzzled Alixanda. Rick's men moved around the tables, collecting glasses and cutlery. They delivered these to the counter, where the barman shoved them into the dishwasher.

Partially consumed meals went into a garbage disposal unit. The dirty plates went into a second dishwasher. Even the table napkins disappeared. The men searched under tables, retrieving any overlooked personal items, while wiping down the polished chairs with heavy cloths. The strong smell of bleach filled the air. There was a quiet urgency about their actions.

Rick emerged from his office with a briefcase. His workers stood to attention. He conducted an inspection and nodded. At that signal, the men marched to the secret door leading to the bedrooms. When the last man left the reception room, that door closed.

Alixanda stared at the wall. A large modern painting concealed where the door had been. She studied the composition for a few seconds before the vision faded.

Disappoint - Fail to Meet Expectations

ॐ ☼ ☙

Hebrews 11:6 Pleasing God is impossible without faith because you have to believe He exists before He can reward you for seeking him.

ॐ ☼ ☙

Jenny was the only passenger to disembark on the fourteenth floor. The lift doors swished open, only long enough to allow her to step forward.

The lights above the door confirmed that the lift continued to ascend. Jenny checked the other three lifts. She had time to move away before anyone else arrived.

Turning from the lifts, Jenny gazed left and right. Long, dimly lit hallways stretched in both directions. There were doors evenly spaced on either side, offset to protect guests' privacy.

Jenny slammed her hand against her thigh. Nadia's clue about the dark-suited sentries was not going to bring her a quick result.

The whole floor seemed deserted.

Perhaps that shifting in the shadows further along to the right was a turning? Was there another hallway branching off from the first? Jenny went quickly, a sense of urgency driving her on. She came to the corner and stepped into the open.

Again, her hopes faltered. There were no sentries. Only more doors, fewer this time and further away. This hallway was shorter, leading to another intersection.

Left or right?

How was Jenny to make that decision?

Both this new hallway and the one she had left behind seemed identical. What if the hallway she had abandoned had other side turnings?

There was a myriad of possibilities. This simple task had taken on the complexity of a maze. She should have made sure she had a floor plan.

Come on, come on – think of something. Jenny faced left, then right, before spinning back towards the direction she had come.

You're wasting time. Go back and ask Piper to get you a map.

Jenny imagined the triumph on Piper's face when she reported her failure. She closed her eyes, taking ownership of her wounded pride.

Why had she been certain Evie's God would help in her search? Jenny was no better than Piper, with his elevated opinion of himself and his endless schemes!

Jenny opened her small bag and retrieved her phone. She paused with her hand over the screen, then wrote quickly.

Evie. I need God's help.

Seconds later, the phone in her hand vibrated.

Jenny jumped. Evie had answered already?

Eagerly, she clicked the notification, and then frowned. All Evie had sent in reply was an image – a little yellow circle with a wide mouth: Pac-Man.

What?

A memory from her early teens flashed into her mind. It had been years since Jenny played that computer game, but the vision was as real as if it were happening now.

Pac-Man raced around gobbling energy balls while monsters chased him. Hurry, get the last one. Too late she saw the glowing ghost appear around the corner. The buzzer sounded. Game Over.

That noise sent tingles down her spine. She recognised it as her body relived the experience. It was the sound of defeat.

Her phone vibrated again. Jenny opened Evie's second message more slowly.

You have to ask to receive.

I just did. I asked you!

Not me. Ask God.

How?

You've been hearing voices. That's God. He's waiting.

"Hey, God!" Jenny said out loud, looking around to make sure no-one was witnessing her insanity. "Evie said You're waiting for me to ask for help..."

> *You have to ask to receive. You have to seek to find. You have to knock for the door to open.*

"You want me to start knocking? Have You seen—"

> *Ask. Seek. Knock.*

Jenny stomped her high heels in frustration.

She walked to the closest door. A band of steel tightened at her temples. Every muscle tensed. The Pac-Man impending-doom music played in her head.

Jenny made a fist and prepared to knock.

> *Not this door.*

Moving on to the next one, she raised her hand again.

> *Not this one.*

Jenny moved to a third door.

No.

"Grrrr! This is NOT helping!"

You haven't asked.

"What? Oh! Okay. Which door?"

The voice inside her head was silent. Was she doing something wrong?

Another childhood memory flashed into her mind. Her adult stepbrother holding out a chocolate bar, and then snatching it way. Tears sprang into her eyes.

Jenny swiped at them angrily. "You didn't say please," had been her stepbrother's favourite taunt. It had been a long time since she had thought of him.

"Please? Please could You show me which door I'm supposed to knock on?"

Run.

This time the vision came with different music: faster and more insistent. It signified the character's turn to chase the ghosts. Pac-Man had gobbled a special energy ball – the one that made the monsters vulnerable.

"You want me to run?" Jenny stood with her hands on her hips, her eyes searching the air around her.

Hurry. You're almost out of time.

߷ ✿ ߷

"What are you doing awake?" Freddie asked as Butch appeared in front of him. "It won't be daylight for hours."

Butch threw himself down on the couch beside his uncle. "You're awake." For a few minutes, they both sat looking at Abigail's drawings taped to the wall.

"You dreamed about her again, didn't you?" the teenager complained. "How long's it gonna take you to accept that she's dead. She's never comin' back. You can't spend the rest of yer life in love with a drawin'. Unless of course, it's one of the *other* women you're dreamin' about?"

Freddie groaned and rose to his feet. "I'm going to bed."

"You do that," Butch said, "but you might wanna check yer messages first."

Freddie slowly faced him again.

The teenager grinned. He waved his uncle's black phone in the gap between them.

"If yer wanted me to sleep, you shoulda brought your phone with yer. It's not my fault your phone waked me. I don't think you're gonna sleep until yer find out why *Evie Romano* phoned yer in the middle of the night."

Cautiously, Freddie accepted the phone. He looked at the screen. There had been six missed calls from Evie, one after the other. He checked the last notification:

Hang Up Message.
Evie Romano reached your MessageBank on 02/01
at 01:40am & did not leave a message.

Freddie faced the mural. His eyes rested on Evie in the middle of the river. Then he looked at Romano, noting the possessive way that man towered over his wife.

There was no way he was going to phone another man's wife, even if she had been trying to reach him.

Butch watched him with interest.

Freddie punched a few buttons on his phone and waited for an answer.

"It's for you," Freddie heard Romano remark before he had a chance to say anything, and then Evie's voice was speaking.

"Sorry if I woke you," Evie began.

Freddie waited, aware that Butch was standing so close he could probably hear her quiet words.

"Sebastian said there's no need to apologise," Evie continued. "Because you were already awake. Did you dream about Abby and Xanda too? I was praying about why God would wake me, and then Jenny sent me a message. She's in trouble. I know Butch is listening too, so I won't say any more..."

Who's in trouble, Freddie wanted to ask. Jenny or Abigail?

His nephew beat him to the first response. "How does she know?" Butch exclaimed. "How does Evie always know? Marco said there's no point trying to keep any secrets from her—"

Freddie pushed Butch away and walked across the room. Away from the drawing on the wall.

Away from the visual reminders of his intimidating boss, and the all-knowing, mysterious Evie.

Away from the missing Abigail, and a dead woman named Xanda...

"I'm sorry, Evie. Butch was talking. I missed what you were saying."

Evie laughed. "Sebastian said, that's enough. I phoned so you could be more intentional with your prayers, and to tell you not to give up hope. Remember this is a spiritual battle..."

Freddie's eyes leapt to the armed warriors in the drawing: Romano, Sigrid, Jenny and Piper. Then he looked at Xanda – she was still alive in his dream.

Finally, he gazed at his representation. Even he was depicted as if he was brave enough to do something – anything – to protect his beloved...

His fingers turned white as he gripped the phone. Freddie shook himself and caught Evie's final words. "...all you have to do is pray."

Distinguish - Recognise the Difference

୬ ☼ ଓ

*Psalm 91:15 God said, "Call on me, and I will answer you.
I will meet you in your trouble and deliver you."*

୬ ☼ ଓ

What should Jenny do? Her heart pounded, and her muscles tensed. Her head throbbed over the impossible decision.

With a sigh, she slipped off her heels. She took a few hesitant steps, inhaled deeply and accelerated. Jenny whipped around the nearest corner, rushing to the next intersection.

She ran here and there, no longer certain which direction she faced.

Where was the "ghost" she was to catch?

Jenny paused. Was it her imagination? Could she hear someone nearby?

No. All she could hear was her own breathing...

Wait – that sounded like a door closing.

Jenny dashed into a side passage. There were only four doors, all towards the further end. Two on either side of the hallway.

Which one?

Jenny studied the doors as she approached. There was light coming from under two of them. She pressed her ear against the door to 1405 and concentrated. No sound came from inside the room.

She went to the furthest door and leaned against the white painted surface: 1408. She was about to turn away when the light blinked out. "Okay, God," she whispered. "I asked, and I sought. Now for the knocking. Please prepare me for whatever I find on the other side of the door."

Knock. Knock. Knock.

She waited with heightened senses. Was it her imagination, or could she hear the sound of heavy breathing?

Yes, there were definitely sounds of movement.

Jenny knocked again, and then stepped back. She smiled towards the peephole.

"Who are you?" a man's voice asked from inside the darkened room.

"A friend of Nadia's," Jenny answered. "Is that Earl? Let me in."

"Nadia doesn't have any friends," the voice growled. "She hooks them up with Rick, and they don't stick around to thank her."

Jenny considered this response. "Okay, so she's someone I met downstairs. She said you could help me. Something about a party?"

"You don't want to go there."

"If you won't tell me where the party is, at least let me in. I don't have anywhere else to go."

"How did you know I was here?"

Tell him the truth.

"My friend is missing. God sent me to find her."

There was a long pause.

Jenny was about to speak again, when he replied, "Did you say *God* sent you?"

"Of course God sent me. How else would I know where to find you? Let me in, Earl."

"How do I know you're telling the truth? How do I know this isn't one of Rick's nasty games?"

"No, Earl. I don't know any Rick, and he certainly didn't send me. My name is Jenny. I'm from Melbourne. I work for Piper Ma—"

With a swoosh, the door swung open.

A strong hand grabbed her. Before Jenny could react, she was inside the room. She recognised her assailant immediately and struggled to control her automatic response. It was too early to reveal she was combat-trained.

Earl slammed her against the wall as the door shut. "Is Piper Maxwell here?"

"Downstairs," Jenny squeaked, prying his fingers from her throat.

He eased off the pressure.

"Tell me where the girl is," she croaked as she rubbed the red marks.

"She's there." He pointed to the main room. "On the bed. You can have her. Make sure you tell Piper Maxwell I had nothing to do with this. I was only following orders. I didn't know Rick was going to kill her..."

"No!" Jenny cried. "She can't be dead!"

Turning the corner, Jenny saw Alixanda lying on the king-sized bed. The agent threw herself beside the still body to check for life signs. Wrapped in a red and gold silk sheet, the young woman was pale, a blue tinge to her lips.

Jenny could find no pulse.

"Don't you die on me!" Jenny pummelled the bed in frustration.

The argument with Piper replayed in her mind. She had been so sure that she would know what to do when she found Alixanda.

Jenny battled her emotions and hardened her heart.

She rolled the body onto its back, checked the airways, and tilted the chin. She blew two quick breaths into Alixanda's mouth, ignoring the stench of stale vomit. Then she began cardio-compressions. One, two, three... concentrating until the rhythm became automatic.

The emergency response trainer had taught her a song. The tune played in the background of her mind. This gave her time to think.

She needed answers.

"Hey, Earl," Jenny called out, turning her head to find him watching her. "How long has she been like this?"

He shrugged. "I don't know. The angel said to bring her here – I forgot to give Rick back the key."

He tossed a key-card onto the bed. "I did what I was told. The angel said she wasn't dead, but she looks dead to me."

Jenny had to keep him talking. The party was somewhere else. She needed that information.

"Did you say an angel? What did this angel look like?"

"Like Genghis Khan in a dress." Earl looked around the room. "A woman with a massive sword that makes blue lightning. She was here..."

He shuffled his feet. "No-one but Kitty and I could see her. I wouldn't have let you in if I'd known she was gone." He glanced at the door. "Didn't you say Piper Maxwell was coming?"

She looked down at her hands. She had forgotten to send a message before she knocked. Jenny feared her face might betray her.

Piper wasn't coming.

But at least he knew she was on the fourteenth floor...

He must have a plan – he always had a plan.

Piper wouldn't let her down...

She had to keep Earl talking, if only to distract herself. "Who is Rick? — Why would he — want Alixanda — dead? Not good — for business."

Jenny paused to give Alixanda the next breath, then the song in her head recommenced on cue with the compressions.

"I'm not a snitch. If you really worked for Piper, you would know." Earl shook his head. "You don't know who you're up against, do you? You're here on your own – like this girl was. Rick knew she was coming. He was ready. He probably knows about you too. You said Nadia sent you?" Earl stared at the door again. "This was a setup."

The suspicious man stepped towards the bed. "Rick poisoned your girl, and she didn't wake up. Then he boasted that he could bring her back whenever he wanted to."

He dropped a small red parcel on the bed beside Jenny. "Here's his rainbow assortment of pills. The instructions are inside, but there's nothing for bringing someone back from the dead..."

Jenny eyed the package, curious about the contents, but her arms kept working. Pins and needles ran through her hands. She longed to stretch. Was she wasting her time? She stared at the body.

Jenny leaned over to administer another breath.

Despite all her efforts, Alixanda's condition remained unchanged.

No – that wasn't correct. The young woman's body was becoming bluer with each passing moment. Jenny had seen plenty of dead people, but never a body that glowed like this.

What kind of poison did they give her?

Earl's next words hissed nearer her ear. "It didn't matter to Rick whether she was dying, because she was going to be dead when they finished with her. Perhaps he'll let me live if I provide him with a replacement."

Jenny's body tensed. If Earl attacked, her instincts would take over. She had to maintain control – she must not act prematurely.

Where was the justice for Alixanda if Earl died without telling Jenny what she needed to know? She had to have the other room number...

Earl grabbed her hands. "Stop trying to save your little friend," he cried, pressing another key-card into her palm. "It's too late for her."

Her fingers automatically wrapped around the object, and Jenny whirled, ready to defend herself.

Both his arms shot up in surrender as Earl backed away.

She relaxed her stance and examined the key-card. To her dismay, there was no room number. Instead, it bore the name "Emperor's Bedchamber".

Jenny winced. Her eyes fell to the golden dragons embroidered on the red silk shroud.

"You have to give me a room number," she said, but Earl was no longer there. She could hear him at the door.

"There's no need," he called. "Rick will come to you."

Jenny ran to the door and looked out. There was no sign of Earl. Was he heading for the lifts? Or was he going to tell this Rick where to find her?

Jenny shut the door. After she activated the deadlock, she pushed the security chain into place. She leaned against the door. She had no choice but to contact Piper. He needed to know what had happened.

The defeated Pac-Man music was back.

Her phone lay on the bed. With a sigh, Jenny sat beside Alixanda. Her back pressed against the body, and she could feel the coldness through her dress. Jenny did not attempt to adjust her position. Picking up her phone, she waited for Piper to answer.

"Report." His voice sounded harsh and distant.

"I have Alixanda." No need to say more. "I-I didn't find out where the party is. Earl got away – he's on his way down—"

Click. Piper hung up.

Jenny stared at the phone. He hadn't asked if her location was secure, or if she was safe. He hadn't even asked where she was.

Piper was still focused on catching the bad guys.

She would have to negotiate this tragedy alone. Jenny shuddered. A blanket of defeat pressed down on her. There was no escape from her failure. Tears filled her eyes...

"Stop this!" she said aloud. "That scared kid who cried when she lost the game vanished years ago."

Jenny faced herself in the mirror, eyes blazing. "You're a battle-hardened mercenary who doesn't surrender. Why are you sitting here wallowing in self-pity? Because Piper Maxwell isn't coming like a knight in shining armour to rescue you?"

She stood and sneered at her reflection. "Soldier, take a good look at yourself. He said he'd trained you to adapt, so adapt. You still have your orders!"

Jenny focused on Alixanda in the mirror. Having heard Earl's prediction about what Rick had in mind, there was no way she was leaving the body behind...

How much time did Jenny have before the enemy caught up with her? She knew she was strong enough to carry Alixanda. But did she remember where the lifts were?

As Jenny wrestled with this problem, she heard that quiet voice again.

Ask, and you will receive.

"Alright! You said to ask, so I'll ask. Give me answers. You're supposed to know everything. I want justice for Alixanda. Show me—"

Someone laughed – the kind of laugh you hear in a child's playground, chuckling and bubbling over with joy. She whirled in search of the source. The sound went on and on until she realised it was resonating from every surface.

A blue light shone around the bed.

Jenny extended her hand. A flash of lightning arced through the air between her fingertips and the body. An explosive jolt hurled Jenny across the room.

ಞ ✿ ೞ

Alixanda waited beside the river. A strong wind ruffled her hair. The waves stirred.

Wisdom appeared on the grassy bank. With her sword raised to the sky, the warrior shouted: "Justice and mercy! In the name of the Lord!"

Lightning flashed. Thunder roared. The sky was ablaze across the horizon.

Then everything went still.

A strange silence spread across the land.

> *Will you answer Wisdom's call? Will you be the agent for justice and mercy for these girls?*

Alixanda quaked. The whispering voice was both inside her, and all around. As she absorbed the words, the warrior with her flashing sword disappeared. The river and the meadow vanished.

All that remained was a dazzling, blinding, all-consuming Presence.

"Yes, Lord."

Return!

Ka-boom!

With a violent blast, the blue lightning coiled around her and lifted Alixanda high. Power resonated within her. Then she plummeted towards the ground...

Dissect –

Analyse and Interpret

ಌ ☼ ಚಿ

Galatians 6:10
When we have an opportunity,
let us do good towards others.

ಌ ☼ ಚಿ

Jenny watched in horror as the lightning raised Alixanda to the ceiling. Moments later, it dumped her to the floor.

The room buzzed with electrical energy as the crumpled body began to move. Jenny cried out and knelt on the floor. She helped the awakening victim to wrestle her arms free of the red sheet. Blue light still sizzled across Alixanda's skin, setting Jenny's teeth on edge whenever she touched her.

Alixanda raised her head and stared. Jenny gasped, captivated by those wild eyes. They were no longer brown, but an intense blue. The colour of Evie's river. Alixanda's lips were moving, but she made no sound.

The young woman shook her head in frustration and lay down. A few minutes later, she lifted her arm, gesturing in the air. A blue haze drifted in front of her.

Jenny frowned. Was Alixanda trying to draw something?

"Paper!" Jenny exclaimed. She scanned the room. There should be a complementary pad of paper, for guests to write notes and leave messages.

Yes! Jenny tossed the folder towards Alixanda, who smiled and waved her arm again. Of course, she needed something to write with. There were two pens. Jenny snatched them up.

She bowed down to press one into the young woman's fingers. The artist's shaking hand wielded the pen. Marks appeared on the paper. The trembling ceased.

Alixanda had been a gifted artist before, but her skills were exceptional now. With a few flashing strokes, a quick sketch of a numbered door appeared on the page.

Jenny stared at the drawing for a second. Was Alixanda providing her with the information she needed? "Is this the party room?"

Alixanda pierced her with those blue eyes before resuming the drawing.

Jenny phoned Piper. "The party is in room fourteen-forty-six," she told him. She heard him relay the information to someone else.

"On our way—" Piper said.

But Jenny was no longer listening. Her eyes had locked onto the paper under the artist's hand. She didn't notice she had ended the call.

Alixanda's pen flew over the page. Jenny witnessed the miracle, a photographic image appearing without a darkroom or a laser printer. Two men emerged on the page beside the numbered door.

Here was the man she had searched for at the bus depot. Alixanda must have recognised Barbara, and fixed the details in her mind. Jenny smiled, comparing the drawing to the digital image on her phone. The surveillance photo was poorer by comparison.

"Gotcha!" Jenny exclaimed. "Alixanda, you couldn't have captured him better if I'd handed you a camera."

Alixanda seemed satisfied with Jenny's response, but she wasn't finished. The first page moved aside. Sketch after sketch appeared with lightning speed. Jenny took photos of each discarded drawing with her phone. She forwarded them to Piper.

She received no reply.

ଽଔ☼ଔ

Piper stood in the fractured doorway to Room 1446.

There were no words to express his frustration. It had taken too long to get permission to search the popular resort. Closing an entire floor had proven impossible. Even commandeering the lifts had brought a nightmare of complications. If Jenny hadn't sent the room number, they would still be waiting.

The police tactical response team had descended on an abandoned room. Someone had tipped off the suspects about the raid.

There was ample evidence people had been here. A service area with the food still hot. Open wine bottles. Tables decorated ready for dinner. Except the plates, cutlery and glasses were missing. The room was not silent. The garbage disposal unit was making a terrible noise. When it ceased, the whirring from two industrial dishwashers still disrupted the silence.

A quick inspection revealed the dishwashers were completing the sterilising steam cycle. There would be no incriminating DNA evidence found there. The room looked as if it had been expertly cleared of anything that might be useful.

The table layout provided an excellent view of a stage which dominated one end of the room.

A speaker's podium sat at the front of the stage. Behind the podium, there was a single row of chairs, some overturned.

201

Piper counted them. Twenty: nineteen unknowns and Alixanda. Where were the girls now? Had Jenny been able to save anyone else?

He stared at a fallen chair, while the police team leader, Nathan Rigg, reported to his superiors. Piper tuned out the one-sided phone conversation.

The security consultant already knew what was to come. He had written the prescriptive document for the police department. An internal inquiry would begin into what had gone wrong. More time-wasting. He had never considered he might one day have to deal with his own protocols.

A forensic team was already on its way to process the room. Piper clenched his fists. He imagined the specialist equipment arriving on wheeled carts to find nothing useful.

Accessing the resort's computer systems required permission, another red-tape delay. Where would they find an analyst at this hour, and how long would it take for them to get here? What he would give for one of Evie's annoying coincidences – to walk out and find an IT expert passing by...

He relaxed his fists, then worked his tense shoulder muscles up and down. The whole mission had been a disaster. The tactical response team had taken too long to deploy.

His greatest regret was not bringing a full team of his own. There had been no-one to assist him in the aftermath. Except for Jenny, and she was busy protecting Alixanda. He reached for his phone and then hesitated. Her anger when she left him on the footpath haunted him.

He didn't want to face her yet.

Piper already knew Jenny's opinion. She had disapproved of authorising the state police to command this joint operation. She had asked him what he'd do if the whole exercise blew up in his face. How would he deal with having to rely on someone else for critical resources?

If she was with him now, he would tell her it felt like wrestling an invisible enemy in the dark. With one hand tied behind his back, and his feet imprisoned by quickset cement.

His decision had been based on Nathan Rigg's attitude during their preliminary negotiations. The inspector had been humble, prepared to surrender the whole exercise to Piper.

They had worked together previously. A successful mission now would open new opportunities for Nathan's career, and render him more useful to them in the future. This was why Piper had relinquished control.

Jenny had an opinion about that too.

As if she knew he was thinking about her, his phone vibrated in his pocket. It had done so at regular intervals since Jenny had phoned to identify the room. He hadn't asked where she was, presuming she would be here when he arrived.

She must have found somewhere safe to hide with the woman she had rescued. There would be time to find out what had happened when they met later to debrief. Piper ignored the vibrations. He would wait until he had something positive to tell her...

಄ ✩ ಜ

In Room 1408, the artist continued her work. Jenny studied each image in amazement. Here were the girls they had hoped to rescue from slavery. The first few pages were filled with group scenes, clusters of girls on a curtained stage. Then followed closer views, so that each girl's face was clearly seen. Nineteen girls. The artist drew another girl – twenty. Wait, this was Alixanda's face, eyes closed and body limp. Jenny looked back at the first sketch – twenty chairs stretched across a stage.

"How—" Jenny began, but Alixanda put her fingers to her lips. There was more work to do, her eyes said. Jenny looked at the pages in her hands.

The girls in the drawings seemed to look back at Jenny. Their expressions hinted at deep emotional trauma. Her heart broke over the recognisable shock, fear and anger. Then there were the few with hardened expressions...

Jenny considered the pairing of two older girls. One frowning and defiant, the other smiling with confidence. She glanced at the artist. The pen hovered over a blank page, and those wild eyes asked a silent question.

"I need to see what happened to these girls," Jenny said.

The pen flashed again, many quick sketches on the same page. A girl, the defiant one – head lowered, weeping. The confident one comforted by other girls, her face outraged. A girl on the floor, with her companions wailing beside her. Jenny could almost hear their cries.

The next drawings showed the same wall. In one, there was an open door. But in the other drawing, that secret door was hidden by a modern painting.

A fresh page, there were only two left. Alixanda again, wrapped in the sheet and held in Earl's arms, in the centre of a crowd of men. A tall, broad-shouldered man stood with his back towards the viewer. There was something familiar about this man. If only he would turn...

The pen hesitated over a blank section. With great care, Alixanda began to draw a giant figure wearing medieval armour. The giant towered over Earl, a flashing sword held high. Jenny gasped in recognition.

"Xanda," Jenny whispered. "Xanda was the angel Earl talked about."

Alixanda shook her head, adding characters to the jewelled breastplate: W-I-S-D-O-M. The artist looked up to make sure Jenny understood. It was Jenny's turn to nod.

Satisfied, the young woman reached for the final page. She drew the stage again. A tall man wearing a fancy jacket held the curtains apart, revealing another door. The girls were being shepherded towards the door by the two men who had been sentries in the earlier drawing. Barbara carried a struggling girl. The other girls were fleeing before him.

Jenny held out a shaky hand to receive the page.

The other drawings would be helpful in identifying the girls, but here was the first to implicate one of the men. The offender was easily recognisable as the man Alixanda had drawn in the first image. The target their undercover operation should have apprehended. Jenny recalled Alixanda had experienced first-hand Barbara's cruelty...

₭ ☼ ⅓

Piper stood in the resort manager's office. He pounded the desk with his fist. "What's taking so long?"

The manager turned towards him. "Until I have written authorisation, I am not permitted to grant you access."

A phone beeped. Nathan Rigg grinned with relief. As the senior policeman present, Nathan was in charge of this interview. He had confided to Piper his sense of being underprepared for the unfolding international implications of this exercise. Piper was the public face for *Operation Phoenix*. Nathan would let Piper make any important decisions.

Nathan waved his phone. "Here is the signed court order."

The manager took extra time reading the electronic document before he stepped aside.

A pale youth lurked in the corner. He leapt across to commandeer the manager's desktop computer. Piper watched as the teenager's fingers danced over the keyboard. The boy muttered to himself as he waited for the three darkened screens to awaken in response.

Declan Stephens was a civilian brought in at Nathan's recommendation – the kid was a relative. The teenager had the reputation of a genius, but that wasn't why Piper had agreed.

Declan was already in Surfers Paradise when Nathan made the call. A quick detour, and the teenager had arrived in less than five minutes.

Piper could hear Jenny's voice rejoicing. Here was another of Evie's answer-to-prayer coincidences. Except Piper hadn't prayed...

Piper profiled Nathan's cousin. The security consultant shifted his feet, troubled by the reminder that Freddie Kidman was also a man more comfortable with the digital world than the real one. The main difference between them was obvious – Declan was following his dreams, already enrolled at university. Circumstances had forced Freddie into an unrelated career. Piper reminded himself the service station manager seemed satisfied with his lot...

Until you ruined his life, Jenny's opinionated voice echoed in his mind. *Thanks to you, he's in love with a fugitive, one that you think you can manipulate to achieve your own goals.*

"I'm in," Declan declared. "What do you want to see first?"

"Room fourteen-forty-six," Piper snapped, leaning over the young man's shoulder.

With a few deft strokes on the keyboard, Declan brought up information.

"It's a corporate suite, with an annual lease. Do you want me to trace the owner?"

"Later. I'm more interested in who's supposed to be there now," Piper said.

Nathan joined him to peer over Declan's other shoulder. The manager hovered in the background, obviously wishing he was somewhere else.

"It's a conference room," Declan announced. "No booking info..." The screens flashed as the whiz-kid opened multiple windows. He clicked and shuffled boxes on each screen.

"Wait. This is interesting." He pointed to an invoice. "Here's an order for catering. Food and drink only – no staff required. Let's pull up the room's entry records..."

Click, click, click. "Here it is." A new digital window opened. Declan swung back and forth between screens as he explained.

Piper and Nathan stepped back to give him room.

"From eight pm, multiple access using the housekeeper key-card. Delivering the catering equipment, setting up extra chairs, decorating the tables. A couple of other entries, no key-card needed, which says someone was in the room to open the door. Did you know there's a record, even if the card isn't used?"

Piper nodded.

"Then here at nine-thirty, the drinks order arrived," Declan continued. "Some expensive wine, but also cheaper beer and soft drinks. Here's the food delivery at ten. From then on, the door opens often until here at twelve-forty. The door remained closed after that. Until an hour ago, when the sensors report a catastrophic failure."

Nathan pulled out his operations schedule notebook. "Piper's informant sent him the room number at twelve-thirty."

"There's a few records around twelve-twenty," the teenager said. "Let me try something else."

Declan minimised a few windows and opened a different database. "There's a phone call from extension thirty-three to room fourteen-forty-six at twelve-thirty. It only lasted for ten seconds. Backtracking, there was a two-minute call from extension one-nine-nine to extension thirty-three immediately before that..."

More clicks. "Extension one-nine-nine is the security phone at the front entrance... and this"—the young man pointed to the telephone beside him on the manager's desk—"is extension thirty-three!"

Everyone turned towards the manager.

The small man grimaced. He reached into his pocket, bringing out a white envelope that bore the crest of the resort on the back. "I had orders. I was to give you this, once you knew about that call. I have nothing further to say unless my lawyer is present."

Piper gestured for the manager to lay the envelope on the desk. Nathan approached cautiously, and Declan swivelled his chair for a better view.

Across the front were two words: Piper Maxwell.

The white envelope bulged in the middle. Piper had his suspicions about what he would find inside. If he was correct, it would confirm a nagging suspicion.

He reached into his pocket and retrieved his leather gloves. Fingerprints, other than the manager's, were unlikely. Yet he must be seen to follow the strict protocol.

Declan handed him a letter opener from the manager's desk. Piper expertly slit the envelope open. He tipped out the contents. An ivory chess piece rolled out and he caught it. Piper displayed it on his palm.

"A white pawn," Nathan said, retrieving an evidence bag from his pocket. "Is there anything else?"

Piper shook his head. He dropped the object into the bag, followed by the envelope. He watched Nathan reseal the bag and write on the label. The policeman passed it to Piper, who checked the details, and added his signature. When the task was complete, Piper turned his stony face to the manager. The man attempted to match his stare, but blinked and looked down.

"Have him taken away," Piper said to Nathan, "but make sure at least two of your people keep him safe."

Nathan frowned and walked to the door. Snatching it open, he selected two officers from those loitering in the foyer. Nathan spoke quietly to them before they escorted the manager from the room. The door closed again.

Nathan strode back to Piper. "Explain yourself."

Piper glanced towards Declan, stepping further away. Nathan followed him, while the teenager swung back to his screens.

The security consultant began. "We don't want a repeat of what happened when your team tried to intercept Earl. I'm still waiting for a satisfactory explanation. How did the doorman manage to approach him without anyone realising what was happening?"

"The paramedics have reported that Earl has a good chance of recovery," Nathan said. "You know these private security guards get carried away. It happens every time they learn there's an official operation on their turf. The doorman landed a lucky punch."

Piper locked eyes on the evidence bag in Nathan's hand. "If the manager hadn't delivered this message, that might be acceptable. But with the phone calls your cousin has uncovered, I'm convinced we're dealing with more than luck."

"What are you implying?" Nathan asked.

"The whole evening has been carefully choreographed." Piper listed the details on his fingers. "One: someone knew I was coming. Two: they were expecting my operative to arrive on the bus—"

The officer tried to disagree, but Piper held up his hand. "Don't try to argue. She is definitely the white pawn. There wouldn't be an undercover agent on your team who fits the profile – unless you make a habit of bringing in young relatives..."

He threw a pointed glance towards Declan before continuing. "They knew I wouldn't risk having another innocent girl disappear if anything went wrong. They knew she was one of mine, and they were ready.

"Three: the false destination, to draw us out of the city."

Nathan stared at him.

"Four," Piper held his fingers high, "they didn't check for a wire. They wanted to make sure we knew about the switch. They knew we were following her."

"Then why did they lead us back here?" Nathan asked, running his hand through his hair.

"They were expecting it to take longer to work out where they were." Piper looked around the office. "The manager had orders not to cooperate, and at least one of the security guards was in on it. I'm betting the one who made the phone call was the same doorman who took out Earl with a 'lucky' punch."

"I'll get Declan to check that out," Nathan said. The boy waved his hand to confirm he was already looking at the security tapes.

Piper continued, "Without Jenny's information we would never have gotten a search warrant. No judge would authorise a search of the whole complex on the evidence we had."

"So what went wrong with their plans?" Nathan asked.

Piper removed his gloves and shoved them back in his pocket. His fingers brushed against another ivory pawn. One more secret he was keeping from Jenny.

This one had been removed from Xanda Jadaran's broken body. Before the police arrived at the Melbourne crime scene.

It was from a unique set. The last time he had seen the chess piece, it had been sitting in Valentino's Sydney apartment. Piper had recognised it immediately and flown to Sydney to see for himself. All the white pieces were missing. Someone had visited his dead cousin's apartment and removed them.

That first pawn had been in Xanda's pocket, accompanied by a pristine note. "Bishop takes pawn. Your move." The handwriting matched.

"What went wrong?" Piper repeated. "They underestimated the faith of a determined woman."

The policeman opened his mouth to ask a question, but Piper turned away. The phone on the desk was chirping.

"I thought you were redirecting all calls," Piper snapped.

"You'll want to take this one, sir." The teenager looked nervous. "It's coming from a room on the fourteenth floor."

"Answer it then," Piper growled.

There were two possible reasons someone would be calling from the fourteenth floor. Either his enemy had left him another message, or Jenny had grown weary of waiting for him to contact her. His money was on the second one.

"Hello?" Declan said, and then held the phone away from his ear.

"TELL PIPER MAXWELL TO LOOK AT HIS MESSAGES," Jenny screamed through the phone.

Her voice carried clearly across the room. "And get him to deliver me paper – LOTS OF PAPER – and pens. I need MORE pens. TELL HIM IT'S URGENT."

Abruptly the call ended.

Taking his phone from his pocket, Piper clicked on one of the notifications. The monochrome image that opened stole his breath.

"How did Jenny get this photo—" The answer hit him hard. He beckoned to Nathan. What had Jenny asked for? Paper and pens? He swore and almost dropped his phone.

"What's wrong?" the policeman asked.

"I'm an idiot," Piper said. "We have a witness, and I've been wasting time. Get your team ready for a briefing. This whole mess has flipped right-side up. The advantage is now ours. You, my friend, had better make the most of it."

Distil – Purify and Transform

℘ ✿ ℘

*Hebrews 12:3 Consider what Christ endured for sinners,
and don't let your soul grow weary.*

℘ ✿ ℘

Jenny paced inside Room 1408. What was keeping Piper? She threw a glance over her shoulder. Alixanda was asleep where she lay on the floor, unable to make any further progress with her drawings. Earlier, when the resourceful woman had reached out her hand towards the bed, it had taken precious minutes for Jenny to understand. The artist had wanted the cotton bedsheet for her next canvas.

The cream sheet beneath her bore testimony to the work she had achieved before the pens expired. It was a miracle they had lasted as long as they did.

Jenny returned to check the artist was still breathing. Was that the third or fourth time? It would be a tragedy if the ill woman was unable to finish her masterpiece. Jenny studied the quick sketches. The section emerging from under Alixanda's prone form showed groups of men. All engaged in ordinary activities, nothing to incriminate anyone here.

Some of the men were at the bar; others helped themselves from the buffet table. They talked in small groups, mingling and mixing. Jenny could almost believe these men were innocent attendees at some corporate function.

If she hadn't seen the girls displayed on the stage.

Clever Alixanda had included details of the room. Enough for Jenny to know all the men watched the stage. That information changed everything. Every sideways glance, each smile, the animated gestures and poses, all told the same tale. The girls on the stage were the main event, the topic of every conversation. The only reason any of these anonymous men were there.

Jenny focused her attention on the one face she recognised. She felt again the dread that awoke with this revelation. "Ricardo Barononi," she had hissed when she realised who Alixanda was depicting. The artist had sighed in reply, then tossed her pen aside. The ink had run out.

Now Jenny wrestled with the meaning of this man's presence in Alixanda's drawings. Piper had kept her in the dark, though she was his second-in-command. He hadn't wanted her to find out about the threats the Sydney businessman had made.

It was Evie who had told Jenny. That in itself was significant. Romano's wife didn't say anything lightly. Jenny had learned to pay close attention to everything that woman said.

If Jenny hadn't listened to Evie's concerns, she wouldn't have conducted her Sydney investigation. She would be clueless about the tension between Piper and Barononi.

Jenny reviewed her information. Barononi was handsome, currently unmarried, in his early forties. He belonged to an influential Italian-Australian dynasty. At first glance, he was a successful businessman. Nothing to mark the respectable man as an enemy. Not even his close association with Piper's grandfather suggested anything more sinister. There had only been a few awkward confrontations with Piper at social events in the distant past. Barononi's hostility towards Piper was no surprise – her boss was an irritating man.

Evie had talked to Jenny because Barononi had shown an interest in Evie's sister Sofia. This happened at the funeral of

Sofia's fiancé, Valentino. Sofia had been too numb to realise anything was happening. Piper had argued that Barononi wanted control over Sofia's inheritance. Romano and John Edwards had both been present. Neither of them would confirm the information when Jenny confronted them.

But what involvement did Barononi have in the current situation? Was he merely one of the "customers" at this party, or did he have a more sinister role? Jenny picked up her phone. She should tell Piper her suspicions...

Her hand froze, and she frowned. What if Piper already knew? She continued pacing.

There came a tentative knock at the door. Tap. Tap, tap.

Jenny tiptoed to the peephole. A nervous teenager wearing an oversized bullet-proof vest stood on the other side of the door. Two armed police officers were standing behind him.

"What do you want?" Jenny asked through the closed door.

"P-P-Piper sent me," the youth croaked. "I-I'm Declan. I-I've b-brought you—"

"You took long enough," Jenny complained. "Hold up what you've brought."

His arms shook as he lifted two reams of A4 copy paper and a handful of pens. Declan's nervous response reminded Jenny of Freddie Kidman. She threw a glance back to the sleeping artist. Would Freddie's uncomplicated life ever be the same? Jenny felt a stab of regret about the way she had teased him.

Jenny unlocked the door. With a smile, she snatched the wrapped paper from the boy's hands. He pulled back in alarm and dropped something. The armed guards didn't move. Declan bobbed down and his fingers chased after the pens.

He handed them to her. Jenny tossed them over her shoulder. They landed with a loud clatter behind her. She kept her eyes on the boy's terrified face. He didn't seem to appreciate her smile.

"I have more pens in my pockets," Declan confessed, fumbling for the rest. "I-I didn't want to drop them."

Jenny's smile became a grin. She couldn't help herself. Just like Freddie, this kid was entertaining. Where did Piper find him?

Jenny snatched the pens from Declan's hands, and tossed them, confident of her aim. She smiled her thanks and dismissed Declan from her mind. She glared at the armed officers. "Are you here to guard the room?"

One of them nodded and was about to speak. "Stay right there," she muttered, pushing the door closed.

At the last moment, she realised what she had said, and pulled the door open again. Declan was standing, pale and shaken, exactly where she had left him – Jenny liked this boy's attitude. She would tell Piper he had to hire him.

Jenny sent Declan on his way with a good-natured shove. "Tell Piper thanks," she said, slamming the door.

୧ ☼ ୨

Missiles were falling from the ceiling. Alixanda opened her eyes. A pen landed in front of her nose. She had it in her hand before she was fully awake. It was easy to draw. She had only one concern. Would the blue energy coursing through her veins wear off before she completed the task?

> Thank You for giving me this gift. Thank You that the images appear in my mind so clearly and it's easy to sketch what I see. Thank You for the energy. Please continue to inspire me, and guide my hand so that I can achieve Your purpose. Lord, thank You for these new resources; and thank You for Piper and Jenny. Without their help, this would be impossible.

"I see you've already found the new pens," Jenny remarked. "You can come back and finish the bedsheet drawings later."

Alixanda looked at Jenny.

Jenny tapped a section of the sheet with her foot. "Show me this man's involvement."

Jenny guided Alixanda to a small table near the curtained window. She propped her on a chair with the paper and pens in front of her. The artist closed her eyes and waited. When she opened her eyes again, she could see Rick's cruel face, as it had first appeared before her. The scene replayed in her mind like a video. She was able to fast forward and rewind it, then pause to capture the right view. Only then did the pen begin to move.

Scene after scene appeared, and she faithfully captured it all.

৪০ ✧ ୬

Freddie couldn't get back to sleep. The words Butch had spoken echoed in his mind. *She's never coming back, never coming back, never...*

> Is that true, God? Is Abigail gone forever? I didn't ask to love her... I'm thankful that I helped her get away from her enemies... I just need to know she's okay...

When there were no more words to express his concerns, Freddie yawned. He hoped she would visit him again in his dreams.

৪০ ✧ ୬

Piper chose to play a secondary role in this phase of the mission. He leaned against the wall, watching Nathan conduct the briefing. Piper was unsure whether any of the assembled men and women worked for his enemies. That made it essential to withhold information about their new evidence. Declan had successfully edited the original images Jenny sent.

The images in this portfolio now resembled hasty shots captured by a hidden camera. Declan was one of four people who knew the truth.

Five, if you counted the artist. Piper looked at the image on the top of the pile, and his heart faltered. He didn't like the questions this image raised. How had Alixanda been able to see herself, and why did she seem so lifeless? He tried to ignore the implications, but this drawing reminded him of the story that Evie Romano told.

In the past, Evie had given detailed descriptions for events she could not have witnessed. Piper had dismissed her account as the ramblings of a critically ill woman who experienced a near-death hallucination...

Piper blinked. He shuffled Alixanda's picture to the bottom of the pile. There were already too many pieces to this puzzle. He refused to entertain any distractions.

He refocused on the briefing.

"Now that I have designated the teams," Nathan explained, "I will detail your assignments. The first priority is to find the girls. The second is to secure a valuable witness. While we were still awaiting authorisation for the raid, Piper deployed another agent. They made it to the fourteenth floor."

An expectant murmur went around the room, lifting the atmosphere.

"The identity of the witness is a closely guarded secret. All I can say is, this testimony breaks the case wide open.

"Look at the thicker folder in front of you. We have to locate these girls. There are twenty of them. We are especially interested in the whereabouts of this girl."

Nathan held up Alixanda's image. The band around Piper's chest tightened even more. It was essential no-one realised she was the witness. "This is Piper's undercover operative..."

Every eye moved to Piper, and he stood taller.

The officer continued, "...and he is eager to have her returned."

Nathan waved another folio. "The second folder includes images of the men allegedly involved in taking the girls. Do nothing to attract their attention, unless you know for certain the girls are with them.

"Turn to the last photo." Nathan held Ricardo Barononi's image high. "Designate this man as 'watch and notify'. Under no circumstances do you approach him. I want to know who he talks to and where he goes.

"Alpha Team, we now know there are at least two secret exits from room fourteen-forty-six. We are going back to open them. We need to identify any other exits and use that information to work out where the missing girls have gone. Hopefully, it will be possible to pick up their trail before they are removed from the resort."

A man raised his hand. "What about the security cameras? Is it true that none of the cameras on the fourteenth floor work? And are there blind spots around the perimeter of the resort?"

"These concerns are already dealt with," Nathan said sternly. "While there *were* blind spots, we have been able to access cameras in the surrounding area. The curfew on service vehicles, which the resort already had in place, worked in our favour. I am confident the girls are still somewhere in this building. We have all the exits covered."

He had their full attention. "The people we are looking for don't know these photos exist. Some of these girls appear on last night's security feed entering the resort in groups under escort. The others may have come in through the service entrance in one of the delivery trucks. For that reason, Bravo Team will stop and search every vehicle before it leaves."

The four members of Bravo Team acknowledged their assignment with a gesture. The remaining teams waited in silence.

"Charlie and Delta Teams, change out of the body armour and monitor the major exits. I'll leave you to work the rotation for yourselves, but at no time do I want any of you to be on your own – stay in pairs."

Piper watched the frowns and whispered comments that followed this instruction. Nathan ignored them, and the hush returned.

"Echo Team, you are to join the pair on the fourteenth floor. There you will assist Piper in removing the secret witness to a secure location. Piper knows the room number. The forensic team are on standby and will meet you near the lifts with their equipment trolley. I never thought we'd be thankful they brought one the size of an elephant!

"The plan is to hide the witness in the trolley, then escort them into the lift. Piper, with some help from our technical genius, will make the witness disappear. When Piper dismisses you from that task, you are to join Charlie and Delta Teams."

After fielding additional questions, Nathan dispatched the teams. He returned to the manager's office, where Declan was learning to master the security camera controls. Piper had already shown him the basic requirements. The teenager was having fun practising his new skills. He grinned as he explored the possibilities, swapping between cameras.

"Make sure you put everything back the way it's supposed to be," Nathan warned him. He sat down to watch this new plan unfold.

Disband - Break Up

an Association

࿇ ☼ ࿇

Isaiah 40:29 God gives power to the weary and strength to the weak.

࿇ ☼ ࿇

Alixanda looked up from an incomplete drawing. She sat at the small table, her body wrapped in a towelling robe. Jenny's shadow fell across the page, making it impossible to ignore her presence.

Something had changed. Alixanda had become increasingly aware of the older woman's tension. Until this moment, the potency of her vision had remained stronger than her curiosity, but she had mentally catalogued the signs for future reference: restless pacing, wild gestures and physical contortions, including some shadow boxing. The unexplained rearrangement of the room's furnishings.

Alixanda had given up trying to speak. Her earlier attempts resulted in nothing more than a hoarse whisper. Jenny told her not to bother. The security consultant understood the artist's requirements from a few simple gestures. The young woman now asked a silent question.

"That's enough," Jenny said, removing the page from the table. She snapped a quick photo before adding it to a pile.

Alixanda blinked. The collection was larger than she realised. Jenny placed the pages on top of the folded, hand-decorated bedsheet. With a quick movement, these items disappeared inside a cream pillowcase. A bathroom robe cord, tied tight, transformed this bundle into a neat parcel.

The red silk sheet appeared on the table, already folded in half. Thud. The unused paper dropped onto the red fabric.

"Give me those pens," Jenny commanded. She tossed them onto the pile, then bound them together within the silk layers. Jenny thrust another cream pillowcase into Alixanda's hands. "Stuff them into this." As soon as Alixanda complied, Jenny seized that parcel. She twisted and closed the opening before hurrying to leave them in the bathroom. She returned with empty hands.

"We have to determine whether you're strong enough to stand. Leaving will be more difficult if you can't walk on your own."

Alixanda froze. She looked across at the bundled drawings on the table. A slideshow of the scenes she still needed to depict flashed through her mind. Jenny's words opened a new portal, one where darkness and danger lurked. Her inner vision trembled as wilder emotions took the stage.

She had been so focused on her creative task she had not thought about what would happen next. Her heart pounded in her chest. Alixanda fought the panic. She closed her eyes, not wanting her protector to know. Her empty hands fluttered, betraying her struggle. The older woman sprang into action.

"You must be hungry," Jenny announced. She returned from the room's bar fridge with an armful of snacks. Alixanda shook her head. The thought of food was abhorrent, hunger the furthest thing from her mind.

"Are you sure?" Jenny asked as she tore the wrapper from a muesli bar.

Alixanda pushed it away with her hand. Jenny shrugged and ate it herself in three quick bites. "I'm starving." The process repeated with the other items. Alixanda's stomach contorted as the older woman wolfed down the food.

She wanted to look away; to hide from the nausea-inspiring activity, but the artist within remained fascinated. Her hands twitched. The desire to capture this scene grew stronger. An understanding awakened.

Her gift was not confined to recapturing her traumatic event. It was active and ready for more adventures. If God was opening a new way for her to experience life, he would protect her. It was time to step out in obedience.

Thank You, Lord. Your presence has strengthened me.

Jenny finished the last of the salted nuts. She licked her fingers and smiled as she tore open the final treat. "I'm not taking 'no' for an answer. Eat this chocolate." Alixanda reached out her shaking hand. Jenny smiled, passing her a bottle of water as well.

Alixanda took a few sips of water then nibbled a corner of the chocolate.

"That's enough," Jenny said, snatching them away again. "You'll have time to finish them later."

The artist puzzled over the sudden urgency, but there was no opportunity to reflect on it. Jenny stripped off the towelling robe from Alixanda's body and pulled her to her feet. The sudden activity disorientated the weakened woman, and she grabbed hold of the table with both hands. Under Jenny's guidance, she found the courage to straighten and let go.

"Excellent," Jenny said. "Now take a few steps."

With a little support, Alixanda managed to walk from one side of the room to the other. Jenny shoved Alixanda back onto her chair.

With her hands idle, Alixanda's mind turned to her present predicament. She looked down at the skin-tight negligee. The thought of stepping from the room dressed like this sent a shiver down her spine. Alixanda frowned at Jenny and stroked her arms. "You're right," Jenny remarked. "If you walk around the resort half-naked, people are bound to notice. I've already prepared a solution. This is not the first time I've had to come up with a dress."

Jenny walked to the king-sized bed. The bed coverings were gone. A rolled bundle the size and shape of a human figure lay upon the mattress. Beside it was a folded sheet. Jenny lifted the fabric, already ripped into sections.

"Stand up, and keep still." Jenny tugged, wrapped and folded the fabric around Alixanda's slim figure. Satisfied with her handiwork, Jenny steered her towards the mirror. The ruined sheet now resembled a stylish dress. "You look like Aphrodite from Greek mythology."

Alixanda closed her eyes. Aphrodite was the goddess of love and beauty. The last thing she wanted was for anyone to look at her with desire. Her inner vision replayed scenes, but this time she was not a remote spectator. She felt again the cruel hands that had abused her. The intensity of the memories made it impossible to stand.

God! Help me!

Whoosh!
The images in her mind were tossed together and caught in a whirlwind. A single figure strode towards her out of the maelstrom. He came with a tender smile on his face. Freddie Kidman was coming to save her. Alixanda gasped.

The hotel room faded.

Now she stood in the meadow awaiting Freddie's arrival. He stopped an arm's length away, and she studied him. He loved her. She could see it on his face.

Freddie opened his arms, and everything changed. Dark clouds filled the sky as the men who had tortured her appeared in a circle around them. They laughed wickedly, taunting her with reminders that Freddie was a man. What made her think he was any different? If she trusted him, he would only abuse and betray her.

As she wrestled with her emotions, the blue lightning tickled her skin again. The desire to step forward into Freddie's welcoming arms became a blazing fire deep within her.

The accusing voices grew louder, their words more vicious and cruel. Alixanda stopped listening. She looked into Freddie's eyes and moved forward. As his hands brushed against her skin, the blue light flared. A flicker of the same fire awakened in his eyes and a song of triumph filled the air. She couldn't work out where the song came from, but it drove the shadows away...

As suddenly as the vision came, the crisis was over. Alixanda regained her senses. Jenny had caught her as she fell and was studying her with a frown.

"Don't do that again," Jenny admonished her. "There isn't time for you to play the helpless maiden. Listen carefully. I'll tell you only once. Then you can rest."

Alixanda nodded, taking the water bottle and chocolate thrust at her.

The agent spoke quickly as she steered her to the bathroom. "It's important that you don't make a sound. No-one can know you're here. Leave the lights off. I've opened the room curtains – sunrise is at five."

Here Jenny paused to ensure Alixanda noticed the clock. "When it is light, go into the hallway to find the lift. I can't give you directions, so you have to trust your God to guide you."

Alixanda nodded again, and Jenny continued. "Take my handbag and the room key. If you meet anyone between here and the lift, pretend you're drunk, and come back here. Wait until the hallway is clear and try again. Make sure you only get in the lift if you're alone. Don't worry about anything else. I will come and get you, and together we will make our escape."

Jenny re-bundled the young woman into the towelling bathrobe, and shoved her onto the tiled floor. The door closed after Jenny left. Alixanda sat in the dark and waited.

She replayed the instructions in her mind like a movie. Comforted, because there was no danger she would forget.

ಶ☼ಛ

Jenny wrenched the hallway door open and stepped back to let Piper in. "Let's do this," she snapped. Piper signalled for the forensic trolley to come closer to the doorway. There was no way it would fit through.

Her eyes widened. She had been expecting a laundry cart. She looked at the armed policemen standing in the hallway. Then she noticed the concerned forensic officers who hovered in the background.

Piper leaned down, opened a wide hatch, and pulled out a stretcher. He tucked it under his arm. Without a word, she led Piper into the room. They rounded the corner to face the bed. He saw the wrapped form lying on the bare mattress. "Good to see you planned ahead," he said. "I knew you would be expecting the usual method. Having the stretcher will make this task easier."

Jenny nodded. They both knew the real witness was safely hidden. When they finished loading the stretcher, they carried it to the trolley. After stowing the bundle away, he closed the hatch. He turned to face her. It was then that she retrieved the wrapped parcel of drawings and shoved it at him.

"Don't lose these," she said. "I've taken photos and sent copies to your email in case it goes missing."

He accepted the fabric-wrapped parcel with a small smile. Next, she passed him the room key for the Emperor's Bedchamber. She handed him the small red pouch containing the incriminating rainbow pills. Piper's smile disappeared. The items went into his pocket.

When his hand re-emerged, he was holding the hire-car key. Jenny looked at it. "You'll want to get changed," he said. "While you're getting your bag from the boot, check my briefcase. I've switched the combination back, so you don't have to waste time cracking the new code."

Jenny raised an eyebrow. Now was not the time to ask how he knew she had been snooping.

"Help yourself to the cash," he said, "and get whatever you need to finish this mission. Then take yourself a little break while I tidy up the loose ends. I'll be in touch when I need you again."

"I'm coming with you now," Jenny said. "There's nothing left for me to do here. I can take a different lift." She picked up her phone and held it in the hand that clutched the car key. Slipping the "Do Not Disturb" sign on the outer handle of the door, she listened for the satisfying click. The lock engaged behind them.

The forensic team took charge of their trolley. With the armed escort, the group went to the lifts. Piper was silent. Jenny reflected on the ease with which the plan had unfolded.

The only surprise was the key Piper had placed in her hand, but it made what came next much easier.

Fifteen minutes later, Jenny sneaked into the manager's office. There was only one person present. Declan sat before the three screens. He played with the master controls for the lifts, too preoccupied to hear her coming. He had accessed the lift video feeds, but Piper and the forensic trolley were no longer his focus. She stood immediately behind him and whispered in his ear, "Caught you."

The teenager knocked over the chair in his haste to get away from the desk. The look on his face reminded her of Evie's nephew Marco, that time she had caught him stealing chocolate biscuits.

"What were you up to?" she asked.

"N-n-nothing," Declan spluttered. "I was just checking—"

Jenny held up her hand. "Save your explanation. I'm in a hurry. Did Piper Maxwell tell you to help me?'

A frown appeared on Declan's face, and he shook his head.

"Oh, dear," Jenny said. "I'll have to go and find him. He won't be happy with the delay..." She turned towards the door.

"Wait," Declan cried. "I know you work for Mr Maxwell. Tell me what you want."

"Thank you." Jenny smiled. "I have to go and get something from the car. Could you please watch room fourteen-oh-eight? I want you to call me – pass me your mobile, and I'll enter my number."

He was quick to obey.

"Call me if the door opens..."

∞ ✧ ∞

Alixanda huddled behind the door of the bathroom. Her hands were restless as she waited. Jenny had made her promise not to turn on the light. She should be resting, but her mind was too active. Her eyes darted to the illuminated clock, plugged in beside the hand basin. Jenny had moved it from the bedside table. The digital numbers glowed, counting down the minutes until dawn. In the dimness, Alixanda found the chocolate and nibbled it. Then she washed away the sweetness with the bottled water.

Her eyes closed, and her mind drifted. She was standing in the meadow with Freddie beside her. "I'll wait for you," he whispered, raising her hand to his lips. The gentleness of his kiss made her heart flutter. "Come to me when you can." As his words echoed in the warm air, Alixanda felt a tug from behind, pulling her out of his reach. The dream meadow faded.

Alixanda sat up with a start and looked at the clock. It was after five. The sun was up! Her heart raced, and she struggled to her feet. Jenny had left clear instructions, and she had failed to follow them. Her hand reached through the shadows, searching for the doorknob. A faint glimmer of blue light twinkled at her fingertips. Reminding her she was not alone.

Alixanda opened the bathroom door and stepped into the empty room. All the curtains were open. The early morning brightness hurt her eyes, forcing her to wait for them to adjust. She stepped back into the darkened bathroom. She must not forget the pillowcase that held her precious art supplies.

Sitting beside it was the small handbag Jenny had left her. She knew that it held the key-card for Room 1408. If she met anyone on the way, Alixanda must pretend she was returning to this room instead of fleeing from it. She dropped the bathrobe to the floor.

Tiptoeing to the external door, she opened it. Jenny had told her to find her way to the lift. She gazed at the number on the door: Flashes of memory flooded her mind, and she sighed. The gift had delivered another benefit. She stepped out with more courage.

Thank You for showing me the way.

Little snippets of recollection were all she needed to walk to the lifts. She pressed the button beside the doors and waited.

Ping.

The lift doors opened, and there was no-one on board. She stepped inside, and the doors closed. The lift began to move before she could select a button. Alixanda watched the numbers count off the passing floors with growing apprehension. Jenny had not told her what came next. When the lift reached the fifth floor, the lift stopped, but the doors kept her prisoner.

Minutes passed. Alixanda's legs ached. She sat down on the floor of the lift, resting her head on her knees. Was this part of Jenny's plan, or had something gone wrong?

Whirr. The lift doors opened, and a single person entered. The doors whooshed closed again, but the lift remained stationary. Alixanda looked at the woman who stood over her. It took a few moments to recognise Jenny because she now had long black hair. Yesterday's jeans replaced the party dress. She also had on a hooded top identical to the one Alixanda had worn yesterday. She wore a pair of dark-rimmed spectacles.

Jenny reached up with a small can. She sprayed something in the direction of the lift security camera.

"I told the new guy to deactivate the cameras," Jenny said, pulling Alixanda to her feet. "Still, I always like to take my own precautions. He was too quick with his offer to help."

Alixanda wasn't sure how to respond. She touched the long wig with her fingers. Jenny smiled and whipped it off. "I always carry at least two in my bag," she said as she ran her fingers through her short blonde hair. Jenny set down her voluminous bag. She reached in and retrieved several items. First came the underwear and shoes Alixanda wore yesterday, followed by her jeans. Finally, the T-shirt emerged.

"I took the time to remove the microphone," Jenny said, "so you don't have to worry. It was a surprise to find your backpack sitting where I could retrieve it. I took what I needed and ditched the rest in a safe place." She was already untying the knots that kept Alixanda's improvised dress in place. "I had planned to swap clothes with you, but I'm happier to give you back your own."

It was a relief to step out of the heavy cream fabric. She was shaking, and Jenny had to help her dress. The older woman handed her the hooded top. Alixanda put it on.

"I've changed my mind about the specs," Jenny declared, putting the glasses back on her own face. She had swapped the first wig for a curly brown one and placed the black one on Alixanda's head. "I think a pair of sunglasses would be better. That way we can pretend you've had too much to drink, to explain your clumsiness." Finally satisfied, Jenny selected a button on the wall panel and pressed it.

The door slid open again. "Put your hand here," Jenny commanded as she stepped out with the redundant fabric. "I don't want the lift to take off without me, while I'm finding somewhere to stash this." Alixanda held her hand over the door sensors.

A few seconds later, Jenny returned and pressed another button. The lift began to move upwards again. She nudged Alixanda to the back of the elevator, handing her the art supplies. "I told Declan to take us up and down to gather as many passengers as possible. The surf is right for a few early risers. I'm hoping by the time we get to the ground floor there will be a nice crowd in our lift to cover our escape."

Alixanda sighed, not sure who Declan was, or why he would be helping them. She wrapped her arms around her bundle and closed her eyes.

The lift went up, stopping occasionally, in keeping with Jenny's plan, and then began to descend. After picking up another passenger on the third floor, it began to ascend again.

People exclaimed in protest when the doors opened at the sixteenth floor. More people entered, and everyone had to shuffle to accommodate them. The disgruntled passengers became quiet when the lift resumed its descent.

"Big night?" a male voice asked. A hand touched Alixanda's shoulder. She shrank closer to Jenny and dug her fingernails into the security agent's arm. She had her hood pulled over her lowered head and was thankful for the sunglasses as an additional layer of disguise.

Jenny patted her hand and spoke to the man, using an American accent, "I'd appreciate it if you could pretend you haven't seen us. I have to get her sobered up before her family discover she's been out all night. Her dad's ex-military, and he'll call out the marines if he finds out about the boy she's been keepin' company with."

The man laughed. "There's an excellent café around the corner," he said. "I'm heading there myself. You might have trouble sneaking past security. There's some kind of police operation going on, and there are armed guards everywhere.

Why don't you allow me to escort you? Your little friend will be less noticeable if they think we're a family group."

"That would be great," Jenny said.

Alixanda looked at her companion in dismay. Didn't she know this was Rick? The last person on the planet – no, the LAST person in the UNIVERSE – Alixanda wanted to go anywhere with.

From somewhere within Alixanda, a deep moan erupted. She brought her hands to her mouth and doubled over in shock. She imagined everyone looking at her. The lift doors opened.

"Let us through," Jenny cried. "My friend needs the restroom."

The crowd parted, and she pushed Alixanda forward. Jenny hustled Alixanda away. As soon as the restroom door closed, Jenny burst out laughing. "I don't know what inspired you, but that was exactly what we needed to get away from *him*."

⁞✧⁝

Nobody tried to stop them from leaving through a side entrance. Jenny guided Alixanda around the corner. They walked away from the police activity. A bus pulled up at the footpath beside them, and Jenny made a snap decision. "Get on." They rode the bus until it stopped at Broadbeach. Jenny took her to a café that was already crowded, despite the early hour.

"Stay here," Jenny said, depositing Alixanda at a corner table. A few minutes later, she returned. "I've ordered two breakfasts. Make sure you don't eat mine while I'm gone."

Gone where? Alixanda wondered. The waitress delivered two heaped plates of food. Eggs three ways – poached, scrambled and fried. Bacon, sausages, hash browns, baked beans, and grilled tomatoes. And massive slices of toasted bread. The waitress returned a few minutes later with a pot of tea and a large mug of black coffee. Alixanda smiled and picked up her fork. There was no way she would be able to eat all the food on the plate in front of her, but she had to make it look as if she was trying. After a few mouthfuls of egg, she nibbled a corner of the toast, before pouring herself a cup of tea.

Jenny returned and looked at both plates. "Good to see you didn't wait for me," she said with a grin as she began to eat. Alixanda watched her companion demolish her food in record time. "Are you finished?" Jenny asked, and Alixanda nodded. Jenny grabbed her plate, replacing it with the empty one. How was it possible that she could eat this much and stay so trim?

"Metabolism," Jenny said with her mouth full. "And the uncertainty about where the next meal will come from. I'm sure you know what I mean. Isn't that how you came to be so overweight when you arrived in Melbourne? You had the look of a woman who knew what it was to be hungry and couldn't believe your good fortune would last."

Alixanda nodded. This was the closest she could come to revealing anything about her earlier life. She looked across the table and saw Jenny pause, her fork halfway to her mouth. "You and me," Jenny said, "are more alike than you know. One day, we'll sit down and swap stories. I'll tell you about someone who had a family and couldn't wait to get away; you can tell me what it's like to lose everyone."

₧✧₝

(Wednesday 24th January)
Jenny returned from the supermarket and unlocked the door to the hotel room. "I'm back."

She knew before she entered the room that Alixanda had gone.

When she left that morning, the artist had been sitting at the table, working on another of her sketches. That chair was empty. A pen lay idle on top of a tall pile of new drawings. She picked up the top one. There was Jenny's face looking back at her, in her current disguise. The assignment was complete.

On the page underneath was a single phrase: "Thank you."

Jenny dropped into the empty chair. She allowed the impact of this abandonment to resonate within her. She had hoped for this moment, had begged God to give the artist the courage to take charge of her own life. Now that it had happened, Jenny found herself unprepared for the sense of loss.

It had been three weeks since Jenny had removed Alixanda from the resort. The two women had settled into a comfortable rhythm. Jenny took care of the travel arrangements and provisions. Alixanda spent her days drawing. She could even sketch while seated in a moving car. The quality of the drawings never diminished. The young woman hardly ate and rarely slept.

They didn't stay in one place for more than a day, and registered in small, out of the way hotels. Jenny was an expert at finding people and knew all the mistakes people made. She hadn't left an easy trail to follow.

Jenny set Alixanda a task, to record the whole adventure as a complete narrative. She also asked for individual stories. The collected drawings catalogued every scene, person by person. They included details remembered with exquisite precision. In this way, Jenny hoped no clue would be missing when it was time for her to report back to Piper. The artist had taken her orders seriously and dedicated herself to the task.

The day after they had walked away from the resort, Jenny had gone shopping. She purchased two pay-as-you-go phones and one of those prepaid debit cards. She sent a message from one phone to the other, saving both numbers. Then she showed Alixanda how to transfer money from one account to another securely, and then onto the debit card. She knew Alixanda only needed to see the passwords and information once.

The artist had accepted the instructions without comment, looking at Jenny for a long time with her strange new eyes. The phone and card weren't referred to again.

Now, Jenny considered rushing out to find the missing woman. She reviewed what she had discovered about Alixanda during the past three weeks. The girl had learned her survival lessons well.

The security agent packed her luggage and left the hotel. She unlocked the small car she had purchased after ditching Piper's rental. It was time to finish her part of the mission and deliver these drawings to her employer. She headed towards the coast.

Turning towards Melbourne was harder than Jenny expected. This was the longest she had been out of Piper's communication loop. Never had she felt so alone.

Discontinue – Bring to an End

🕉

Galatians 5:1a Christ set us free to enjoy liberty.

🕉

Last night's dream had been more intense than usual. Freddie dragged himself upright from the couch. He had stopped trying to sleep in his bed. The last time he tried, he had woken on the floor beneath the drawing – stiff and sore.

He stumbled through his preparations for work. He made sure his nephew and niece were both awake. They got ready for school while he cooked their breakfast. Nikki had come to live with them three weeks ago. The shadows under her eyes haunted him. Sigrid was doing her best, but she seemed better at fighting bad guys than dealing with a troubled child.

Freddie smiled. He had to concede Sigrid's angry approach had worked wonders with Butch. The teenager had improved the way he spoke. Apart from a small scuffle at the start of the year, there had been no further trouble at school.

After the playground fight, Sigrid had dragged Butch to the *Maximum Security* training facility. She was still working to regain her strength, but she proved to be more than a match for Butch. The belligerent teenager did not appreciate being repeatedly thrown to the floor. Especially by a woman he considered to be an invalid.

"Where's your self-respect?" Sigrid had asked him. "If you can't take out your opponent in the opening moves, then you deserve to lose. Don't start something unless you're certain you can win."

Freddie wasn't sure whether to be worried or relieved by her philosophy.

At least Sigrid no longer had Freddie in her sights. Jenny had reappeared at the end of January and taken the angry operative aside. Since then, his adopted cousin's attitude had changed. Sigrid had a new assignment – she hadn't been happy shadowing Evie while Jenny was away.

Since her interview with her superior, he often found Sigrid staring at the wall mural. Something significant had happened, but he wasn't going to ask. If he needed to know, someone would tell him. He had enough to keep his mind busy.

The other big lifestyle change related to his work for Romano. He was still the manager at the service station, but his hours had reduced. The Boss insisted a family man must spend more time at home. Freddie's working day didn't start until nine. He no longer worked weekends either. At first, Freddie tried to argue. But now, he had to admit the changes helped him manage his complicated household.

Today, as he walked to work, his life felt more settled.

His monthly security screening would happen at noon. Freddie calmly performed routine tasks until Evie and Jenny arrived to take over. He was halfway across the car park to the main compound when his phone rang. He glanced at the screen.

His heart raced in anticipation. The unfamiliar number didn't concern him – it was nothing new for either school to phone him from a different line. But he would have to tell the caller he couldn't deal with their emergency until Piper and Romano released him. "Freddie Kidman, how can I help you?"

"Hello, Freddie Kidman," the female caller replied, and said nothing further.

Freddie stopped walking and frowned. "Who is this?"

Laughter came to him through the phone. It began as a small chuckle. Then it grew louder until it sounded as if it was behind him. Freddie turned.

A small woman approached him from the street, giggling as she came. He saw her put her phone in the large bag she carried over her shoulder. She kept coming. He admired her graceful, confident movement, as recognition awakened in him. This was the woman who haunted his dreams.

Freddie shoved his phone in his pocket and ran to close the gap between them. She stopped then, putting down her bag. Her face was radiant. He lifted her from her feet and spun her around, his arms hungry to hold her. He could feel her heart beating as he crushed her to his chest.

"Welcome home," he whispered, leaning back to gaze into her eyes. She stared back at him, the hint of uncertainty shimmering in their indigo depths. He dropped her back onto her feet before releasing her. "Your eyes were brown, but now they're blue," he said in wonder. "You're exactly how I imagined you. I've seen you in my dreams."

She raised her hand to caress his face. "You're not dreaming now." He thought he'd stopped breathing, but when she took her fingers away, he was still alive. Freddie reached for her hand, wanting more, but he didn't want to frighten her away.

He remembered where he was and where he should be.

The doorway to the workshop called him. God's timing was perfect.

❧ ✿ ☙

Alixanda stepped into the workshop. She paused to take in the new environment. Her smile widened. Freddie was so

239

sensitive to her mood, he stopped walking, without her needing to ask. What would he say when he learned she could draw the entire scene, exactly as she saw it now? She spun around, taking it all in.

Two huge black and tan dogs loped towards her. Freddie gasped. He relaxed when the dogs licked her face and danced around them. Alixanda leaned closer to pat them. When she had satisfied their curiosity, she sent them away.

"Ready?" Freddie asked. "I wish I could guarantee a warm welcome when we get to Romano. He's not expecting you, so I don't know how this is going to go."

She patted his hand. "Please don't be afraid for me. I'm stronger now."

Freddie nodded. He straightened his shoulders. Then he boldly led the way across the industrial maze that was familiar territory for him. She smiled, pleased he had become more confident during their time apart. A door on the further side of the workshop was partially open. He rapped loudly before pushing into the room.

Alixanda paused to memorize the scene. Six identical couches arranged in a rectangle, with tables in the central space. Three familiar men occupied the couches on the right. Not one of them looked up at their entry.

"Take a seat, Freddie," the smaller of the three men called out. He sat beside the tattooed giant Alixanda knew was Romano. "We'll be with you in a moment."

The documents in their hands distracted them.

Freddie led her to the couch, opposite the man who had spoken. They stood waiting.

Freddie's employer was the first to look up. He sprang to his feet. "You've returned," Romano remarked, speaking to Alixanda. She nodded.

"I didn't recognise you," he continued, "but I can tell by Freddie's grin that it must be you. He looks as if all his dreams have come true."

She turned her attention to the others. They responded differently. The first man stood to acknowledge her presence. Dave Henderson's eyes were alert, his expression welcoming. Alixanda acknowledged him with a smile before focusing on the third man.

Piper Maxwell remained seated, and would not look at her. No emotion registered on his face. She studied his stiff posture, and the contours of his face. He continued to stare at the table, filling the space between them. Was he trying to hide something from her gift? Neither of them said anything.

Romano broke the awkward silence. "Evie told me you would be back before her babies were born, but she didn't tell me about the changed appearance."

"Did you find the answers I need?" Piper asked. Romano frowned at him. Piper dismissed his concern with a gesture. "Jenny delivered the drawings you left with her, but you sent nothing more. As one of my employees, I expected you to keep me updated with your progress."

Freddie tensed beside her. Alixanda squeezed his hand.

"Sit down," Piper commanded. "Dave, go and postpone the rest of the interviews. I'm not letting her leave until she's made a full report."

Dave stood. "I'll stay out in the workshop. I've witnessed what happens when you take on Evie in a debate. It's obvious that A-Alixanda – is that right? Alixanda has the same look in her eyes. I don't want to be caught in the crossfire."

Freddie still held Alixanda's hand. He pulled her down beside him onto the couch to face her inquisitors. They had barely taken their seats when the door Dave had disappeared through re-opened. Evie, now heavily pregnant, came bursting in with Jenny close at her heels.

"Welcome home," Evie said, coming to hug Alixanda. "Jenny said she saw you in the car park."

Standing to receive Evie's embrace, Alixanda looked past her towards Jenny. The bodyguard struck a valiant pose. "This is always my best profile," Jenny said, her head tilted at a ridiculous angle. Then her face broke into a grin. She vaulted the couch. Evie stepped out of the way with seconds to spare.

"Make sure you do me justice in your next report," Jenny said. She wrapped one arm around Alixanda's shoulders and punched her arm. "No more of that sentimental softness Piper has been teasing me about since I came back." Then Jenny leaned closer. "You didn't answer my messages," she whispered. There were tears in Jenny's eyes as she turned away towards a coffee machine on the far side of the room. She spoke louder. "And if you try to convince Piper I have a gram of compassion, I'll deny it."

"You'd better get Alixanda a blindfold then," Piper told Jenny, as she dropped onto the couch beside him. Jenny put her cup on the table in front of them. She smiled sweetly at him before launching her attack. He ducked, avoiding the blow she aimed at his head. Neither of them seemed to find anything unusual about their behaviour.

Evie waddled around the other table to sit beside Romano. Alixanda noted the care that her husband showed the pregnant woman as she settled on the couch. Such great devotion to each other. So this was love!

Alixanda considered how she would portray her princess now. She longed for the sketchbook hidden in her bag. Evie's rounded belly was a reminder that these babies would soon be born. A small cloud of sorrow touched the artist, at the reminder that her own baby had died. Evie stared at her, understanding in her eyes.

Alixanda blinked. She remembered the promises God had given her, and she sighed.

"I'm still waiting," Piper grumbled.

Alixanda nodded, reaching for the bag at her feet. "I came prepared."

Jenny clapped her hands in delight. "You have a new voice. I wondered how you would manage on your own without one."

Alixanda withdrew a cream pillowcase. A red silk-wrapped bundle emerged from within. The artist laid it on the table. As her hands unfolded the layers, she flicked quick glances towards each of her audience. It was important to remember all the details...

From the red wrapping, she removed a pile of large yellow envelopes and hugged them to her chest. Different emotions pushed for domination. Her heart pounded, and her smile faded. She bowed her head and prayed silently:

> Lord, You brought me here. Please keep me from distractions. Help me to say as little, or as much, as You require for this moment. Make me sensitive to Your leading and guard my heart...

When she looked again, Piper had moved to the edge of his seat. His powerful arms extended to receive her work. Jenny was setting up a small document camera on the table – she must have had it in her ever-present bag. Romano had moved towards the wall-mounted television and switched it on. He passed Jenny the remote control as he resumed his seat.

Alixanda leaned forward to deliver her precious files. She looked across the room at the four people who were waiting for her to reveal these secrets. Her eyes lingered on Evie. At that moment, she made a decision and removed one of the envelopes. She dropped it into Freddie's hands.

"This one is incomplete."

Piper frowned. He looked from Alixanda to Evie. He glared at the envelope Freddie tucked beside him on the couch. The artist kept her eyes fixed on Piper. When he returned his attention to her, she passed over the remaining files. He flicked through the pile, examining the drawings on the outside of the envelopes. Finally, he put them on his lap, leaning back against the couch.

"How do you want to play this?" Piper asked. "Do you intend to explain yourself? Or am I supposed to guess what's in each envelope based on the cover illustrations?"

"It's your game," Alixanda replied.

Piper smiled. With the action of someone examining a hand of cards, he rearranged the envelopes. He selected one and lifted the flap. His hands flicked through the pages, but he didn't remove any of them. He laid the envelope on the table. Jenny moved her gadget so that the illumination fell on the line drawing on the outside. Piper kept his eyes on Alixanda.

She had to look away.

Everyone else was gazing at the screen mounted on the wall. The display filled with a detailed drawing of a ferocious face: half-man, half-wolf.

Jenny adjusted the focus, then reached out and patted the envelope. "If the drawings inside are even half as good as the cover, Piper won't ever complain that you don't earn your pay."

Piper scowled at Jenny, and she grinned in reply.

"You're always quick to tell me what I think," Piper told Jenny. "Now, I find my newest recruit has taken your lead by presenting a report that contains no text. You're the expert; you tell us what's in this envelope."

Alixanda watched the air around Piper and Jenny sizzle and pop. His intense glare had moved from the artist to his usual sparring partner. Deep gratitude towards the older woman bubbled inside her.

Alixanda sighed. She nestled herself beside Freddie. He slipped his arm around her shoulders as if to protect her.

Everyone waited.

It wasn't Jenny who spoke first.

"Clayton Wolfe," Freddie said, his attention fixed on the screen. The pressure of his arm intensified. He dropped his eyes to look at her. "I knew he wasn't someone I could trust."

Alixanda smiled at him and nodded.

"You're right," Jenny said, with confidence. "He's the Judas who betrayed the witness he should have protected. This file will contain enough background information to pin that man down. Now we'll know how connected he actually is."

"An easy guess," Piper said. "With her new face, going after him was a predictable first choice for Alixanda." He laid down a second envelope beside the first. Jenny adjusted the camera. Three men standing outside a burning house replaced the man-wolf image on the television screen.

Alixanda waited. She was sure Jenny would be quick to respond.

"We know these faces," Jenny said. "These are the men she was to testify against. Alixanda has revisited her old home, and used that location to capture her memories of the traumatic events."

Jenny tapped the envelope with her finger. "This one, Constantino Barbara, implicated himself in the Surfers Paradise incident. The other two are unknowns."

"Not anymore," Piper snorted. "Another easy guess. Now, for something harder." He laid out the third and fourth envelopes in quick succession. "These two belong together, both sides of the one story."

The projected image switched again. This time it showed three children crying, with a police car in the background.

"The children whose rescue was the catalyst for her troubles," Jenny said, not even looking for confirmation. "We needed to know when they became targets, how long they were in danger and from whom. And what happened to them afterwards."

Jenny pushed the envelopes along the table. Now the fourth cover illustration appeared on the screen.

"The school and the community where the scene played out." Jenny flashed Alixanda a quick look. The artist nodded. "To build a complete incident profile, we needed the before and after details."

"Excellent, Sherlock," Piper said, as the fifth envelope slammed onto the table. "What do you deduce from this one."

Jenny worked without hesitation. "This is Alixanda with her old face. She went backwards in time, then drove to each of the places she remembered. She retraced her history back to the day she entered the foster care system."

He laid the next envelope down and leaned back. Jenny busied her hands. She stared at the image of two children in a small bush clearing.

"Two girls – one looks to be three or four, and the other one much older. The older girl is looking at me, but I can't see the little one's face. It's as if Alixanda can't see what she looks like, so she drew—" She stared at the artist.

Jenny's face lit up. She continued with confidence. "Your earliest memories led you back to the physical location. New eyes, fresh evidence." She patted the file with both hands. "From the thickness of this file, I'd say you found plenty."

Another envelope landed on the table. Jenny looked from the cover illustration to the widescreen television.

"Two drawings of the same man, but he's much older in the second one. This is the man who appears in the story twice. Here in the recent event"—she pointed to the burning house envelope—"and a lot earlier, in the bush scene with the two girls.

"This man realised our witness had put the puzzle pieces together. He intended to silence her forever. He was so certain he'd won, he made a critical mistake. He decided to extend her torture. If he'd killed her immediately, we wouldn't know he existed."

Jenny scrutinised Alixanda. "He believes he's free to continue his long reign of terror, but justice is heading his way."

Alixanda watched as her small audience absorbed this information. The envelopes lined up in a row, like the opening moves for a game of Solitaire. Nobody attempted to examine the contents. The detailed drawings, and the stories they would reveal, were still unseen.

How would Piper proceed?

Bang. Piper dropped the final envelope onto the table.

Jenny had the image on the screen before she realised what she was seeing. A collective gasp arose from the others. There were children's faces on this cover. One familiar teenager dominated the foreground. Alixanda watched them closely as they each turned from the screen to look to her.

Freddie dropped his arm and pulled away. "Why is my nephew Butch in your report?" he asked.

Piper spoke with sarcasm. "That's a question for Evie to answer."

"Why would Evie know anything about this?" Romano growled, alert to the hint of danger. "Is this another coincidence, or did Alixanda find a connection?"

Evie placed her hand on her husband's arm and smiled at Piper. "Alixanda came to us for a special purpose," she told Romano. "It's indisputable that Freddie's nephew was also sent to us. We've all listened to Butch tell his story"—Evie gestured with her other hand around their group. "Now we've seen enough of Alixanda's report to make an assessment. Butch is in this file because the same organisation was responsible for his sister's trauma."

"Which one of these files will we discuss first?" Jenny asked. Her hands hovered over the row of yellow envelopes.

"None of them," Piper said. He moved with lightning speed. Before Freddie realised his intention, Piper snatched the forgotten envelope from beside him.

Alixanda leapt to her feet. "No!"

It was too late.

Piper tore open the envelope. Illustrated pages spread out over the tables. One drawing landed at Evie's feet. Romano retrieved it.

Jenny snatched it from his hand to place it on the table. She adjusted the camera.

The image of an unsmiling woman filled the screen.

The room went still.

Alixanda sat with her head in her hands.

"I don't understand," Freddie said. "What's so important about this file that you didn't want Piper to see it?"

Alixanda sifted through the scattered drawings. She searched for one that would clarify everything. She stood as she placed the sketch in his hands.

"That's my brother with this woman," Freddie cried. "Are you telling me my brother's implicated in this criminal activity? There has to be some mistake..."

"It's not your brother I went looking for, Freddie," Alixanda said. "Your father showed me this photo. This woman is your brother's wife. I believe she's my sister."

Freddie opened his mouth, his eyes telling her he knew nothing of this marriage. She put her fingers to his lips. "I kept this file separate because everyone here knows her by another name."

The silence was heavy. It was Jenny who supplied the name. "Jezebel – the woman who abducted Evie and then escaped."

"Do you know where she is?" Romano asked as he towered over Alixanda. His smile had vanished.

Freddie stood and placed his arm around Alixanda's waist. She trembled as she shook her head. "I can't see into the future. She has disappeared again."

"So Alixanda's long-lost sister married Freddie's brother," Jenny remarked. "Now that's a coincidence I didn't see coming. That's going to make for an interesting family dynamic if Alixanda marries Freddie."

"You may be premature in planning their wedding," Piper retorted. "Freddie might not want to marry someone who invites trouble to the ceremony."

Jenny challenged him. "The only trouble on the invitation list is you! Alixanda is one of your agents now. Perhaps she'll decide not to tie herself to a man who can't protect her from you?"

"There's only one way to determine whether either of you is right," Freddie said. He raised Alixanda's chin, and gently brought his lips to hers. She allowed the kiss to linger, as his arms wrapped around her. When Freddie released her, she smiled at him and reached for her bag. He nodded as he turned to the others in the room. "Alixanda and I are leaving now," Freddie announced. Surprise seemed to keep everyone quiet.

Freddie turned to Piper. "Take all the time you need to work through her report. When we've made up our minds whether there's going to be a wedding, we'll let you know."

Freddie took her bag. Without a backward glance, he led her through the door. It was a relief that no-one tried to follow them. They left behind raised voices as they hurried away.

When they were safely on the footpath, Alixanda spoke. "It's not going to be easy."

"I know," he said, "but I love you too much to let you deal with this alone."

"Knowing you were waiting for me sustained me."

His smile grew. "Race you home."

Alixanda laughed as she ran. Hand in hand, they turned the corner.

Freddie led her past the apartment building's main door. When they arrived at the private entrance to the corner apartment, he became solemn again. Alixanda stood facing him.

"Do you need Piper's permission to get married?" he asked.

"Only if you need Romano's permission."

"Let's ask neither of them. I have a friend who can get us a license. I asked months ago, but there's a four-week wait after you sign the forms. Until you're ready, you can have my room, and I'll sleep on the couch. It's been my resting place since you went away." He reached for her hand. "Are you sure about this? About wanting to marry me? Jenny warned me you might never be ready."

Alixanda stepped closer and hugged him. "The shadows of my past still linger, but I want to replace them with new memories. I've learned to wait for God to sort out the details. Being married to me won't be easy…"

"I'm up for the challenge," he assured her. "I was about to tell you the same thing. I come with a ready-made family. There's Butch, and his sister Nikki lives with us now, too. Sigrid's in our apartment more than she's in hers on the fourth floor. Then there's Marco and his two stepbrothers popping in to visit all the time. They live upstairs. Marco's mother, Sofia, bought the apartment building. That was before she married my friend, John Edwards."

"I've always wanted a big family."

Freddie stared into her blue eyes before scooping her off her feet. He opened the gate and carried her into his apartment, then set her down on the couch in front of the artwork that had been rescued from her old apartment.

"You saved it!" she exclaimed, bouncing on the cushion beside him. She reached for his hand as she stared at the drawing of the princess and her entourage in the meadow.

"You have Butch to thank for that," Freddie said. He looked at the drawing. "I've longed for you to explain it all to me. I've spent so much time studying it, I go there in my dreams."

"I know you do," she said, squeezing his hand. "I've met you there. There are times when that imaginary world seems more real than this one…"

For the next few hours, they talked about the artwork, which led to discussing the shared dreams.

"In those dreams," she whispered, "you took care of me when I didn't think I could go on."

Freddie stood, still holding her hand. He led her across to the artwork. Taking hold of her shoulders, he placed her in front of her image. He arranged himself to stand in the hero's position and waited. Alixanda looked to the drawing, moving her hands to his chest to match the heroine, and she dropped her head to hide her flustered face.

Together they faced each other, a living re-enactment of her earlier vision. Her heart beat faster as his arms wrapped around her waist. The memory of other hands flooded her mind with the first stirrings of distress. Being confronted with the reminder of what those wicked men had done made her knees weak. She raised her chin, not wanting to be alone with those memories.

"I love you," Freddie said, staring into her eyes. Alixanda wondered if he could see what she could see. He continued to speak. "I believe God can set you free to love me in return."

He kissed her. It was not an unassuming token of his affection, but a firm declaration of his love for her. In that instant, something unlocked deep inside her. Alixanda knew she didn't want him to stop. There was no comparison between the horror of her past, and the future he was offering her. She kissed him in return. With that simple action, she made a crucial decision. She would give away the nightmare in exchange for a lasting promise.

Their moment of passion was short-lived. The apartment door banged open to announce his nephew and niece arriving home from school. It would take some time to explain to the outraged teenager why his uncle was "making out" with a stranger.

Alixanda sat down on the couch and watched the drama unfold.

How wonderful it was to be home.

Timeline

June 30 (Chapter 1) *White Rose of Promise*
August 25 (Chapter 1) *When Promises are Broken*
October 30 (Chapter 1) *When Freedom is Promised*
        Introducing Abigail, Butch and his uncle Freddie
October 31   Abigail's enemies arrive; Introducing Evie &
        Romano, Piper, Jenny, Sigrid & Xanda
        Abigail's new friends promise to help her
        Freddie makes a difficult choice
November 2   Abigail's artistic talent flourishes
November 5   Abigail's enemies return
November 6   Abigail escapes; Freddie is arrested
November 15   Freddie is released to rebuild his life
November 16   Abigail changes her name to Alixanda
January 1   Alixanda goes to Queensland
January 2   Another narrow escape
January 24   Alixanda disappears
April 24   Alixanda returns to be reunited with Freddie

Character List

St Jerome's Boys Junior School:

Abigail Golding - the new teacher
Principal Cameron Melrose - Head teacher
Butch Cassidy Kidman (15) - grade 9 student
Freddie Kidman - Butch's uncle, works for Sebastian Romano
Marco Fontana (13) - grade 8 student, Evie's nephew
Tyler Kelly (14) - grade 9 student

Abigail's associates:

Dr Anderson - A&E resident doctor
Louise Silverton - woman in witness protection
Clayton Wolfe - Sydney witness protection agent
Alixanda Jadaranata - aka Xanda, *Maximum Security* operative
Ruthie - Alixanda's missing sister
Evie Romano - Marco's aunt, Sebastian Romano's wife
Jenny Prescott - *Maximum Security* deputy commander,
      Evie Romano's body guard
Sigrid Ericson - *Maximum Security* undercover operative

<u>Freddie's associates:</u>
Blake Remington - Freddie's co-worker
Sebastian Romano - AKA the Boss, AKA Romano
         Freddie's employer, Evie's husband, Marco's uncle
Dave Henderson - Romano's deputy, Marilyn's husband
Marilyn Henderson - Evie Romano's friend, Dave's wife
Lilly Henderson (5) - Marilyn and Dave's daughter
Piper Maxwell - *Maximum Security* owner,
         Operation Phoenix Commander
Xanda Jadaran - *Maximum Security* undercover operative
John Edwards - friend to Romano and Freddie
Leonardo Fontana - Marco's brother, Evie's nephew
Sofia Fontana - Marco and Leonardo's mother, Evie's sister
Nikki Kidman (12) - Freddie's niece, Butch's sister
Samson Davidson - Freddie's half-brother, Butch's uncle

<u>Melbourne Adventure:</u>
Mike Kelly - ex Romano employee
Nelson Felmingham - *Maximum Security* operative
Oliver Johnston - *Maximum Security* operative
Patrick Sims - *Maximum Security* operative
Vincent and Trey - *Maximum Security* operatives
Brian Grovener - Victorian witness protection agent
Officer McCormick - policeman
Officer Vitali - policeman
Gabriel Messinger - lawyer
Nancy - nurse
Valentino Horatio - Piper's cousin (deceased)
Ricardo Barononi - Sydney businessman

<u>Queensland adventure:</u>
Earl - a man in Surfers Paradise
Nadia - a woman in Surfers Paradise
Kitty - a girl at the Surfers Paradise party
Scarlet - a girl at the Surfers Paradise party
Wisdom - a messenger
Inspector Nathan Rigg - Queensland task force leader
Declan Stevens - Nathan Rigg's relative, technical whiz-kid
Constantino "Barbie" Barbara - a man in Surfers Paradise

River Wild Series

Book 1 (2019) *White Rose of Promise*

Book 2 (2019) *When Promises Are Broken*

Book 3 (2020) *What Price My Freedom?*

Book 4 (later in 2020) *Which Promise This Time?*

Book 5 (2021) *When Promises Are Forever*

These books can be read in any order. Each story stands alone, but some of the characters make an appearance in every story.

Available at <u>www.chrissygarwood.com</u>

White Rose of Promise

A prophetic dream she can't remember. A shameful past she can't forget. An impossible future she dare not cherish.

Maria Evangelina Fontana comes home from twenty years in exile. She is looking for reconciliation but her family refuse to acknowledge the secret that keeps them apart. They cannot accept that the lost years have changed her forever. Her hope for a new beginning fades.

Sebastian Romano has no time for women and abhors weakness. The wealthy businessman is uncertain why he offers Ria a way out of her dilemma, but it is too late to change his mind. If only he had understood the risk.

Ria's innocence turns his orderly world upside down. Her faith challenges his values as she steps into her destiny. He thought he was done with his violent past, but his enemies have found her. Romano watches helplessly as the prophecy unfolds...

When Promises Are Broken

A family curse, an evil plot, an unlucky coincidence. Three destinies entwined.

Sofia sits in angry isolation at the wedding reception, unspoken secrets and broken promises her only consolation. No-one will listen, and now it is too late. Her innocent sister has married a very bad man.

Pastor John Edwards is puzzled by Sofia's animosity. Her emotional outburst drives him to prayer. When a sinister stranger warns him to keep his distance, he wonders if it is already too late.

Valentino makes clear what he wants from Sofia. He is rich, handsome and available. So why does she question his motives and reject his advances? He laughs at her assertion that trouble pursues her, but then he disappears...

Which Promise This Time?

Jezebel, Evie's enemy from *White Rose of Promise*, makes an unexpected return. A shadow of her former self, she is running from Samson Davidson, a man of prayer who has promised her a future she doesn't deserve. But more than one enemy has vowed to pursue her until she loses either her freedom or her life. Alixanda and Freddie, Evie and Romano, together with Piper, Jenny and the *Maximum Security* team, are all drawn into the adventure.

When Promises Are Forever

Sara Messinger has a crush on her boss, Nero Mariani. When she meets Oliver Johnston, a *Maximum Security* agent, he warns her to be careful. Oliver knows that Nero's family business is not what it seems. Has Oliver's warning come too late? Nero's influential family want to find him a replacement wife, and Sara seems like the perfect candidate.

Fantasy River Series

Phoena's Quest: First Spark
(later in 2020)

The quest begins with a first spark. It flares in isolation, untended and unknown. Too late, the darkness tries to smother it...

The Westernbrooke Academy for Young Noblemen has always been Phoena's home. An orphaned servant without a past, the teenager lacks magical talent and protections. She is often targeted for magical experiments. After years of torment, she longs for invisibility. The other servants think her luck is running out.

Lord Karilion, the Academy's best magic-user, has beaten all challengers. The wealthy heir is also the champion swordsman. Viscount Baraapa, secure in second place, has no magic but his scientific mastery outweighs that disadvantage. The foreigner, Lord Oramis, threatens the balance when he refuses to be tested. What is the Ambassador's son hiding?

The quest selects its champions: a servant girl and three noblemen who think winning her loyalty is a game. And there's a dragon in the back garden...

Other titles in this series:

Phoena's Quest: Second Flame
Phoena's Quest: Third Fire

Acknowledgements

This book could not have been written without the support and encouragement of many people.

Firstly, I am grateful to God for inspiring me, for giving me the time and the persistence to bring this story into life.

My writing adventure has not been a solitary one. God provided me with a supportive team - determined to ask the right questions, demand the next instalment and keep me moving forward. Thanks to Gillian Perrett, Naomi McGlone, Belinda McGuire, Donna Bullen, Tim Berry, and Eva Bitterova for your help with *When Freedom is Promised*.

I am thankful for you, dear reader. I am especially grateful for your gentle reminders to keep writing because you want to know what adventures are in store for your favourite characters.

A special thanks to Belinda Pollard, publishing mentor and editor, for taking me under her wing and for the professional advice that has helped make this book better than I could have imagined.

Last but not least, thanks to my patient husband Tony, for his constant encouragement, and ongoing support.

Chrissy

A Note From the Author

Greetings from Tasmania, Australia.

Thank you for reading my book. I hope you enjoyed it. If you are able, please leave a brief online review, as this will help other readers find my work.

If you would like to receive updates on my progress with other books in the **River Wild Series**, please visit <u>www.chrissygarwood.com</u> and complete the form. Links to social media can be accessed from my webpage.

Publishing a novel was a childhood ambition, one that I set aside a long time ago. Since then, I have added wife and mother, student, childcare educator, visual artist and chaplain to my list of achievements. To help me appreciate the brighter moments, God has guided me through dark days in the wilderness, where my faith has been tested.

I have learned a lot about myself and my ambitions while writing this series of books. The confidence I have gained as a storyteller has enriched my character. I believe it has made me a humbler disciple of Jesus Christ, a more determined encourager, a better friend.

When I first lost myself to the rediscovered joy of writing, my horizons expanded. My fictional world became populated with characters who whispered their stories to me.
This was how The River Wild series was born.

Chrissy